SAM
GUNN
JR.

BOOKS BY BEN BOVA:

SAM GUNN JR

JR

A NOVEL

BEN BOVA

NEW YORK TIMES BESTSELLING AUTHOR

BLACK STONE
PUBLISHING

Printed in the United States of America
Originally published in hardcover by Blackstone Publishing in 2022

First paperback edition: 2023
ISBN 979-8-212-18466-3
Fiction / Science Fiction / General

Version 1

Blackstone Publishing
31 Mistletoe Rd.
Ashland, OR 97520

www.BlackstonePublishing.com

To Don, Dave, Sonny, and the other guys I grew up with in South Philadelphia

Never stand begging for that which you have
the power to earn.

                              –Miguel de Cervantes

BOOK ONE: AN ENDING

"He's dead."

The medical examiner was bent over the body of Sam Gunn, who was sitting in his office chair, his jaw hanging open, his hazel eyes staring at nothing.

Frederick Mohammed Malone, executive vice president of S. Gunn Enterprises, Unlimited, puffed out a grunt. Malone was a large Black man with a shaved bald scalp and a tiny Van Dyke beard adorning his chin. He was staring at Sam.

"You're sure?" he asked.

"Quite dead," said the medical examiner. "Massive infarction. Must have popped off just like *that*." And he snapped his fingers.

Malone said, "He kinda looks surprised."

"I'll bet he was."

The office was surprisingly small, unadorned, considering the interplanetary scope of S. Gunn Enterprises, Unlimited. The plain utilitarian desk where the corpse sat was its major piece of furniture. On the wall behind it was a montage of photographs of Sam Gunn, many showing rockets standing tall and erect in the background, more of them showing Sam with beautifully smiling young women in skimpy attire.

The medical examiner was a small, pale man; next to Malone he looked like a wizened child. Looking up at the massive Black man, the examiner asked, "How old was he?"

"Who knows? Sam never gave the same answer twice."

"I've got to put something down for the examination report. It's official business."

Malone almost grinned. "Sam never bothered much with official business."

"But—"

Turning his gaze back to Sam's inert body, Malone grumbled, "Say a hundred and twenty-five. That's close enough."

For the next several minutes, the examiner asked questions and Malone made up answers.

"Can't you be more specific?" the medic pleaded, waving his handheld computer in Malone's face.

"'Fraid not," said Malone. "When people questioned Sam, he never gave the same answer twice."

With that, Malone turned and tenderly closed Sam Gunn's staring eyes. Then he gently pushed up his chin. It sagged open again the instant he removed his hands. Malone tried again, and again the chin sank, opening the deceased's mouth.

"It won't stay shut," the examiner said. "Not without surgical intervention."

Malone huffed. "Just like Sam," he said, almost grinning. "Nobody could get him to shut his mouth. Not ever."

With a weary sigh, the examiner complained, "Look here, I've got to get all the details straight. For the official record. It's important."

Malone sighed back at the small man. "And I'm gonna have

to face ten zillion lawyers, former girlfriends, and god knows who else—all of them looking to tear off a chunk of S. Gunn Enterprises, Unlimited, for themselves."

The medical examiner shrugged his frail shoulders and snapped his handheld shut.

BOOK TWO: EARTH

JACKPOT, NEVADA

The farm was a lonely green spot in the middle of the surrounding dust-brown semidesert. In the distance, cars and trucks whizzed along Highway 93, most of them heading south, toward Las Vegas at the other end of the state.

Junior stood by the door of the bedroom and stared at his mother's emaciated figure. She hardly made a wrinkle in the bedcovers, her once-glamorous figure had shrunk so much, eaten away by cancer.

He was well-built lad, nearly six feet tall, athletically slim, with restless hazel eyes and a head of thick, ungovernable red hair. A sprinkle of faint freckles dotted his snub nose and cheeks.

Should I phone the doc again? Junior wondered. *He said he'd be back this morning, but Mom is just lying there like she's already dead and . . .*

As if to contradict her son, his mother opened her bright blue eyes and fixed them on him. It made Junior's heart leap. *She's still alive! The cancer hasn't beaten her yet.*

Mom slowly pulled one arm from under the bed covers and motioned for Junior to sit beside her. He crossed the bedroom on his long legs and sat on the edge of the bed.

"There's something I've got to tell you, Samuel."

"Don't try to talk," he whispered. "Save your strength."

"No, I've got to tell you." The woman's voice was so soft that Junior had to bend closer to her lips to make out her words.

"It's about your father . . ." she whispered.

"My father?" All his nineteen years Junior had wondered who his father might be. He had never seen him, and his mother had sternly avoided all mention of his identity.

"Sam Gunn," she breathed. "He's your father."

Junior felt his eyes go wide. "Sam Gunn? The space guy?"

"Yes. I met him when I was performing at Selene City, on the Moon. I fell in love with Sam and I thought he was in love with me too." She shook her head slightly, as if remembering those days when she was a star dancer in a traveling troupe of performers.

"Sam Gunn?" Junior repeated. "*The* Sam Gunn?"

"He gave me this farm—this worthless piece of dung. Left me here and zoomed away, out to the Asteroid Belt, I think."

Junior straightened up on the bed. "Sam Gunn is my father?"

His mother nodded, then closed her eyes.

"He's rich!" Junior exclaimed.

"Find him," his mother whispered. "Find him and show him what a fine young man he fathered."

Visions of space adventures filled Junior's mind. Sam Gunn! One of the pioneers of the human race's expansion into space. He built whole cities on the Moon! He was the first man to get to the Asteroid Belt! He created the first space habitat to orbit Jupiter!

He was rich! *And I'm his son!*

"Mom, when did you know him? How did you meet him? What was he like?"

But his mother could not answer her son's eager, excited questions. She lay silent and still on the bed, her eyes closed forever.

LAWYERS

Junior felt his heart break. He phoned the doctor who had been attending his mother, who sternly commanded him to, "Touch nothing! Leave her exactly where she is. I'll be over at your place in an hour or two."

He took more than two hours.

Junior wandered through the tiny farmhouse, the only home he had ever known, tears in his eyes and wild visions of space adventures blazing through his thoughts. All his life his mother, his friends, even the teachers at the regional school had addressed him as "Junior." The family doctor called him "Samuel."

Now he knew his real name: Sam Gunn Jr.

All he had to do was prove it.

The day after his mother's burial—in the scrubby field in back of the farmhouse—Junior put on his best (and only) suit and drove into the town of Jackpot, to the office of Grabbitt and Runn, Esq.

The office was on the top floor (the second) of one of Jackpot's seedy plastic downtown buildings, across Main Street from the county courthouse. Junior parked the family sedan in front of the building, paying no attention to the fact that the street was almost empty of parked vehicles.

He took the stairs three at a time on his long legs and rapped at the door of Grabbitt & Runn, Esq.

A lean, bald, cranky-looking man in a dark three-piece suit opened the door. Looking up at Junior, his wrinkled face eased into a toothy smile.

"Mr. Gunn, I presume!"

Junior dipped his chin in acknowledgment and stepped into the office. It was a largish room, with an unoccupied desk next to the door, a railing cutting the floor space in two, and a pair of dark, formidable desks on its other side. Bookshelves crammed with loose papers and bound volumes lined the far wall, except for the two windows that looked out onto Main Street and the courthouse.

"Come in, young man! I am Elmer J. Grabbitt, attorney at law."

"Pleased to meet you," said Junior, extending his hand.

Grabbitt, whose spindly frame reached only to Junior's shoulders, ignored the extended hand. Instead, he pointed to the sturdy desk on the left side of the room and gestured Junior past the dividing railing.

"We were all very saddened to hear of your mother's passing," the lawyer said, shaking his head sympathetically. "She was a fine woman."

Junior wondered how much Mr. Grabbitt knew of his mother. He could not remember ever seeing him before. He'd only found the lawyer's name when he sifted through his mother's meager collection of papers.

But he kept his silence as he sat in the stiff black wooden chair in front of Mr. Grabbitt's desk.

"Now then," said Grabbitt, unconsciously rubbing his

hands together as he sat behind the desk, "how can I help you, young man?"

Junior squirmed uncomfortably on the hard chair, trying to arrange his thoughts. "Well, I guess the first thing I need to know about is the mortgage on the farm. Mom always kept the financial matters to herself—"

"She was in over her head," Grabbitt snapped, his voice suddenly hard, almost bitter.

"Over her head?"

"She owed a half-dozen back payments on her mortgage. I tried to keep the bank from foreclosing on her, but now that she's dead, they want their money. You know how bankers are."

"No, I don't know," said Junior.

"Well, they want their money. They're going to foreclose. Right away."

"What does that mean?"

"It means you'll have to leave the place. The bank will try to sell it to somebody else, although who'd want to buy it is a mystery to me."

"Leave it!" Junior yelped. "But where do I go?"

Grabbitt shrugged his frail shoulders. "That's up to you. Did your mother leave you any money?"

"She didn't have any to leave. She—"

Grabbitt interrupted, "You can't stay at the farm. It doesn't belong to you anymore."

"But—"

"Sorry, son. The world can be cruel sometimes."

Junior nodded, his thoughts in a whirl. Grabbitt got up from his desk chair and gestured toward the door. "That's all I can do for you, young man. Goodbye."

Junior slowly rose to his feet and shuffled toward the door. Grabbitt stayed behind his desk.

"Go out and get yourself a job," the lawyer advised. "A healthy young man like you should be able to find a job somewhere."

"Thank you," said Junior, as he reached the door. He left the law office and went slowly down the steps and out into the brightly sunny street.

He had no place to go, no one to turn to.

He drove slowly home, packed his few belongings and tossed them into the sedan's trunk, then started down the highway.

To where? he wondered.

HEADING FOR VEGAS

As he drove the aging sedan southward, Junior wondered what he was going to do. He had no job, and not enough money to rent a hotel room. Everything he knew, everything he had experienced in all his life, had been in the area around the town of Jackpot.

He felt like crying, but he was too proud, too determined to let the tears even start.

What would my father do? he asked himself as he drove along the highway toward Las Vegas. And he realized he had no answer to the question.

But he had a diskette from his mother's meager belongings, a diskette labeled simply, "Sam." Junior put the car on automatic steering, then slid the diskette into the slot beneath the dashboard TV.

As the old sedan rolled south on Highway 93 Junior watched a series of news stories about the fabled Sam Gunn, space entrepreneur. The Sam Gunn who built an entertainment complex on the Moon, at Hell crater. The Sam Gunn who led the first expedition to the Asteroid Belt. The Sam Gunn who wooed beautiful women while he built an interplanetary corporation and then went broke pushing the frontier of human habitation farther and farther into the edges of the solar system: Mars, the asteroids, Jupiter, Saturn . . . The Sam Gunn who sued the Pope and claimed he had encountered an alien civilization beyond the orbit of Pluto.

By the time the diskette ran out of news stories about Sam Gunn it was getting dark and car's fuel gauge was trembling near empty.

And Junior was trembling with excitement about his father's fabulous career.

All right, he said to himself. First things first. He pulled into the next gas station along the highway and filled the car's tank, using his mother's credit card. He used the card again to rent a seedy motel room for himself. He felt a little stir of conscience, knowing that he wouldn't be able to pay the credit card bill. But then he thought that the bill would go to Mom's address at the farm, and he was never going to see it.

He felt a pang of apprehension at the thought of cheating the credit card company, but he quickly realized that a billion-dollar international corporation wasn't going to fret over the few dollars he was spending.

His motel room was hardly grand, and there seemed to be a party of some kind going on in the room next door. Junior could hear the thumping beat of neopop music vibrating through the thin wall separating the rooms, and raucous, high-pitched laughter.

Annoyed, he phoned the desk clerk downstairs to complain.

"People come here for a good time," the clerk told him, his voice sharpish, cranky. "Jam a pillow over your ears if you want to sleep." With that, the clerk hung up.

Junior sat on the thin mattress of his bed, trying to think of what he should do. He decided to wait out the noise.

So he bent over the meager package he had made of his mother's papers and started reading through them. Bills, bills, and more bills. Except for one little sheet; it looked like a page torn from a tablet.

At its top was a heading written in pencil. Mom's handwriting, Junior recognized. It said, "Sam's accounts (some of them)." And a triple row of numbers ran down the length of the scrap of paper.

Junior studied the numbers. Some of them were accompanied by notations: "Third National Bank, Las Vegas, Nevada." "Golden Gate Savings and Loan, San Francisco, CA."

"Penn Central, Philadelphia, PA."

The numbers were considerable. And they were accompanied by dollar signs. Thousands of dollars in some places. Tens of thousands in a few.

Most of the entries had nothing more than question marks next to them.

Junior looked up from the list. *Sam's accounts*, he repeated silently to himself. Some of them, at least.

Does this mean that my father opened accounts in these banks? Suddenly Junior wanted to leap to his feet and whoop deliriously. I'm rich! My father deposited money in these banks. It belongs to me! All of it!

He was so excited that he jammed the paper into his pants pocket and got up from the bed. He no longer wanted his raucous next-door neighbors to stop their noise. He wanted to join them! He wanted to celebrate!

Junior went out into the dimly lit hallway and rapped on his neighbor's door, which was shuddering from the reverberating music roaring inside the room. No answer. *They probably can't hear me*, he thought. So he knocked harder, pounded on the flimsy door with both his fists.

The door opened a bit. A narrow-eyed, hard-faced guy in a dirty undershirt looked Junior up and down, then asked, "Whattaya want?"

"I'm your next-door neighbor," said Junior, forcing a smile.

"So what?"

"So your noise is keeping me awake."

"Tough."

"The least you can do is invite me in to join your party."

The guy's eyes flashed wide for a moment, surprised. Then he broke into a gap-toothed grin and swung the door wide open. As Junior stepped into the room, the guy shouted over the strident music, "Fresh meat!"

The room was jammed with nearly a dozen people, about half of them women, two of whom wearing nothing but underclothes. They all stopped their writhing attempts at dancing and stared at Junior.

"Come on in!" shouted one of the girls. She was wearing only a bra and panties and had a glass of some vile-looking liquid in one hand.

Junior stepped into the room, smiling. A smashing blow to the back of his head knocked him to the floor and he slid into unconsciousness.

POLICE . . .
AND BANKERS

Junior tried to open his eyes. They fluttered briefly but refused to open all the way.

A voice, seemingly from far, far away, called out, "He's comin' out of it."

He felt as if he were enmeshed in cobwebs. Junior's legs, arms, even his eyeballs all refused to obey his brain's commands.

"How ya feel, kid?"

With an enormous effort, Junior slowly peeled his eyelids back. He was on the floor of his own room, on his back. Strangers' faces hovered above him.

"Wha . . ." He tried to speak, found that his tongue was just as hard to control as the rest of him.

The man bending over him almost smiled. "You'll be okay, kid. They socked you pretty hard."

Junior blinked several times, then pushed himself up on his elbows. He was in his own room, but the place looked as if a tornado had ripped through it. His clothes were thrown all over the floor. Papers littered the bed. The meager night table's little lamp had been knocked over. Morning sunlight streamed painfully through the room's only window.

Squinting as he sat up slowly on the floor's thin carpeting, Junior asked, "Wha' happened?"

"You got mugged."

"By the people in the next room," Junior said, his voice little more than a pained croak.

"Yep." The man bending over him was thickset, balding, obviously a plainclothes policeman. He helped Junior to his feet. "They gave your room a good going over."

Junior started to nod, but it only made his head hurt more. There were two uniformed police officers in the room, together with the hotel's manager, whom Junior remembered from the night before, when he registered for the room.

"I'm sergeant Malverson," the plainclothes policeman said. Pointing to the two uniforms, he added, "That's Officer Gaines and Officer Abrams."

Again, Junior tried to nod. This time he almost made it.

The police sergeant helped Junior sort through his meager belongings. His wallet was the only thing missing.

"They took your cash and credit cards," said Sergeant Malverson. "Anything else missing?"

Junior shook his head. "There wasn't anything else to steal."

The two uniformed cops left, with the motel's manager. Sergeant Malverson sat on the bed while Junior picked up his scattered clothes and hung them back in the closet.

"Did you put anything in the drawers?" the sergeant asked.

Junior shook his head, wincing. "Didn't have anything to put in them."

They walked out into the bright, warm morning and checked Junior's car. It was still where he had parked it the night before, locked up tight. But there was a scuffed dent in the driver's side door.

"Kicked it when they couldn't get it open," Malverson noted, almost smiling. "Frustrated, I guess."

"I guess," Junior agreed.

The police sergeant left Junior at the old sedan and drove off. Junior went back to his hotel room and used its phone to generate replacements for the credit cards the thieves had taken. Once the phone printed out the new cards, Junior stuffed them into his back pants pocket, zipped his clothes into his hanger bag, went downstairs, and checked out.

He headed south once more, toward Las Vegas and its Third National Bank.

─────

The bank manager looked more like a suspicious troll than a businessman: he was short, portly, with a thick head of dark hair and a skeptical scowl on his heavy-jawed face.

Junior had spent nearly an hour in the Third National Bank, being passed from teller to chief teller to assistant manager to—at last—the manager himself.

He was seated before the manager's wide, handsome desk, in a little cubbyhole of an office partitioned off from the rest of the bank by shoulder-high dividing walls. It was late afternoon, the bank was practically empty of customers. Junior had the feeling that the whole staff was staring at him from their places at the silent, empty counters.

"Sam Gunn was my father," Junior was explaining. "He died a few days ago."

The bank manager nodded, the suspicious scowl on his face unchanging. "I saw the news broadcast."

"He has nearly thirty-three thousand dollars deposited here, in your bank."

The manager glanced at his desktop screen. "Thirty-two thousand, seven hundred dollars, and eighteen cents. It's been sitting with us, in this bank, for nearly twelve years. Drawing interest every month."

Junior said, "I'd like to close the account."

With a sad shake of his head, the manager said, "We can't just turn over the money to you, not without firm evidence that you are his inheritor."

"I've shown you my driver's license and my Social Security card!" They were reproductions of the originals, Junior knew, but he felt they should do.

The banker shrugged his padded shoulders. "That's not sufficient identification, I'm afraid."

Junior felt his brows knitting. "What do you need?"

The manager leaned back in his swivel chair and looked up at the ceiling. "Mr. Gunn, we need some unequivocal proof that you are indeed Sam Gunn's offspring."

"A blood sample?"

"We don't have a sample of Mr. Gunn's blood to compare it with."

A flash of a memory of Mrs. McNiff's fifth-grade English class lit Junior's mind. The man had just ended a sentence with a preposition, he thought.

But he let that pass. Leaning forward in his chair, Junior said, "I am Sam Gunn's son. My mother told me so."

"And where is your mother?"

"She died two days ago. She told me on her death bed."

With a sad shake of his head, the manager said, "We'll need something more substantive than that, young man."

Feeling a helpless sense of frustration taking hold of him, Junior said, "Pull up an image of my father's face. You'll see the resemblance."

"That would hardly be proof."

"He was my father!" Junior insisted. "Are you trying to tell me that my mother lied to me?"

"Nothing of the kind, young man. But this bank requires substantive proof of your claim to be Mr. Gunn's son."

"A DNA comparison?"

"Comparison to what? We don't have Mr. Gunn's DNA on file here."

Junior sank back in his chair. It's like talking to a blank wall, he thought.

"So what happens to my father's money?"

"It continues to accrue interest," said the banker. "until someone presents us with unequivocal proof of a family relationship."

Junior pushed himself to his feet, muttered, "Thanks for your time," and walked out of the bank on trembling legs.

L'AUDACE, L'AUDACE . . .

Blinking in the late afternoon sunshine, Junior walked up the street from the bank to the curbside stall where he'd parked the sedan. A bright orange parking ticket was affixed to the car's windshield-wiper.

The end of a perfect day, he growled to himself as he yanked the ticket from his windshield and crumpled it into his pocket.

Where to? he asked himself as he slid in behind the steering wheel.

And answered, The public library.

———

It was an impressive building, looking more like an ancient Roman temple than anything else. But once inside, Junior found that the library was quite modern, with individual booths lined with electronics systems where a visitor could delve into just about any subject under the sun.

Junior closed himself into one of those booths and started looking up whatever the library had about his father.

Which was considerable. There were seemingly thousands

of magazine articles, television interviews, film clips of Sam Gunn and his exploits along the frontier of space. There was Sam building his pleasure palace at the Moon's Hell Crater; Sam the explorer leading the first human expedition into the Asteroid Belt, Sam the tycoon of industry starting up the first transportation line to the asteroids, Sam the wild man who, when his insurance carrier refused to pay for rocket accidents that were deemed "acts of God," sued the Pope!

Junior spent hours in the cubicle, watching his father's antics with a mixture of pride and revulsion at the way Sam Sr. skirted the edges of interplanetary law.

But it was one television interview, in particular, that caught Junior's attention. Sam was being interviewed upon returning to the Earth/Moon vicinity after towing a mile-long asteroid from the Belt and parking it in a sun-centered orbit.

The interviewer—a comely young woman who obviously relished Sam's every exploit—asked him, "What's the secret of your success, Mr. Gunn? What makes you succeed so spectacularly?"

Sam broke into a gap-toothed grin. "George Danton," he answered.

The interviewer was obviously puzzled. "Danton? Wasn't he some Frenchman?"

"Right," Sam answered. "He was a big force in the French Revolution . . . until they chopped his head off."

"But how . . . ?"

His grin growing wider, Sam told the interviewer, "Danton said the secret of his success was *'L'audace, l'audace, toujours l'audace.'*"

Sam's pronunciation was terrible, but the interviewer grasped his meaning. "Audacity?" she asked.

"Right," said Sam, patting the woman's knee. "Audacity. Go where no man has gone before. Do things no man has done.

Be the first. Lead the charge and don't bother to look behind you to see if anybody's following you. As the American Civil War general Nathan Bedford Forrest put it, 'Git there fustest with the mostest.'"

Junior stared at the screen mounted on the library's table. "*L'audace, l'audace,*" he whispered to himself.

———

The bank was closed by the time Junior left the library. He ate a greasy dinner in a rundown restaurant, slept in his car, woke with the sun, and washed up in a public lavatory. Then, wishing his suit didn't look so rumpled, he headed back to the Third National Bank.

The bank manager looked displeased that Junior had returned. He sat behind his desk, the expression on his face sour enough to curdle the weekly output of every one of Campbell's soups factories.

With obvious distaste, the manager asked, "And what can I do for you, Mr. Gunn?"

He knows I'm Sam Gunn's son, but he won't let me take out my dad's money, thought Junior.

Trying to hide his resentment, Junior said as pleasantly as he could, "I realized that when we talked yesterday, I forgot to mention the finder's fee."

The banker's brows rose half a centimeter. "Finder's fee?"

"Yes," said Junior, as pleasantly as he could manage. "I believe the usual finder's fee in cases such as this is ten percent. That would be slightly more than thirty-two hundred dollars, wouldn't it?"

The bank manager nodded. Then, "And to whom would this finder's fee go?"

Junior tried to look surprised. "Why, to you, I suppose."

"Thirty-two hundred dollars? To me?"

"It's not all that much, I realize. But it's better than nothing, don't you think?"

For an eternally long moment the manager said nothing. But Junior could fairly hear the wheels spinning inside his head.

At last the man whispered, "I believe the finder's fee is usually twenty percent."

"Ten. I checked the standard references."

"Twenty."

With a great show of reluctance, Junior said, "Let's not argue. We can agree on fifteen percent."

"Make it an even five thousand."

It was Junior's turn to hesitate. He realized that the bank manager could do arithmetic in his head much faster than he could himself.

At last he broke into a genial grin and capitulated. "Okay. Five thousand it is."

The manager smiled broadly and extended his hand over his desk. Junior grasped it firmly while figuring that he had slightly more than twenty-seven thousand dollars coming to him.

A little less than twenty minutes later, Junior loped down the sunny street to his car with the cash in his pocket, grinning from ear to ear as he muttered, "*L'audace, toujours l'audace.*"

LEAVING EARTH

For the next six weeks, Junior drove across the nation, stopping for a day or so at each of the banks mentioned in his mother's penciled list.

He was piling up a substantial treasure. Plus learning how to convince hard-eyed bankers that he was indeed the son of the famous Sam Gunn.

In Des Moines Junior traded in the old family sedan for a stylish convertible. In Chicago he bought himself some new clothes.

When he reached Philadelphia, though, he didn't withdraw money from his father's waiting account. He deposited most of the funds he'd wheedled out of the other banks he'd hit. A few thousand here, he told himself, a few thousand there—and pretty soon we're dealing with real money.

But as left the Penn Central Bank in Philadelphia, with an account book that tallied close to a million dollars, a voice in his head asked Junior, "Okay, now what are you going to do with all this money?"

Standing on the sidewalk just outside the bank, Junior squinted up at the late afternoon sky. The pale ghost of the Moon was hanging up there, grinning at him.

He answered himself aloud, "I'm going to go to Dad's company headquarters, on the Moon."

So Sam Gunn, Junior, walked to the nearest travel agency office and booked a flight to Selene City, at the mammoth crater Alphonsus, on the Moon.

———

The Moon-bound rocket was mounted atop a jet-powered airplane, a completely reusable first stage that lifted the aptly named *Lunar Express* to the high stratosphere, then released it to fly on its own to Selene.

Junior felt excited as he waited in the passenger lounge for the booster-and-spacecraft combination to begin boarding. He remembered from his study of Sam Gunn's well-documented exploits that Sam had pioneered the double-decker lifter and spacecraft concept years before he himself had been born.

But Sam's hardware was actually a fake, of course. The spacecraft never left its booster plane. Sam sold the experience of spaceflight to gullible tourists, raising enough money in the process to build an actual spacecraft that really did take tourists into space—briefly.

His flight was apparently fully booked, Junior saw as the people lined up to board the spacecraft. Dad could have made honest money on this system—if he'd had enough money to actually build the hardware, back in those early days.

The Moon-bound passengers filed through the handsomely decorated waiting room, through a slightly claustrophobic tunnel and at last into the luxuriously appointed passenger compartment of the spaceplane itself.

It was easy for Junior to spot the workers from the tourists. Male or female, the regular workers shuffled quietly along the ship's central aisle to their seats, while the tourists oohed and aahed at everything they saw: the sleek interior of the spacecraft, the commodious reclinable seats, the sharply uniformed crew members who smilingly directed the passengers to their assigned places.

Junior had a window seat and, much to his delight, the aisle seat adjoining his own was taken by a good-looking young woman.

Junior glanced at her, then—embarrassed by his good fortune—found that he couldn't speak to her. To cover up his awkwardness, he leaned forward and turned on the spaceplane's orientation lecture.

"You first flight to the Moon?" the young woman asked. Her voice was low, soft. It sounded like an angel's call in Junior's ears. And she was really beautiful: slim, shapely figure, lustrous dark hair falling to her shoulders, sparkling gray-green eyes.

He nodded, unable to force a word past his lips.

"Mine too," she said, smiling appealingly.

Say something! Junior's brain demanded. But his voice was beyond his conscious control.

"I'm Deborah Salmon," she said, thrusting her hand toward Junior.

He stared at it for what seemed like a century and a half, then took her hand briefly in his own. It felt warm and altogether wonderful.

"Samuel Gunn Junior," he managed to croak out.

Deborah smiled prettily. "I've got a job waiting for me at Selene," she said. "I'm a physical therapist."

Junior nodded numbly, thinking, *I wouldn't mind being a patient of yours.*

But before he could force a word past his lips, the uniformed flight attendant on the spaceplane's orientation lecture advised,

"We're all set for takeoff. Please be sure you're strapped in and have a pleasant flight."

"Here we go," said Deborah, leaning slightly toward Junior.

He sensed the plane starting to roll forward. *I'm on my way to the Moon,* Junior told himself, *with a beautiful young lady sitting beside me and smiling at me. Me!*

He leaned back in his comfortable seat and tried to relax. But he couldn't.

BOOK THREE: THE MOON

IN SPACE

"Seatbacks down, please," called the flight attendant.

The double plane's takeoff had been quite normal, but now they were reaching the altitude where the spaceplane would separate from its carrier.

"Here we go," Deborah said again, smiling as she lowered her seat back nearly flat.

Junior nodded and managed to say weakly, "Yeah."

He tensed as he waited for the crushing force of acceleration to squeeze him down into his seat's cushions. Instead, all he sensed was a gentle nudge. He felt almost disappointed.

The roar of the spaceplane's rocket engines was muted by the plane's heavy acoustic insulation. Outside the small oval window next to him, Junior saw the blue sky deepen swiftly until it became quite black. He felt a twinge of disappointment because he couldn't see any stars.

Leaning toward him, Deborah gushed, "We're in space!"

"Yes," said Junior. "We are."

There was really nothing to see out there, nothing but utter blackness. Junior remembered an old Air Force aphorism:

"Flying for the Air Force is nothing but hours of boredom, punctuated by moments of sheer terror."

But he didn't feel terrorized. Or bored. Deborah was leaning his way, her eyes wide with delight, her lips parted temptingly.

Without thinking, Junior slid his hand behind her head, drew her to him, and kissed her.

"Welcome to space," he breathed.

She looked surprised for a moment, then her smile returned. "Same to you, Mr. Gunn."

"Sam."

"Sam," she said, still smiling.

Junior lay back on his chair and smiled back at her.

Suddenly Deborah's eyes went so wide he could see white all around her startlingly gray-green irises.

"Look!" she yelped.

Junior turned his head to look out the small, oval window.

And saw the Moon, almost full, its oddly lopsided face grinning at him.

Turning back to Deborah, he said, "Looks like he's welcoming us."

"I hope so," said Deborah. For the first time, the eager smile disappeared from her beautiful face. She looked worried, almost frightened.

"What's the matter?" Junior asked.

"Oh, it's nothing," she replied, still looking nervous, apprehensive.

"It must be something."

She bit her lip, then answered, "I . . . I'm worried about my job. A little."

"Your job?"

Deborah nodded. "I'm something of a dancer. I signed up for a six-week tryout with Hell's Belles."

Junior felt his face warp into a puzzled frown.

"That's the dance group at Dante's Inferno," Deborah said.

"Dante's Inferno?"

"It's the nightclub at Hell Crater," she explained, as if she were confessing to a crime.

She went on, "Dante's pays way better than anything I could find in the States. I've got my mother and little brother to support, and a job at Dante's is the best I can do for them."

"Oh."

"I'm not a whore," Deborah said, in an urgent whisper. "I'm a trained physical therapist. And I'm trying to become a professional dancer. I have responsibilities."

"Dancing in Dante's Inferno."

"That's right." She looked almost angry now, righteously incensed.

Junior didn't know what to say. He heard his mouth murmur, "I understand. I see."

But he wondered about what he understood, and he tried to blot out the vision of what his mind saw.

SELENE CITY

Most of the flight was monotonously uneventful. Junior chatted haltingly with Deborah as the spaceplane made its way to Alphonsus crater and the mostly underground city of Selene.

She's a physical therapist, he kept telling himself.

He remembered reading somewhere that such a term was sometimes used as a euphemism for a sex worker. For all the long, boring hours of the spaceplane's approach to the Moon, Junior wondered about that question. He found that he wanted to believe Deborah, wanted to take her at her word—but a lingering doubt in his mind warned him to be careful.

Still, the memory of their one brief kiss seemed wonderful. Junior decided to take Deborah at her word and leave all doubts behind. That's what Dad would do, he told himself.

At last the spaceplane came down at Selene's landing area—tail-first. Junior hardly felt the bump when its landing struts touched the circular pad on the Moon's barren, dusty surface.

"We're here!" Deborah almost shouted. "We're on the Moon!"

Junior grinned and nodded at her. "We sure are."

The viewscreens on the backs of the seats in front of them started to show a safety lecture that began with, "Welcome to the Moon. Remember, the gravity here is only one-sixth of what you've experienced on Earth."

Junior realized the safety lecture was actually a thinly disguised pitch for renting weighted boots that were advertised as "helping you to adjust to the lower lunar gravity." He decided to rent a pair from the flight attendants who were pushing a cartload of boots along the aisle between the seats.

He rented a pair for Deborah too.

"Ooh, thanks," she cooed. "But you really didn't have to."

Junior grinned at her. "If I *had to*, I would have resented it," he said.

Deborah smiled back at him as she tugged the weighted boots over her shoes.

Weighted or not, it still felt strange to stand and try to walk in the lunar gravity. Junior waited for Deborah to step out into the aisle, then he slid out cautiously beside her.

With a smile, he took her hand and started to guide her up the aisle to the plane's exit hatch, very conscious of the difference in gravity. He felt as if he were gliding on ice, the way he used to skate on the farm's pond on those rare winter days when the pond froze over.

"Easy does it," he said, inching his way toward the hatch, with Deborah in tow.

The aisle was crowded; there wasn't any space to fall into if he stumbled, but still Junior made his way up the aisle, slowly, patiently.

He glanced over his shoulder at Deborah, who was visibly tense, white-faced.

"Almost there," Junior said reassuringly.

He ducked through the hatch and suddenly realized the

passengers were lined up in an almost claustrophobic tunnel that curved up ahead so that he couldn't see how long it was or where it ended.

"Almost there," he repeated, more weakly.

Deborah started to nod, caught herself, and forced a smile.

Peering past the people lined up ahead of him, Junior saw at last that the tunnel ended at a hatch, very similar to the hatch they had gone through when exiting the spaceplane.

"Just a few more steps," he told Deborah.

"Yes, I see."

Stepping through the hatch was like entering Wonderland. They were suddenly in a vast, brightly lit dome, with seemingly millions of people shuffling, striding, even dashing all over the crowded floor. High up, near the dome's apex, a huge curving sign greeted the arrivals with WELCOME TO SELENE flashing on and off.

Attendants in bright coral-red uniforms directed the arriving passengers to walk through the check-in inspection arches that scanned each person with x-rays, heat sensors, and neutrino beams.

Junior happily led Deborah through the detectors and to a booth beyond them where a bored-looking inspector flipped through their papers and asked a few routine questions, ending his cursory examination with a deadpan, "Welcome to Selene."

On the far side of the inspection booths, Deborah stood uncertainly, glancing at the small groups of people waiting for the new arrivals.

Looking at Junior, she said uncertainly, "Somebody was supposed to meet me here . . ."

Junior shrugged good-naturedly. "I don't have anybody waiting for me. I'll stay with you until—"

"Deborah Salmon?" came a flat, unemotional voice.

Junior looked down and saw a stunted mechanical apparatus, no taller than his hips, with a round dome that featured a pair of blood-red optical sensors, and a half-dozen jointed metal arms folded tightly against its cylindrical body. DANTE'S INFERNO was printed down its side, in devilishly red letters.

Deborah stared at the robot for a moment before answering, "Yes, I'm Deborah Salmon."

"Follow me, please."

Junior tagged along, to the baggage area, where Deborah retrieved a smallish pink suitcase. The robot extended one of its arms and said, "I will handle that for you."

Then it pivoted on the trunnions at its base and headed off to what seemed to be an underground parking area, where several golf cart–sized vehicles were taking on passengers.

Deborah watched it uncertainly, then looked up at Junior. "I guess that's my ride to Dante's Inferno."

Feeling torn, Junior said, "You don't have to go if you don't want to."

"Yes I do," she replied, tightly.

And she walked away, following the stumpy robot, leaving Junior standing alone in the midst of the throng.

THE PLAZA

For long moments Junior just stood there, amidst the hurrying, chattering crowd, and watched Deborah board the tram—with the robot—until it whisked her away, out of his sight.

She didn't want to go, he told himself. But she let the robot lead her away. Like a prisoner being taken off to jail, he thought.

Shaking his head to clear his thoughts, Junior told himself that he was here at Selene to find the headquarters of his father's company, the center of S. Gunn Enterprises, Unlimited.

Deborah's going to Dante's Inferno, he reasoned. *I'll be able to find her there.*

So he squared his shoulders, hoisted his pitifully small travel bag, and headed for one of the giant-sized information screens mounted against the curving wall of the reception center.

He found S. Gunn Enterprises, Unlimited easily enough. There was a cluster of other names beneath it: Vacuum Cleaners, Inc., Asteroidal Resources, Ltd., Sunsat Power and Light, Vesta Jewelry, and several others.

Junior pulled his phone from his jacket pocket and tapped out the code for S. Gunn Enterprises' location, then used the phone's data system to guide him to a tram that would carry him from the arrivals' reception center into Selene City itself. He hoped.

The tram whisked Junior—and a couple of dozen visitors, residents, students, retirees, workers, and excited, chattering children who could hardly sit still in their seats—along a lengthy, brightly lit tunnel. Most of Selene was underground, Junior knew. The Moon's airless surface was bathed in hard radiation from the Sun and distant stars and peppered with occasional meteor showers. You could go from a few hundred degrees Kelvin to a couple of hundred below zero simply by stepping from sunshine into shadow up there. Belowground was far safer. And easier to maintain in comfort.

The tram's first stop was at a huge station, where many trams were disgorging passengers and taking on new ones. Junior saw signs where the trams were stopped for loading and unloading: Administrative Headquarters, Farside Express, Spaceport, Factory Complex. Checking his handheld, he saw that S. Gunn Enterprises was listed among several other corporations in Selene's main administrative building, up in the Plaza—wherever that was.

Fortunately, there were detailed electronic maps of Selene on the walls of the busy, noisy station. From there, Junior located the main administrative building and started out for it on foot.

He rode an automated moving stairway up toward the surface and got off at its final stop. He stared at the huge expanse of the plaza.

It was the closest thing to an Earthly outdoor environment that could be found on the Moon. Junior stood surprised, awed really, as tourists and workers surged past him. The plaza was under a huge concrete dome that extended from the moving stairway out so far that its gray vastness almost curved over the short lunar horizon.

There was greenery everywhere. Junior saw trees, shrubs, and colorful flowers lining the sinuous paved walkways that extended in every direction. People strode along those walkways. Families of tourists with excited, happily shouting children; workers in various color-coded uniforms; and squat little robots rolling along on tiny, seemingly frictionless wheels.

People were talking, laughing, shouting. Junior saw a youngster soaring high overhead on outstretched plastic wings. In the low lunar gravity, one could fly like a bird, or at least glide pleasantly.

The greenery opened in places, and Junior saw stores and restaurants. In the distance stood what looked like a band shell, with rows of seats arranged in front of it. And farther, an actual Olympic-sized swimming pool, with divers jumping from a thirty-meter-high platform and performing acrobatics as they slowly, leisurely, plunged toward the water.

He spotted two stout, gray concrete pillars that supported the arched dome covering the entire plaza. Beyond the dome, Junior realized, was the harsh airless surface of the Moon. But here inside this magnificent dome, human minds and hands had built an environment that was as Earthlike as they could make it. Junior felt awed.

He stood there at the head of the moving stairway that connected to the tram line below and drank in the sheer human magnificence of the plaza. But only for a few exalted, exhilarating moments. *Come on*, he said to himself. *You're here to find the headquarters of Dad's company.*

Hefting his meager travel bag onto his shoulder, Junior marched determinedly toward the nearer of the two stout pillars supporting the dome.

The pillars were like the skyscraper buildings Junior had read about at school. Nowhere near as tall, but sturdy, wide and high enough to house several floors of offices, Junior saw as he approached the nearer one. A check of his handheld showed his father's headquarters was in the farther one, of course.

S. Gunn Enterprises was on the top floor of the building.

S. GUNN ENTERPRISES, UNLIMITED

The ground floor of the building housed a reception area and four elevators. No humans manned the reception area, only stumpy little robots.

Junior went to the counter and one of the robots asked, in a pleasant—almost sultry—voice, "May I help you?"

"S. Gunn Enterprises," Junior replied crisply.

The robot extended a spindly arm. "Elevator two, behind you. Top floor."

"Thank you."

"You are entirely welcome. Have a pleasant day."

As Junior approached the elevator its door slid open. It was empty. He stepped in and murmured, "Top floor, please."

The same warm voice as the reception robot's replied, "Top floor. Express."

The door slid shut and Junior felt a slight surge of acceleration as the elevator rushed upward.

He got out when the door opened again and saw he was facing another receptionist. At least this one was human: a very attractive young blond woman in a glittering metal jacket.

With a certainty he didn't actually feel, Junior announced, "I'd like to see the president of the corporation."

The blond looked up at him with large, purple eyes. "And whom may I say is calling?"

"Sam Gunn Junior."

The blonde's lovely face contracted into a frown, but only for a moment. She put on a smile and said, "One moment, please." Then she turned slightly and said into a phone screen, "A Mr. Sam Gunn Junior is asking to see Mr. Malone."

For the next half hour, Junior was shuttled from one underling to another. Each of them asked for some evidence of his identity. Junior showed his Nevada driver's license and insisted that he was here to talk to no one less than the corporation's president.

Patience and persistence paid off. At last Junior was escorted by a pair of midlevel flunkys to an office whose door read Frederick Mohammed Malone, President. The sign looked sparkling new.

One of the flunkys opened the door and gestured Junior through it. The office of President Malone was small, almost entirely taken up by a single modest-sized desk that bore an old-fashioned computer screen on one side of it. A broad-shouldered Black man was sitting behind it.

Frederick Mohammed Malone looked up at Junior, his face stern, almost scowling. Slowly he got to his feet. He was a large man, tall and heavy. He did not extend a hand.

"You're Sam Gunn Junior?" His voice was a low purr, almost a growl.

Junior answered, "Yes, I am."

Malone focused on Junior's face. "Those freckles real?"

With a smile and a nod, Junior replied, "Had 'em all my life."

Gesturing to the one leather-upholstered chair in front of the desk, Malone slowly sank back into his own swivel chair.

As he tapped at the keyboard on his desk Malone asked, "You know how many guys have come up here claiming to be related to Sam?"

Junior shook his head.

Peering at the computer screen, "You're the . . . thirteenth, so far."

Lucky thirteen? Junior asked himself.

Leaning back in his swivel chair, Malone said, "Okay, prove you're Sam's kid."

"My mother told me. On her death bed."

Malone grunted, unimpressed. But he said, "You look kinda like Sam. If those freckles don't scrub off. Too damned tall, though."

"My mother was almost my own height. She was an actress, years ago. A dancer, really. When she met my father."

"You got his hair, sure enough."

Unconsciously smoothing his unruly red mop, Junior said, "My mother wouldn't lie to me. Especially not on her death bed."

"Yeah, it's a heart-wrenching story. I've heard a dozen of 'em, so far."

"This one is true!"

Malone pushed himself to his feet once more. Junior saw that it seemed to take him a considerable effort.

As he edged slowly, deliberately, around the desk he crooked a finger and said, "Come on, kid. We're gonna see if you're telling the truth or not."

Junior shot to his feet.

"I got a sample of Sam's blood in storage. We'll compare yours with his."

"Good," said Junior.

In complete silence, Malone led Junior along a corridor that seemed to wind around the building. Junior couldn't help noticing that the big Black man limped noticeably as he walked. *He seems to be in pain*, Junior told himself. *Even here on the Moon, in one-sixth normal-g, walking is painful to him.*

As if he understood what was going through Junior's mind, Malone broke his silence. "Bionic legs. Grown in a lab back Earthside. Sam got 'em for me."

"But . . ."

"Yeah, yeah, I know. My own damned fault. Let myself get too heavy, even for the Moon. I ought to slim down some."

"Bionic legs?" Junior asked.

Malone nodded as he walked—limped, actually—along the corridor. Through the windows on one side of the passageway, Junior could see the greenery and crowds of people thronging the Plaza down below. *They've worked hard to make it look like Earth*, he told himself. *Like home.*

"Here we are."

Malone had stopped in front of a door the bore the title of Medlab. Nothing else.

Malone tapped on the keypad mounted on the wall beside the door, and it clicked open. With a shooing motion, he gestured Junior inside.

It didn't look like a medical facility. It was a smallish room. No examination table, no rows of bottles on the bare walls, no doctors staring at him. Just a rather pretty, pert, redheaded young woman in a nurse's white uniform sitting behind a modest-sized desk.

"Mr. Malone!" she said, apparently surprised. "What can I do for you?"

Easing himself into one of the straight-backed chairs along

the wall, Malone sighed gratefully, then said, "I want to compare this young man's blood to Sam's."

The redhead's chirpy young expression morphed into a semi-frown. "Another one?"

With a deeper sigh, Malone replied, "Another one."

The nurse touched a button on her desktop console and a section of the wall to her left slid upward, revealing a row of glassware.

"How many does this one make?" she asked.

Malone said, "Thirteen."

Lucky thirteen, Junior repeated to himself. *I hope.*

TESTING

The nurse told Junior to sit down. There was only one other chair in the tiny reception room. Junior sat on it, next to Malone, who loomed over him like a dark thundercloud.

"Whatever happened to the fella that you brought in here last week?" the nurse asked, as she picked various bottles from the shelves where they rested.

"We ran a security check on him. Turns out he was wanted in Peoria, back Earthside."

"Wanted?" the nurse asked, as she gestured for Junior to roll up his sleeve.

"Extortion. Theft. Half a dozen petty crimes."

Shaking her head as she shook a bottle of reddish liquid, the nurse said, "Too bad. He was kind of cute."

"But not very smart."

"Too bad," she repeated.

Junior tensed as the nurse approached him, expecting a needle. Instead, she pressed an adhesive pad against the inside of his elbow and then picked up a small cylindrical object and held it before his left eye.

"Try not to blink," she said.

Junior stared into the cylinder. It sort of looked like a miniature telescope. He heard a faint buzz.

"There," said the nurse, moving back to her desk.

Junior blinked.

The nurse tapped a few more buttons on her desktop keyboard. The desktop slid open, and a complicated array of glassware rose up from it.

Murmuring, "This'll take a few minutes," the nurse plugged the mini-telescope device into one end of the elaborate network of interconnected glassware.

Sitting next to Junior, Malone looked like a man who had been through this routine before. Twelve times before, Junior reminded himself.

Pointing at the gleaming glass arrangement, Junior asked, in a semi-whisper, "What's this all about?"

"Comparing your blood to our sample of Sam's," Malone replied softly.

Junior nodded.

The nurse pecked at the keyboard again, then swiveled her desk chair slightly to peer at the computer screen that had risen out of the desktop. For a moment she looked surprised. Then she punched a button and sat back once again. The glassware array burbled and beeped.

Looking across her desk at Junior, she almost smiled. "Checks out," she said to Malone.

Malone glanced at Junior, then said to the nurse, "Run it again."

After three tries, the nurse said, "Mr. Malone, the results aren't going to change, even if you run the analysis a hundred times."

"You're sure?" Malone said, in a voice that sounded to Junior like the rumbling of a distant volcano.

She nodded. "Positive. This young man is a blood relation to Sam Gunn."

Malone still looked unconvinced. "Nobody's jiggered your sample of Sam's blood?"

"It's been under the security system's seal since the last guy you brought in here."

Junior studied Malone's face. He had seemed surprised at first. Maybe shocked would be more accurate. Now he appeared to be leery, unconvinced, unwilling to accept what the nurse was telling him.

"What's the degree of certainty?" Malone asked.

"Better than ninety-seven percent," answered the nurse.

Malone heaved a monumental sigh. With obvious reluctance, he turned to Junior and forced a smile. "I'll be damned. Looks like you really are Sam's son."

Junior grinned. "My mother wouldn't lie to me. And I haven't lied to you."

"I guess not." His tentative smile slowly evaporating, Malone stuck out his hand. "Welcome to the funeral, kid."

═══════

Junior obediently followed Malone back to his office. The big man sank onto his swivel chair like a tired laborer after a hard day's work. Junior took the chair in front of the desk again.

"You said funeral?" he asked.

Malone nodded morosely. "We got sixteen different banks tryin' to foreclose their loans to the corporation. Eleven women suing us for breach of promise, child support, emotional distress, whatnot. The government of Selene says we owe them more'n six years' worth of back taxes . . ."

"Six years?"

With a weary nod, Malone went on, "And two of our ships have been impounded at the Valles Marineris base on Mars until we pay their goddamned fees on the incoming cargo."

"Wow."

"This corporation is heading toward receivership. We're strapped for cash, and everybody this side of heaven is squeezing us for money that we don't have."

"Sounds pretty grim," said Junior.

"That's not the half of it," Malone grumbled. "Sam always ran things on a shoestring. He'd put incoming profits into new ventures while he stalled the creditors. How he got away with it, I don't know. He was always a smooth talker, a fast operator. I'm not, and the vultures are circling over this corporation's dying body."

Junior saw true sadness on the Black man's face. "Can't you declare bankruptcy? Or something like that?"

Malone said, "Then the vultures would grab all the corporation's assets and we'd be out in the cold with nothing but the clothes on our backs."

"So you start over."

Malone's eyes went wide. "Start over?"

"Let the creditors take over. We go out and start a new operation."

"We?" Malone bleated. "What's this 'we,' white man?"

Junior thought that Malone's question was the punch line to an old joke, but he didn't know what the joke was. So he said, "We start a new corporation: S. Gunn and Company."

"A new corporation. Doin' what?"

"What was my Dad trying to do?"

Malone's brow furrowed. "What wasn't he tryin' to do? Sam always had at least half a dozen irons in the fire."

"So let's take a look at them. At least one of them ought to be worth developing."

"That's crazy."

"Just because it's crazy doesn't mean it won't work," Junior insisted.

Malone stared at him. "Christmas bells! You sound just like your old man."

S. GUNN AND COMPANY

The next week zipped past in a blur. Junior watched as Malone filed bankruptcy papers—and an application for a new corporate startup: S. Gunn and Company.

Under the heading asking for business description, Malone tapped in "to be determined."

Junior thought there were several possibilities. His father's operation had found that the nickel-iron asteroids orbiting out in the belt between Mars and Jupiter often contained gem-quality diamonds and other gemstones buried in their metallic bodies.

But when he excitedly suggested to Malone that the new corporation should make diamond mining its prime business, the Black man shook his head wearily. "And go into competition with DeBeers and the cartel? That's crazy."

"Who's DeBeers?" Junior asked.

"The diamond cartel back Earthside," Malone explained. "They've got the gemstone market tied up just the way they want it, and they don't take kindly to newcomers tryin' to get into their game."

"It's a real cartel, then?"

With a quick, sharp nod Malone said, "Guys have gotten themselves killed trying to break into that market."

Disappointed, Junior dug deeper into the reports that the old corporation's exploratory ships had sent back to headquarters. Among the millions of asteroids floating around out there were vast amounts of metals, minerals, jewels, and—most valuable of all—oxygen.

"O2 is vital, isn't it?" Junior asked Malone.

The two of them were sitting in Malone's cramped office. The wall screens showed abstracts of the old corporate reports, which legally belonged to the corporate combine that has bought the old S. Gunn Enterprises, Unlimited assets for a pittance.

"If you want to breathe, yeah, oxygen's vital," Malone answered, with a wry grin. Then he added, "And mix it with hydrogen and you get a reasonably good rocket propellant."

"I thought we used nuclear rockets, mostly."

Another nod. "Mostly. But hydrogen and oxygen make good propellants. And they're a lot cheaper than the nukes. And not radioactive."

"As long as you can dig them out of the asteroids."

"There is that," Malone agreed.

Junior felt puzzled. "Where does the hydrogen come from?"

"Water. Break it out of water molecules."

"There's water in the asteroids?"

"Some," Malone answered. "Most of what we use comes from the water that's trapped here on the Moon, underground."

Junior thought about that. "What about comets? They're mostly frozen water, aren't they?"

"Yeah, but they come zoomin' through the inner solar system at a damned high delta-V. Cost too much to go chasin' after them."

"Really?"

"Really."

"Couldn't we pre-position a ship at a spot where the comet will come through and chip off the ice from it?"

With a slow, heavy shake of his head, Malone countered, "Yah. You sit out there and wait for the comet. It comes zooming in like a bat out of hell. You've got to match its velocity if you want to work on it, and matching its velocity takes a lot of energy."

Nodding his understanding, Junior said, "And energy means firing up your rockets."

"And firing up the rockets means using your propellants. Ain't no free lunch out there."

Junior felt as gloomy as Malone looked.

The two men spent the rest of the week scouring the old corporation's reports. Nothing came to light. No bright *aha!* moments broke their deepening gloom.

Finally, Malone heaved himself to his feet and said, "We stay at this much longer, we're both gonna turn into pumpkins. Let's get some dinner."

Pumpkins? Junior wondered. But he got up from his chair and said merely, "Good idea. Where do you want to go?"

"Pelican Bar."

Junior had heard of the place. Owned by a fugitive from drowned Miami, Florida. Decorated with half a zillion photos, paintings, and statuettes of pelicans.

But he said, "How about Dante's Inferno?"

Malone scowled. "That's a couple hour's tram ride from here. Out in Hell's Crater."

"Yeah, but there's somebody there I want to see."

"A woman, huh?"

"That's right."

"Easy way to spend money, kid."

"I'll pay for our dinners."

For a few seconds, Malone stood behind his desk, silent, appraising Junior with a skeptical expression on his dark face. At last he shrugged his bulky shoulders and said, "Okay. Why the hell not?"

"Thanks!" said Junior.

"You're payin'."

"Right!" said Junior happily. But as they made their way toward the tram system's terminal, he wondered if he had enough credit in his account to pay for an evening at Dante's Inferno.

GOING TO HELL

The tram was built like a bus, except that it had no wheels and was instead hanging from an overhead cable that whisked Junior and Malone over the ringwall mountains circling Alphonsus Crater and out across the Mare Nubium toward Hell Crater.

Junior spent the two-hour-long ride goggling at the view as they sped toward Hell.

"That's the Straight Wall!" he marveled as the tram hurtled along.

Malone, who had spent much of his life on the Moon, was nowhere near as impressed.

The tram was half-filled with passengers, mostly men of various ages, who joked loudly about "going to Hell."

Malone asked Junior, "Did you know that this whole Hell Crater complex was Sam's idea?"

"Really?" Junior asked.

"Yep. The little SOB thought it would be funny to build a Sin City complex in Hell."

"But there's nothing illegal about it, is there?"

"Nope. The New Morality hasn't been able to clamp their

mother-lovin' controls on the Moon." Then Malone grinned and added, "Thank God."

"So Sam's operation is legitimate."

"So far. The crater was named after a Catholic priest, some Austrian dude named Maximilian Hell, or something like that. An astronomer."

"And now it's an entertainment center," said Junior.

"Sex palace," Malone corrected. "Sam went broke building the joint. He sold it to Rockledge Industries for peanuts."

"Just like him," Junior muttered.

At last the hurtling bullet-shaped vehicle slowed noticeably as it climbed the mountains circling Hell Crater and glided into the dome that covered the "recreation" center there.

Malone heaved himself to his feet and Junior stood up beside him. They joined the other passengers exiting the tram and entered the dome that housed the Hell Crater entertainment complex.

The dome's decor was far from subtle. Its interior was painted a lurid red, with a huge sign overhead that flashed the message, WELCOME TO HELL!

Junior felt his face pulling into an unhappy frown. "They're not very subtle about it, are they?"

Malone shrugged. "Pays to advertise."

Most of the tram's passengers trooped directly to Dante's Inferno, the entrance to which was a couple of dozen meters from the tram station. Junior saw a blood-red building designed like a fantasy palace with another garish sign blinking on and off. A huge Asian in a costume designed to look like traditional garments stood at the door, grinning and offering each arriving customer a repeated, "Welcome to Hell" greeting.

Junior found the greeting obnoxious, almost disgusting.

But the men shuffling through the entrance grinned and made loud jokes about it.

Inside, the nightclub was arranged like a smallish auditorium, with rows of seats stacked up around a central open stage. An orchestra was seated to one side, already playing reedy, seedy tunes.

Malone and Junior were escorted to a pair of seats halfway between the entrance and the stage. The seats were banked up steeply enough so that their view of the stage was unobstructed by the men sitting in front of them.

Their seats had little arms on them, almost like the desks Junior remembered from school in Nevada. Scantilly clad waitresses glided among the rows of customers, who were almost entirely males ranging in age from sixteen to bald and wizened. The theater was abuzz with expectant chatter.

DANTE'S INFERNO

Suddenly the band exuded a blaring fanfare, and a single male personage—in a red devil's costume, complete with twitching tail, cape, and pitchfork—came prancing out to center stage.

"Good evening!" he shouted, his voice amplified almost painfully. "Welcome to Dante's Inferno! You're gonna have a helluva good time tonight!"

The audience cheered lustily.

The emcee promised "unearthly delights" and "voluptuous beauties to entertain your every desire." The nearly entirely male audience cheered and hooted. Junior glanced over his shoulder at Malone, who sat quietly in his seat, looking almost bored.

Is he a homosexual? Junior suddenly wondered.

"Let the show begin!" the emcee shouted. Junior winced at the sound volume but the rest of the audience yowled with delighted expectation.

And from the wings on both sides of the stage pranced twenty naked women.

Junior blinked and realized that they weren't totally naked. But their costumes—such as they were—left very little to the imagination. They writhed and wriggled across the stage, showing their considerable physical assets to the howling, exuberant audience.

Junior stared at the dancers, trying to find Deborah's face in the chorus. They were all done up in piled-high blonde wings, decorated with blood-red lightning bolts. He saw that they wore impossibly high-heeled thigh-high boots, also blood-red, and longish gloves of the same color. But the rest of their costumes were close to nonexistent.

Their dance was erotic and very provocative: waggling bosoms and rhythmically swaying hips. Junior unconsciously licked his lips and felt perspiration beading on his upper lip. He strained to catch sight of Deborah, but none of the dancers looked like her.

She's not here! Junior realized. He almost felt relieved. Then he thought, *Well, maybe she'll come onstage later on.*

So he sat through the opening dance routine and the mini-drama that followed it: a three-person comedy that featured a top-heavy heroine pursued by an earnest young man and a roguish villain—who ended by triumphantly carrying the squealing heroine over his shoulder offstage while he cackled evilly.

Then the stage went dark. The show can't be over already, Junior told himself.

It wasn't. It was intermission. The theater's side lights came on, and another bevy of scantily-clad young women came prancing along the aisles, selling everything from aspirin to zinc-enriched "performance pills."

And there was Deborah!

Like all the other Belles, Deborah was practically naked: a tiny bikini-style bottom and nothing but lurid red pasties over her nipples. *They don't leave much to the imagination*, Junior thought as he goggled at her.

But she was beautiful: slim-waisted, long-legged, with a generous bosom and those sparkling gray-green eyes.

With an artificial smile pasted across her face, Deborah worked her way along the aisles of seated men, offering the wares from the tray fastened to her bare midriff.

As she made her way up the rows of customers toward the area where Junior was sitting, one of the seated men grabbed Deborah's arm and pulled her onto his lap. The goods on her tray spilled to the floor as she struggled, and the crowd roared. Junior saw red. He leaped to his feet and clambered over the men sitting between him and Deborah.

Deborah fought against the guy who was holding her, but he was laughing as he wrapped both his arms against her practically naked body. The men around him were laughing loudly, too, and shouting encouragement.

Furious, Junior grabbed the man by the back of his neck, shouting, "Let go of her!"

Surprised, the man released Deborah—who slid off his knees and bounced her rump onto the floor—and turned to face Junior. He rose up from his chair like a smoldering volcano, his face twisted with surprise and anger.

"Who th' fuck are you, shithead?" he growled as he pried Junior's fingers from his neck, then lifted him completely off his feet.

For an eternally long moment, the guy held Junior in midair, his dangling feet churning helplessly. Then the guy balled one of his massive fists and cocked it, his face grim, furious.

Junior felt something hard touch his back, then an instant of unbearable pain, then nothing. The blackness of oblivion.

MANAGER'S OFFICE

Junior awoke slowly. He blinked several times before his eyes could focus. He was in an office of some kind, with a bland, blond middle-aged man bending over him.

"He's coming out of it," the man said to someone standing behind him.

The other man was small, dapper, bald with a trim little dark mustache.

And standing in a corner of the office was Deborah, looking frightened, worried. She had an oversized coat draped over her bare shoulders. It covered her down to her knees.

The dapper little man stepped up to the couch on which Junior was lying.

"We do not tolerate rowdyism in this club!" the man said sharply.

A door opened and Malone stepped in. Suddenly the office felt crowded, with the big man looking sternly down at Junior.

"He was trying to protect me," Deborah said, in a quavering voice.

"Protect you?" the dapper man snapped. "This is Dante's Inferno, not a Sunday school!"

"That guy was pawing her," Junior growled.

"So?"

"He's new here," Malone tried to explain. "He didn't know what to expect."

The dapper man turned out to be the club's manager. And he was very angry. "You could have started a riot!" he exclaimed. "You're lucky the man you attacked refused to press charges against you."

"He was pawing her," Junior repeated.

Exasperated, the manager snapped, "What's that got to do with it? What did you expect? A fucking ballet recital?"

Junior hung his head.

"He was trying to protect me," Deborah said again. "He didn't know the rules."

The manager fussed and fumed for several long moments. Junior almost thought he could see steam venting from his ears.

Finally, he pointed a stubby finger at Junior and said, "You're banned from this club. For life! I don't want to see your face again. Ever!"

Before Junior could think of anything to say, the manager whirled to face Deborah. "And you're fired! I don't want to see—"

"Fired?" Deborah looked shocked. "Why? What did I do?"

"You nearly started a riot!"

"It wasn't her fault," Junior said, pushing himself to his feet.

"I don't care! She's fired and you're banned. Now get out of here, both of you. I don't want to see your faces again. Ever!"

Malone, looking grim, opened the office door. Junior crossed over to Deborah, who said, "I'll have to change."

The manager stood in the middle of the office, next to his elaborately decorated desk, pouting angrily.

"Come on," said Malone, gesturing for Junior and Deborah to leave.

The three of them walked down a short corridor to the troupe's dressing room. Junior could hear the band's music blaring from the club's stage. The show was going on, in the finest old show biz tradition.

Deborah hesitated in front of the dressing room door. "Ladies only," she said to Junior, in a near-whisper.

"Oh," he said, reddening slightly. Stepping aside, he added, "We'll wait for you out here."

Deborah entered the dressing room and shut its door firmly behind her. Junior fidgeted out in the hallway.

"You okay?" Malone asked.

Junior thought a moment, then replied, "I feel kind of stupid."

"This isn't your type of place," said Malone.

"I guess not."

"Your father would have loved it."

"I'm not my father," Junior replied. Somehow that realization made him feel even lower.

Malone seemed to run out of words. The two of them stood in the hallway, fidgeting, waiting.

At last Deborah reappeared, wearing a knee-length mauve dress and clutching a portfolio-sized bag in both her hands.

Malone led them along the hallway, to a door that opened onto the wide public space of the Hell Crater dome. People were walking by, couples, singles, even a few families with small children.

And standing less than a dozen meters in front of them was the guy Junior had attacked in the nightclub. With two other men behind him.

"I thought you'd sneak out this way," he said, almost sneering at Junior.

Spreading his hands, palms outward, Junior said, "I want to apologize about what I did in there."

"Yeah."

"I'm sorry about it."

"Sure." The guy jabbed a forefinger in Deborah's direction. "And you, cutie, you owe me a good time."

Deborah stood frozen, eyes wide, gasping.

Malone took a step toward the three of them. "Now look, buddy—"

"Naw, you look. Your friend made me look like an asshole in there. He's gotta pay for that."

"How much?" Junior asked.

The guy blinked. "How much?"

With the beginnings of a smile, Junior said, "How much money will soothe your hurt feelings?"

"Money? I don't want money. I want your blood."

Shaking his head, Junior stepped closer to the guy as he said, "Money's more practical. How much do you want?"

With a tight grin, the guy said, "I just want to pound your head into the pavement, kid."

"I wouldn't like that."

"I figured. It's kinda painful."

"You need the three of you to accomplish that?"

Looking Junior's spare figure up and down, the guy answered, with a smirk, "Nah, I ought to be able to do it all by myself."

Malone started, "Now wait a minute—"

The guy turned his eyes toward Malone. "Shuddup, gimpy."

Junior's right foot flashed out and caught the guy's knee. He hollered "Ow!" and collapsed to the ground. His two friends looked startled, uncertain.

His voice suddenly strong, commanding, Junior told the two of them, "Pick your friend off the pavement and take him to the nearest infirmary. He won't be able to walk for a few days."

Malone's eyes goggled as the two of them did what Junior

told them. He turned toward Junior, who stood with his fists clenched and Deborah standing behind him.

"What the hell was that?"

"Street fighting," said Junior tightly, his eyes still on the retreating trio. "I took video lessons back home—when my mother wasn't watching."

Deborah clutched Junior's arm, and he went with her and Malone back to the tram station and Selene City.

THE DIAMOND CARTEL

The calling card read, *Chou Chang, Manager, Shepard Golf Course.*

Puzzled, Junior looked up from the card to the Chinese gentleman who was sitting in front of his desk. The man was dressed in dark gray slacks and a checkered jacket with a flower in its lapel.

"Golf course?" Junior asked. Malone had given Junior this bare little office, next to his own, shaking his head unhappily at the realization that S. Gunn Enterprises, Unlimited, was still steadily sinking into a sea of red indebtedness.

Chang smiled minimally. "Sam gave me the golf course as a wedding gift. Actually, he gave it to my bride and me. She's the course's pro, of course."

Puzzled, Junior echoed, "Of course."

"I understand you are Sam's son," said Chang.

Junior nodded. Then, "What can I do for you, sir?"

Chang's smile changed. Just a bit, but it was different from what it had been a moment earlier.

"I have an uncle, back Earthside . . ."

"And?" Junior prompted.

"One of his oldest friends is a jeweler," Chang said as he

reached into his jacket's side pocket. "He asked me to give this to you." He pulled out a small, dark box.

"A gift?" Junior asked.

"A token of his esteem."

"Esteem?" Junior echoed. "From a man I've never met?"

Chang dipped his head slightly. "And from the organization he represents."

Junior reached out to Chang's extended hand and took the jewel box in his own hand. He opened it, and saw a gleaming, beautifully worked ring inside, with a large diamond sparkling at its center.

"Wow!" Junior exclaimed, then immediately frowned at his sudden, surprised lack of self-control.

Chang sat there before Junior's desk. The office suddenly looked shabby, threadbare.

"I'm overwhelmed," Junior said, with an honest smile.

"I am pleased," said Chang.

Junior's mind was racing. The organization that the jeweler represents must be the ever-loving diamond cartel. Has to be!

He had spent the previous week and a half wondering how he could contact the diamond cartel. And now the cartel had contacted him!

Still as calm as ever, Chang said, "My friends understand that your company has found gemstone-quality diamonds among the asteroids you are mining."

Trying to control his excitement, Junior nodded and said, "Yes, we have."

Reaching down to the bottom drawer of his desk Junior touched the fingerprint-sensitive button that unlocked it, then opened the drawer and pulled out an oblong box. He placed it on his desktop and opened it.

Chang's eyes widened. The box was filled with more than

two dozen gem-quality diamonds, beautifully cut and polished. *I didn't have to contact the cartel*, he said to himself. *The jeweler who worked on these made the contact for me.*

For what seemed like an eternity, Junior and Chang stared at the glittering stones. At last Junior broke the silence:

Pointing to the diamonds, Junior explained, "We found these in a few of the asteroids we've been mining."

"So many," Chang breathed.

"Yes. And there are millions more such asteroids out in the Belt."

Chang couldn't seem to take his eyes off the diamonds. Junior reached into the box, scooped up a few of them, and handed them to Chang.

The man raised a hand in protest. "I couldn't."

"Sure, you can," said Junior. "Send them back Earthside and let your friends examine them. I'm sure they'll be interested."

"You don't seem to understand."

"Oh?"

"The cartel does not want more diamonds. That would only drive down the price for the stones."

"Oh?" Junior repeated, trying to make it sound surprised, uncertain.

"A vast increase in supply would destroy the market value of the gems we find on Earth."

"I hadn't thought of that," Junior lied.

For several long, silent moments the two men stared at each other, both of them trying to pry into the brain of the other.

At last Chang said, "Your father was very generous to me."

"He was a generous man, I'm told."

"The men who manage the diamond cartel can be generous, also."

"They can?"

"Make no mistake," Chang went on, his tone changing, suddenly hard, dangerous. "Men have been killed over precious stones. Whole cities have been ravaged."

"In the past," Junior amended.

"In the present," Chang corrected. "And perhaps in the future."

"Sounds brutal."

"It can be. The cartel has operated peacefully, for the most part, over the past few generations. But they have claws. And teeth."

"And they don't want their nice little operation threatened by an influx of stones from space."

"Exactly so."

Junior studied Chang's face. The man wasn't perspiring, he didn't seem to be nervous at all. But there was iron in his voice as he said, "The cartel will not tolerate a sudden influx of gem-quality stones from space."

Junior hesitated a moment before answering, "I suppose I can't blame them. It would destroy everything they've worked for over so many generations."

"Exactly so," Chang repeated.

"So what does the cartel propose to do?"

Now Chang hesitated. Junior thought he could see the wheels spinning inside his head.

At last he said, "You must not offer your gemstones to the Earthside market."

"And what will the cartel offer me if I agree to make such a sacrifice?"

Again Chang hesitated. Then, "You understand that I am not authorized to make a formal proposal."

"But an *in*formal proposal?" Junior prompted.

Chang cast his eyes to the ceiling, took a deep breath, then replied, "Ten million New International Dollars."

"Over what period?"

"Per year, as long as no gemstones from space are marketed Earthside."

"Ten million," Junior said, trying to sound disappointed.

"Ten million," Chang echoed.

"Per year."

"Each and every year."

It was Junior's turn to stare at the ceiling. Mentally he counted the seconds, . . . *five . . . six . . . seven . . .*

"Make it fifteen million."

"Twelve."

"Fifteen."

Chang sighed heavily. "I'd have to get authorization from Amsterdam."

Junior pushed his phone console across the desktop to Chang's reach. Then he sat back and tried to look calm as Chang phoned the cartel's headquarters.

It took nearly half an hour, but at last Chang made a half-hearted smile and agreed, "Very well. Fifteen million per year."

Trying to contain himself, Junior slowly rose from his desk chair and extended his hand toward Chang. "Thank you, sir," he said.

Chang allowed a genuine-looking smile to form on his face. "You are a wise man, Mr. Gunn. Much like your father."

Junior smiled back. "I couldn't think of higher praise. Thank you."

Junior walked Chang to his office door, said a gracious goodbye, then closed the door and leaned against it, breathless.

After nearly a full minute he went back to his desk, slid the phone console back to its regular spot, then raised his face to the ceiling and yowled a heartfelt, "YAHOO!"

"ALL WE'VE GOT . . ."

Malone was scowling as he asked, "Fifteen mil?"

"Per year," said Junior, nodding happily.

The two of them were seated in Malone's office, which was much bigger and more handsomely decorated than Junior's cubbyhole.

"And you agreed to it?"

"We shook hands on it," said Junior.

Malone shook his head unhappily. "You gave in too easily. They would've prob'ly gone a lot higher."

Junior shrugged and grinned at the older man. "Fifteen million a year should help you dig out from under our problems."

For a moment Malone said nothing. Then he conceded, "Might make the banks more willing to loan us some real money."

Junior nodded.

"But you could've gotten more from the bastards."

"Maybe."

"No maybe about it," said Malone, looking unhappy, disappointed.

"It's a good deal," Junior insisted.

Hunching his massive frame over his desktop, Malone

explained, "But you've cut us off from the market. We can't peddle the stones Earthside."

"So what?"

"So what?" Malone snapped. "So we've got a fortune in diamonds and other gems and no place to sell 'em."

"There's Selene."

"Selene's a dinky little frontier town! Less'n five thousand men, women, and children."

"Now," said Junior.

Malone's expression morphed into a puzzled frown. Before he could say anything more, Junior explained, "Ten years from now Selene's going to be a thriving metropolis. Maybe a million inhabitants. More. Plus, orbital cities in space between Earth and the Moon."

"Ten years . . ."

"And there'll be settlements on Mars—"

"Research bases."

"Towns," Junior corrected. "Cities. And orbital cities around Jupiter. Plus settlements in the Asteroid Belt. And maybe on Venus too."

Malone said sourly, "Pie in the sky, kid."

"Sure," said Junior, grinning. "So was living on the Moon, a few years ago."

Malone shook his head unhappily.

"Don't you get it? Don't you see? We're on a frontier here! We've already got a half-dozen bases here on the Moon."

"And they're gonna buy diamonds? Get real."

"You get real, Freddie. Cities are going to grow here. And on Mars. All across the solar system! In ten, twenty years there'll be more people living off-Earth than on-Earth!"

Malone's brow furrowed unhappily. "From your mouth to god's ear," he muttered.

"Trust the future, Fred! So the cartel has the Earth market to itself. All we've got is the rest of the blessed solar system!"

"I'll be damned," Malone muttered. "You're just as crazy as your father was."

Junior threw his head back and laughed heartily.

═══════════

The following week a private rocket landed at Selene's spaceport, bearing a solitary passenger, a Mr. Dano Barneveld, from Amsterdam. His only luggage was a briefcase which bore an agreement on a single sheet of paper, and an electronic bank transfer note for fifteen million New International Dollars.

He went straight from the spaceport to Frederick Mohammed Malone's office in Selene, saw that the agreement was properly signed and witnessed—by Sam Gunn Jr. and Malone, respectively—and passed the bank transfer document to Junior's waiting hand. Then he left to return to Earth.

Malone and Junior danced around the big man's desk, then repaired directly to the Pelican Bar, where the revelry lasted far into the night.

The Pelican Bar was thronged with people. True to its name, the place was festooned with pictures of pelicans, statues of pelicans, and behind the bar a constantly running video of pelicans gliding over the waters of the Atlantic Ocean lapping against Miami's bright sandy beach.

All gone now, Junior said sadly to himself. All drowned by the greenhouse flooding. Scuba divers swim in those hotels now.

Two robot bartenders trundled back and forth behind the actual bar mixing drinks for the loudly celebrating customers. The owner—jowly and fat but smiling happily—wormed his

way through the crowd to the bar, personally congratulated
Junior, then hurried off to deal with new arrivals.

Malone was quickly surrounded by a bevy of young women
who cast admiring eyes upon him. Junior was accompanied by
Deborah Salmon, who made certain that no other female got
closer than arm's length.

"You're going to have to be very careful," Deborah warned
Junior—shouted it into his ear, actually, over the uproarious
din rattling the glassware behind the bar. "Lots of women will
be coming on to you."

Junior grinned at her. "I only have eyes for you."

She cast him a worried look. "From what I've heard about
your father—"

"That was my father, Debbie. Not me."

Smiling at Junior, she asked, "So what are you going to do
with the money?"

Junior hesitated a moment as a pair of half-drunk engineers
pushed through the crowd thronging the bar and shouted loudly
enough to attract one of the robot barkeepers.

"So?" Deborah repeated.

Ticking off on his fingers, Junior said, "Use the money to
convince bankers to loan us enough to pay off the old corporation's debts and get out of this bankruptcy situation. Then
look for new ventures where we can make indecent profits.
Oh—and get married."

"Married?" Deborah looked surprised. "Sam, nobody gets
married these days."

"I do."

"But—"

Junior grasped her free hand. Her other was holding a
multi-hued concoction. "I love you, Deb."

She stared into his eyes. "I . . . I think maybe I love you too."

Junior's face broke into a wide grin. "So let's get married!"

She swallowed visibly. "Not yet. Not so soon. We hardly know each other, really."

"I love you!"

"Sam, love is a big word. And marriage is a life sentence."

"You don't want to?"

"Let's try living together first. See if we can really stand being together."

Suddenly the blare of all the conversations and music felt like a thunderous headache to Junior. It must have shown on his face, because Deborah reached out and touched his cheek.

"Did I hurt you?" she asked.

He shrugged. "A little . . . no, a lot."

"I'm sorry."

Grasping her wrist, Junior said, "Let's get out of here."

She nodded. "Good thinking."

They left Malone with the crowd at the bar and weaved through the boisterous crowd, then rode the moving stairs up to the big dome on the surface. The Plaza was very quiet. Most of Selene's residents were home in their beds at this wee hour of the morning. Wordlessly, Sam and Deborah walked out the very end of the dome, and the big curving windows that looked out at the bleak crater and its surrounding mountains. In the distance an automated tractor was methodically scooping up lunar regolith at its front end and depositing freshly-made solar cells from its rear.

"I'm sorry, Sam," Deborah whispered. "I'm just not ready to make a lifetime commitment. Not yet. I've got to take care of my mother and my little brother . . ."

He nodded wordlessly. Then he pointed toward the window. "There's the universe, out there."

She looked at the myriads of stars gleaming against the

blackness of space. "It's so big. It makes me feel like a teeny little ant."

"Makes me feel like there's a zillion places to go. To explore. To build."

For a long moment, Deborah was silent. At last, "Let's go to bed, Sam. Let's explore each other."

PIERRE D'ARGENT

Tired but happy, Junior left Deborah sleeping in bed. Quietly, quietly he showered and dressed, then made his way to his cubbyhole office, next to Malone's bigger, swankier lair.

He had no secretary, no office assistant, but his desktop computer screen showed a message in bold letters: SEE ME PDQ. MALONE.

Curious, Junior ducked out into the corridor and walked the few paces to Malone's office. He rapped on its door once, then stepped in. Malone was sitting behind his desk, staring off into the distance, looking thoughtful.

"You rubbed the lamp?" Junior asked, with a smile.

Malone stirred and looked puzzled.

"What lamp?"

"You summoned me."

Malone's perplexed scowl morphed into a begrudging smile. "We're gonna have a visitor this afternoon."

As he took one of the two cushioned chairs in front of Malone's desk, Junior asked, "Who?"

"None other than Pierre D'Argent."

Junior's eyes went wide. "The president of Rockledge Industries?"

"None other."

"He's coming here?"

"This afternoon. Arrives on the noontime shuttle."

Junior recognized the name. D'Argent and his father had tangled many times over the years. Rockledge owned several of the operations Sam Gunn had started; once Sam got an operation running profitably, he used the profits to start some new venture and sold off the older company—more than once to Rockledge.

"What does he want?" Junior asked.

Malone shrugged heavily. "Looks like he wants to meet you."

"He could have done that with a phone call."

"Don't get your back up," Malone advised. "Be nice to the man. He's the heavy-money man."

Junior nodded, but he was thinking of the stories he'd read about Rockledge's bamboozling his father out of several profitable endeavors—including the Hell Crater operation.

"Be nice to the man," Junior muttered. But in his head, he heard, *And keep your powder dry.*

———

Once they got confirmation from the spaceport that the noon shuttle would land on time, Malone went out to meet Pierre D'Argent.

"You stay here," Malone advised Junior. "Let me bring him to you."

So Junior sat in Malone's office, twiddling his thumbs and trying to stay calm. But he kept asking himself, Why's he coming here? What's he after?

Eventually, the office door slid open, and Malone ushered Pierre D'Argent in to meet Junior.

The word for Pierre D'Argent was *elegant*. Tall, slim, silver-haired, his face was smooth and unlined, a monument to cosmetic surgery, his smile warm and almost genuine. He was wearing a knife-edge-creased pair of pearl-gray trousers topped by a royal blue sports jacket, with a small but bright silver Rockledge Industries pin on his lapel.

Junior shot to his feet as the two men entered the office. Gesturing toward Junior, Malone introduced, "And this is Sam Gunn Jr."

His smile widening enough to show perfect gleaming teeth, D'Argent extended his hand. Junior took it in his own. D'Argent's grip was firm but not too much so. Just right. *Well practiced*, Junior thought.

"You're quite a bit taller than Sam," he said, in a smooth, careful baritone voice.

"My mother's genes, I guess," said Junior.

"Same hair, though. And freckles. How *Huckleberry Finn*."

Somehow, Junior detested the man.

Turning to Malone, D'Argent asked in a matter-of-fact tone, "I presume you've checked out his genetic background."

"Quite thoroughly," Malone replied.

Still smiling, D'Argent said, "I can't get over your height, young man. Why, you're almost as tall as I am. Sam was a runt."

Junior wisecracked, "And I reach all the way down to the floor."

Malone started to laugh, but quickly stifled it.

Without being asked to, D'Argent took one of the chairs in front of Malone's desk as he said, "When I heard that Sam had fathered a son, my first instinct was to ask, 'Only one?' But then I realized I had to meet you for myself, face-to-face."

Junior lowered himself tensely into the other seat while Malone limped around the desk and sat on his swivel chair.

A taut silence enveloped the room. D'Argent stared at Junior, as if he were mentally trying to peel back a mask—or perhaps peering into the past, trying to recapture his earlier dealings with Sam Senior.

Junior spoke up. "You and my father had several encounters in the past, didn't you?"

"Yes," said D'Argent, unsmiling. "The little so-and-so tried to snooker me fairly often."

"But you always made money on the deals he brought you."

"Often. Not always."

The silence fell again, briefly. Malone broke it with, "So why did you come all the way up here? Not just to see Junior, I imagine."

Carefully, D'Argent responded, "That was part of it, to see Sam Gunn's offspring."

"And the other part?" Malone prompted.

"Mars," said D'Argent.

"Mars?"

"Mars."

MARS

Junior asked, "What about Mars?"

D'Argent hesitated, his pale eyes focused on Junior like a pair of laser beams. At last he replied, "You know that the scientific team exploring Mars has discovered living creatures there."

Before Junior could respond, Malone scoffed, "Microscopic bugs, living deep underground."

D'Argent nodded. "Correct. But a few days ago, I found myself wondering what Sam would make of that discovery."

"And?" Junior prompted.

A broad smile spread across D'Argent's handsome face. "And I thought that Sam would be opening a museum on Mars, a museum dedicated to the discovery of life on the Red Planet."

Malone huffed, "You need a microscope to see the little buggers."

"The museum would be dedicated not merely to the life that's actually been found there," D'Argent quickly corrected. "The museum would have exhibits about all the fantastic ideas people have written about possible life on Mars. From H. G. Wells's Martian invaders of Earth to the many different ideas of possible Martian life from the plentiful fiction on the subject."

Junior said slowly, "Exhibits about fictitious inventions of Martian life."

"Not fictitious," D'Argent corrected. "Imaginative."

"Phony," said Malone, with more than a little disgust in his voice.

But Junior breathed, "Dejah Thoris."

"Huh?" D'Argent and Malone uttered simultaneously.

"A princess of Mars," Junior explained, "from the novels that Edgar Rice Burroughs wrote, back in the early twentieth century."

"Didn't he write the Tarzan books?"

"Yes," Junior said, "but he also wrote about John Carter, Warlord of Barsoom."

"Barsoom?"

"That's the Martian name for Mars."

D'Argent said, "I presume she was a beautiful young woman."

"And very human in appearance," Junior added.

"A worthwhile addition to our museum," D'Argent said, with a chuckle.

"We could build an animatronic robot of her. Make it look completely human," said Junior.

"And scantily dressed," D'Argent quickly agreed.

His brow furrowing slightly, Junior said, "If I remember Burroughs's novels correctly, she didn't wear much more than weapons and jewelry."

"Wonderful!" exclaimed D'Argent.

Malone brought them back to reality with, "So you want to build a museum—on Mars itself?"

"And bring tourists to it," said D'Argent, nodding happily. "Rockledge will provide the transportation."

"Good idea," Malone agreed. "Only one thing wrong with it."

Looking suddenly peeved, D'Argent snapped, "What's wrong with my idea?"

Leaning back in his creaking swivel chair, Malone answered, "The IAA won't let you do it."

"The International Astronautical Authority?" D'Argent growled. "What do they have to do with this?"

"They control all the work bein' done on Mars," said Malone. "And they don't allow any commercial developments."

D'Argent sputtered, "No commercial developments? None at all?"

Before Malone could reply Junior said, "But this wouldn't be a commercial development. It'd be educational, inspiring, intellectual!"

"Educational?"

"Intellectual?"

Bobbing his head up and down, Junior explained, "Our exhibit would show how human beings imagined Martians might be. So in our museum, we'd include exhibits about the natural conditions on Mars, how they shape the planet's environment."

"Alongside an animatronic doll of Dejah whatever her name is," D'Argent agreed.

But Malone shook his head wearily. "The IAA won't allow it. They'll see right through our scheme."

D'Argent's grin faded, and he closed his mouth with an audible click of his teeth.

But Junior said, "Then we'll just have to change their minds."

PARTING

It took several days for Junior to wangle a meeting with the chairman of the IAA's Mars committee. But once his request was confirmed, he had to tell Deborah that he'd be going Earthside for a few days.

He took her to dinner at Selene's Earthview restaurant, the finest eatery in the lunar city.

Earthview was several levels deep, built around a central spiraling staircase that curved downward from the restaurant's entrance, with intimate dining tables spaced at each level. Its walls were hung with oversized view screens that showed views of the barren plain and ring-wall mountains of the crater Alphonsus up on the surface, with the blue-and-white ever-changing Earth hanging against the darkness of space.

Junior picked up Deborah at the one-bedroom apartment they shared and the two of them walked to the moving stairs that led down to the restaurant.

Deborah seemed strangely silent as they made their way down to the Earthview's entrance. Junior had little to say, as well. He was trying to figure out the best way to tell her he was leaving for his trip to IAA headquarters in Amsterdam.

Once they were seated at an intimate table for two, Junior started to say, "I'm going Earthside in a couple of days."

Deborah's eyes flashed wide. "So am I," she said.

"You are?"

"My mother's taken a turn for the worse. The doctors aren't very optimistic about her chances."

Junior suddenly realized why she'd been so quiet. "I . . . I'm sorry to hear that."

"So am I," she said, in a barely audible whisper.

"Is it really serious?"

"Terminal, they think."

Deborah looked stricken, as if she herself were dying. Junior heard himself ask, "Is there anything I can do? Anything you need?"

She shook her head.

Pushing his chair back, Junior said, "Let's get out of here."

She nodded in agreement. Their robot waiter trundled to their table with the drinks they had ordered and stood there in mechanical astonishment as the two of them left their table and headed up the spiraling staircase to the restaurant's exit. Junior pulled a hundred-dollar note from the wad in his pocket and handed it to the astonished head waiter as they left the restaurant.

He led Deborah up to the Main Plaza and they walked in silence to its end.

Once they seated themselves on one of the stone benches and looked through the sweeping window at the desolate crater outside, Deborah broke into sobs.

Junior slid his arm around her shoulders. After holding her in silence while she wept, he whispered, "Do you want me to go with you?"

She raised her tear-streaked face to him and shook her head. "What good would that do?"

He felt his face pull into a frown. "She doesn't have to really die. We could have her frozen—"

"Frozen?"

"Until the medical profession learns how to cure what's killing her. Then we could revive her and—"

"No, Sam!" Deborah hissed, pushing away from him. "We don't believe in that."

"But it could save your mother's life."

Shaking her head almost violently, Deborah said, "When God calls you, it's wrong to try to evade His wish."

"God's got nothing to do with it," Junior said.

"He's got *everything* to do with it! My mother has been a good Christian all her life. It would be a sin for her to try to avoid God's calling her home."

Junior stared at Deborah. A thousand arguments rose in his mind, but he saw in her eyes, her rigid posture, her stubborn refusal, that she was horrified by his suggestion.

"All right," he said softly. "All right."

They sat there, gazing out at the star-spangled universe, for nearly an hour. Deborah's tears stopped flowing. Junior's mind kept spinning with the thought, *She's willing to let her mother die, rather than break her religious belief.*

It was a lesson he would never forget.

THE INTERNATIONAL
ASTRONAUTICAL
AUTHORITY

"A museum on Mars?" said Phillip Cranston. "That's impossible, I'm afraid."

Cranston was chairman of the IAA's Martian committee, a man with the power to quash Junior's request. He was a bland, inoffensive-appearing man, just about Junior's height, lean but slightly potbellied, with thinning light brown hair and strangely piercing dark eyes.

The two of them were alone in Cranston's spacious office, on the top floor of one of Amsterdam's tallest skyscrapers. Through the floor-to-ceiling windows that took up one whole wall of the office, Junior could see the streets of Amsterdam far below and the river Amstel and several canals cutting through the busy city blocks.

Somewhere children laugh and sing, Junior misquoted to himself, *somewhere hearts are light . . .* But there is no joy in Mudville—or Amsterdam, dammit.

Sitting before Cranston's broad desk, Junior asked, "Why is it impossible?"

Ticking off points on his long, lean fingers, Cranston explained in a carefully modulated tenor voice, "First, the IAA has declared the whole planet a scientific preserve. No commercial development is allowed anywhere on Mars."

"But—"

Without taking a breath, Cranston continued, "Second, if we did allow you to build your so-called museum, it would be a distraction to the workers who are patiently uncovering the history of the native Martian life forms and their deep underground ecological environment."

Junior started to object, but Cranston barreled on,

"Third, we cannot allow a stream of visitors to set foot on Mars. Who knows how their presence might affect the existing natural Martian environment?"

Trying hard to keep from frowning, Junior countered, "But if you let us have just a tiny portion of the Martian landscape, we could operate the museum without disturbing your work in any way."

Cranston shook his head. "No, no, no. Your so-called museum would be just a foot in the door. Soon you'd want to lead guided tours through the digs and allow tourists to take souvenirs home with them. It would be a disaster, a fiasco. True scientific investigation would be smothered by hordes of tourists . . . honeymooners, families with little children! Impossible."

Junior thought hordes of tourists would be very profitable, but he could see what Cranston was afraid of. How to change his mind?

"We're willing to donate the profits we make to the IAA," he said.

Still shaking his head, Cranston replied, "Crass commercialism! Never!"

For a long, silent moment the two of them sat facing each other, with Cranston's commodious desk—and his inflexible attitude—separating them.

As he stared at the uncompromising bureaucrat, Junior heard his father's voice whispering inside his head, *Make the victim a party to the crime.*

Leaning forward in his chair until he was practically nose-to-nose with Cranston, Junior said, "I'm not trying to ruin your work with crass commercialism. What I want is to show the people of Earth how important your work is, how vital to our understanding of the universe."

Cranston backed away a bit, actually rolling his desk chair slightly back from his desk. "Then you can understand why our work can't be disturbed by hordes of tourists gawking over our shoulders."

With the slightest shake of his head, Junior replied, "There won't be hordes of tourists. The trip would be too expensive for that. Only the very wealthiest people would be able to afford a visit to Mars. The elite. The cream of the crop. Business leaders and government officials. Heads of charitable organizations."

Cranston didn't reply for several breathless moments. At last he repeated, in a near whisper, "The cream of the crop."

"The *creme de la creme*," Junior whispered back to him.

Before Cranston could respond to that, Junior went on, "We could set up a review board that inspects the backgrounds of each and every person who applies for a visit to Mars. You would be on that board, of course, probably its chairman."

"Chairman . . ." Cranston breathed.

"You and your board would have absolute control over who is allowed to visit Mars and who is not. It would be an extremely prestigious position."

"Yes," said Cranston, nodding, "Prestigious."

"Rockledge Industries would provide transportation and build the museum—under your supervision and control."

"Rockledge."

"If you'd like to meet their CEO, I could arrange that for you."

Cranston hesitated a fraction of a second. "That would be necessary, I should think."

"Of course."

"The museum should be sited some distance away from where the science team is working," Cranston said. "We can't have their research work interfered with."

"We'll put it on the other side of the planet, if you like."

Nodding, Cranston said, "Not *that* far away, I should think."

"Whatever you believe would be best."

Straightening up in his chair and easing into a weak smile, Cranston said, "Young man, I think it could work! A museum on Mars, dedicated to the significant work we are doing there!"

Junior stuck out his right hand and Cranston gripped it firmly.

"You know," Cranston said as they shook hands, "I've never been to Mars myself."

Grinning happily, Junior said, "You'll be on the first ship we send there. You'll be their leader."

Cranston smiled back at Junior, visions of Mars dancing in his head.

BOOK FOUR: MARS

NANOSUITS

The expression on Junior's face showed considerable disbelief.

He and Frederick Malone were in the corporation's warehouse, in one of Selene's upper levels, standing in front of lockers that held a row of nanofabric spacesuits hanging limply in them.

Somewhat uncertainly, Junior said, "I've heard about nanosuits, of course, but I've never seen one before this."

With a weary sigh, Malone eased his bulky form onto the bench that ran in front of the row of empty suits. "Well, there they are. Just about the only product that's bringin' in any money to us."

Junior reached out and grasped one of the suits' limp, transparent arms.

Turning back to Malone, he asked, "And this protects you just as much as a regular spacesuit?"

Nodding, Malone answered, "Better. Been usin' 'em for damned near ten years now. No complaints."

Fingering the slightly slippery nanofabric, Junior muttered, "Hard to believe."

"No complaints," Malone repeated. "The team on Mars uses 'em. The Rock Rats, out in the Belt, they're our major customer."

Junior nodded.

"I know, it's hard to believe," Malone said. "But these damned tissue-paper suits give you just as much protection as the old-style triple-layer ones."

"The wonders of nanotechnology," Junior muttered.

"They're self-sealing too. Get a rip in one of 'em, and the damned stuff seals itself up before much air can leak out."

"Really?"

"Really."

"How can they do that?"

"Damned if I know. You can talk to the people in the nano-lab if you want details. Christine Cardenas came up with the stuff, back when she worked for Sam."

"She won the Nobel Prize, didn't she?"

"Yep. Smart cookie."

Junior knew that everything Malone was telling him was true, but he couldn't get past the feeling that these suits were too light, too fragile, too thin to protect somebody out in the radiation-drenched vacuum of space.

Malone broke into a wide grin. "Your father damned near won the first international golf tournament we held out on the course he built over at Hell Crater, wearing one of the first models of this kinda suit."

"Came in third, didn't he?"

Malone nodded.

"Everybody else was wearing regular types of suits," said Junior. "Cumbersome. Not much flexibility."

"With one of these nano types it's like wearing a sports coat," said Malone.

"With a bubble helmet," Junior added.

"You only need the helmet if you want to breathe," Malone joked.

Junior forced a smile.

"C'mon," said Malone. "Let's find one your size and go try it outside."

Junior nodded. But something inside him was hollering, *Hell no, I won't go.*

=====

Junior had never been outside before. He had come to the Moon in a commercial rocket—owned and operated by Rockledge Industries—and walked from its passenger compartment through an access tube into Selene's arrival port, built well beneath the Moon's stark, airless surface.

Now, as he squirmed into the gossamer nanosuit, he was about to step out onto the airless, radiation-drenched surface of the Moon. He felt only slightly comforted by the fact that Malone was coming with him—also protected by a sheer, flimsy, filmy, transparent nanosuit.

But he couldn't back away from this ordeal. Malone was watching him like his old high school principal, waiting for him to hesitate, to call a halt to this test.

That's how Junior thought of this business; it was a test. *Malone is trying to see if I have the guts that my father did.*

Okay, Dad, Junior said to himself as he and Malone pulled on the nanosuits and clumped to the airlock in Selene's bustling transportation center. *Here we go.* And, side-by-side with Malone, he stepped across the hatch's coaming and into the constricted, windowless airlock chamber.

The nanosuit was actually comfortable, Junior thought. Lightweight, flexible, it was like wearing a raincoat. He remembered from his schoolbooks how the earlier astronauts had to wear those heavy, ponderous suits and helmets like upside-down fishbowls. This nanosuit was much easier to wear, and quicker to pull on.

Still, he held his breath as the outer hatch of the airlock slowly slid open. And there stood the universe: the pockmarked barren floor of the crater Alphonsus, its weary, slumped ringwall mountains, and then the black eternity of the universe spangled with countless clouds of bright, untwinkling stars. Junior felt the stars were staring at him, waiting to see how this stripling would react to the real world.

Junior tripped slightly over the hatch's coaming as he stepped out onto the bare lunar regolith. Malone grabbed his arm and steadied him.

"Careful, man," Malone said.

Junior heard his voice in the earphones of his bubble helmet.

"I . . . I'm okay," he said, unable to move his eyes from the gleaming stars that swarmed above him.

"Gets you, don't it?"

"It sure does."

"Me too," said Malone.

Together they strode out across the barren dusty surface of the Moon, the massive Malone plodding slowly, leading Junior carefully out onto the wide expanse of the huge crater.

"Look!" Malone pointed upward.

Hanging above them, in the midst of the silent stars, was the curving blue-and-white slice of Earth, gleaming, beckoning, the home of humankind.

Our cradle, Junior thought. *But we're moving beyond it now.*

"O Lord," Malone recited, "I love the beauty of Thy house, and the place where Thy glory dwells."

"I didn't think you were religious," Junior said.

"I'm not," said Malone. Then, raising his arms heavenward, he added, "But this . . . this always gets me."

"Me too," Junior admitted.

For half an hour, Malone led Junior out across Alphonsus's barren expanse. Junior watched the remotely controlled tractors that patiently, endlessly scooped up the topmost layers of the sandy regolith and converted them into solar panels that they deposited on the ground to feed Selene's ever-growing demand for electricity. Off in the distance—almost past the short lunar horizon—Junior could see one end of the huge catapult that launched spacecraft into the wild black yonder.

And there was Selene's astronomical observatory, the big optical telescopes and rows of radio receivers standing uncovered in the vacuum of space, all pointed toward the heavens.

"A lot going on," he said to Malone.

"A lot," the big Black man agreed.

As they returned to the airlock, Junior saw his own bootprints next to Malone's. *They'll remain there for centuries!* he marveled. But then he realized, *Or until a tractor chugs over them.*

Once they got safely inside and started to peel off their nanosuits, Malone asked, "How'd you like it?"

"Terrific," Junior enthused. "I could stay out there all day."

Nodding, Malone muttered, "Raptures of the deep. Like seamen felt back when they were crossing oceans in sailing ships."

Raptures of the deep, Junior thought.

"Don't get too carried away, kid. Guys have killed themselves that way."

Junior bristled at "kid," but he said nothing.

ON TO MARS

The next few days were lonely. Deborah had left for Earth and Junior realized that Malone was the only friend he knew in Selene. He spent most of his time studying educational videos about conditions on Mars, trying to prepare himself for his upcoming trip there. But time and again he found himself thinking about Debbie, wondering how she was, where she was, if she was wondering about him.

He phoned her every day but got nothing except an automated voice saying that she would return his call as soon as she could.

Yet she never called back.

Junior began to realize how most of his father's female friends must have felt: seduced and abandoned.

But he sternly pushed those dreary thoughts aside and concentrated on preparing for his flight to Mars. Pierre D'Argent called him once, the day before his flight, to offer his best wishes. Junior chatted with the Rockledge president for a few minutes, but then D'Argent had to answer an urgent call from New Zealand and bade Junior a hasty "Bon voyage!"

Alone.

Malone went with Junior to Selene's spaceport and saw him off with a sudden bear hug.

"You call me soon's you get there," said Malone.

"Right. Sure."

"Gonna miss you, man."

"Me too," Junior said, surprised at the turmoil he felt inside as he untangled himself from Malone's grasp.

So, alone, Junior walked the length of the slightly spongy access tube and into the shuttle rocket that was to lift him to the spacecraft in orbit that would fling him to the planet Mars.

The journey took four days.

Junior tried to relax in the commodious seat he was assigned to. Takeoff from lunar orbit was mild, a mere puff of thrust and they were hurtling away from the Moon. He strained to feel some excitement, some sense of adventure. *You're going to Mars!* he told himself, time and again. But he felt only sadness to be leaving the Moon, leaving big, gruff Malone—leaving Deborah.

Junior shook his head. *I'm not leaving her. She left me. I told her I loved her, and she went flying back to her home on Earth. She left me alone.*

That evening, following the instructions playing on the screen in front of him, Junior unfolded his seat, which turned into a reasonably comfortable bed. He drifted into sleep, and if he had any dreams, he didn't remember them when he woke up.

The other passengers on the transport ship were mostly scientists on their way to conduct studies of or from Mars. Mainly two varieties of specialists: geologist types intent on digging into the Martian ground in search of microscopic life forms, and astronomers looking outward to study Mars's two tiny moons and the heaven-spanning stars.

Only a few of the passengers were not scientists. One was a bookish-looking young man, an accountant, intent on keeping the scientific studies within their assigned budgets. Another identified himself over the first night's dinner as a "groundhog," an expert, experienced tunneling engineer who intended to help the geologists study the Martian territory "as deep as my equipment can penetrate."

The third was a beautiful young woman, dark of hair and eye, a face that might have been sculpted in ancient Athens, and a long-legged, full-bosomed body that made her the center of attention of the mostly male passengers.

That first night of the flight, she sat across the dining table from Junior. Like a magnet surrounded by iron filings, she was quickly the center of everyone's attention—even the few women among the passengers.

Her name was Linda Venture, she announced in a slightly hesitant, utterly feminine soft voice. She was an archeologist, she said.

"Archeologist?" snapped the man sitting next to her, one of the geologists. "Nobody's found a trace of any intelligent species on Mars. What're you going to do when we get there?"

Her soft voice was firm and undaunted. "I'm going to study the people working there. I'm doing an investigation on how non-terrestrial conditions affect human relationships."

One of the engineers sitting several chairs down the long table spouted, "I volunteer to be one of your study subjects!"

"Me too!" several others chimed in.

But Junior, who was staring at Linda with wide eyes, found himself thinking, *Dejah Thoris! She'd be perfect to play the beautiful Princess of Mars.*

For nearly the whole flight to Mars Junior tried to work up the courage to speak to Linda Venture about posing for a portrait of Dejah Thoris. But he couldn't get her alone, away from the salivating scientists and engineers who made up the bulk of the ship's passengers.

The folding seats that the travelers slept on were hardly private, separated from one another each night by nothing more than flimsy mesh screens that dropped down from the overhead. The ship's videos called the screened-in sections "privacy cubicles," but Junior could hear whispered conversations and groaning snores as he tried to get to sleep. Not very private.

How to get Linda alone? he wondered. *I can't talk to her about posing for an image of Dejah Thoris with all these other guys crowding around us.*

What would Dad do in a situation like this? he wondered.

It was the night before their ship took up orbit around Mars that the answer came to Junior. Linda herself provided it.

As Junior was leaving the dining table, Linda got up also and walked out of the eating area a few steps behind him.

He noticed her as he opened the hatch that connected to the ship's central passageway, which ran the length of the passenger section. He held the hatch open for her.

"Thank you," she said in her semiwhisper as she stepped through.

"De nada," Junior replied.

"You speak Spanish?" she asked as they started along the passageway.

"Only a few words."

"I've always wanted to learn Spanish," she said. "Never could find the time."

Junior asked, "Have you tried the sleep learning systems? They're supposed to be pretty good."

Linda shook her head. "I heard they plant unholy suggestions in your mind while you sleep."

Unholy suggestions? Junior asked himself. Then he asked Linda, "Are you a church-goer?"

"Not really," she replied as she walked alongside Junior. "But a girl can't be too careful, you know."

By the time they got to the section of the ship where the passengers' seats had been converted into their nighttime beds, Junior and Linda were chatting amiably.

"So if you're not a scientist or an engineer," she asked, "what are you going to be doing once we land on Mars?"

"Building an educational center," Junior answered. "For tourists."

"Tourists? I thought Mars was restricted. No tourists, only scientific investigators."

Trying to look and sound professional, Junior explained, "Tourism will help pay for the scientific work."

"Really?"

"That's what we're planning for."

"That's fascinating!" Linda said, her eyes gleaming.

They had walked the length of the passenger compartment. Linda pointed to one of the screened-off bunks.

"This is my place," she said.

Junior heard himself say, "I'm not sleepy."

"Me neither."

"Let's go exploring," he suggested.

She hesitated long enough to make Junior think she was going to turn him down. Instead, her beautiful face broke into a warm smile and she said, "Sounds like fun."

EXPLORING

One end of the ship's central passageway stopped at a closed airlock marked in all caps with the message, "to be opened only by a crew member." Junior shrugged, turned Linda around, and headed in the other direction, forward, toward the ship's bridge.

There was another airlock hatch there, similarly marked. But to one side of it was a smaller hatch, with no warning prohibition on it.

His brows raised questioningly, Junior gestured toward the closed hatch. Linda hesitated a moment, then nodded her approval. Junior tapped on the electronic buttons set in the middle of the hatch. His first two combinations he tried brought no results, but then—using a simple "one, two, three" sequence—the hatch popped open.

Junior stuck his head in. It was a small enclosure with a domed top, lit only by tiny red guidance lights. Empty. No furniture at all. But when Junior helped Linda over the hatch's coaming, the cramped space brightened with soft white light.

And the dome's cover slid back, revealing a panoply of stars, strewn across the blackness of space like scatterings of dust.

"It's an observation port," Junior realized.

He heard Linda's breath sigh. It was like standing in the middle of creation, surrounded by the glories of heaven.

He pointed to one spark of light brighter than all the others. Circular. And red.

"Mars," Junior whispered.

In her little-girl voice, Linda said, "It looks awfully far away."

"Tomorrow it will look a lot closer. We'll go into orbit around it."

She nodded.

On an impulse, Junior slid his arms around her waist, pulled her close, and kissed her. Linda made no resistance. She melted into his arms and twined her own arms around Junior's neck.

"You're very beautiful," he whispered.

She said nothing, leaning her head against his chest.

For the next half-hour Junior pointed out the few constellations he could recognize against the swarms of stars clustered above their heads. Orion. Hercules. The Twins.

Then Linda asked, "Tell me about this museum you're going to build."

Junior hesitated a moment, then began, "Well . . . it's going to be all about Mars, how we humans have imagined Mars to be over the years, and what we've learned about the planet's actual condition."

"Fiction and fact," she said.

"Yes. And I thought . . . well . . . I hoped . . . that you would agree to help me."

"Help you?" Linda sounded genuinely surprised. "How could I help you?"

"By being the model for Dejah Thoris."

"Dejah who?"

For the next half-hour Junior explained about Edgar Rice

Burroughs's novels and the ravishingly beautiful Princess of Mars. Linda listened, fascinated.

Finally, she asked, "And you think I could play her part?"

"Just pose for a 3-D portrait of her, that's all you'd have to do."

She cocked a brow. "And what would my costume be?"

Junior swallowed hard. "Not much, really."

"Bare boobs?"

Swallowing again, Junior admitted, "I guess so."

"You said she wears nothing but weapons and jewelry."

"That's the way Burroughs described her."

Linda's semifrown dissolved into a warm smile. "Sounds like fun!"

"You'll do it?"

"For you, Sam. I'll do it for you."

Junior suddenly felt as if he were in zero-g, floating weightlessly, soaring among the stars.

"Wonderful!" he gushed. "I'll get the artist to alter your face, so you won't be so recognizable—"

"Oh, no!" Linda snapped. "What's the use of being the princess's model if nobody can recognize me?"

"You want people to know you posed for the animatronic model of Dejah Thoris?"

"I sure do. I want people to know when they meet us."

"Us?"

She twined her arm in his. "I'll do anything for you, Sam. Anything at all."

Junior's knees suddenly went weak.

MARSBASE

The next morning their spacecraft took up orbit around Mars. Junior stared at the video images of the planet: it was a world of reddish dust, peppered with craters from meteoric impacts, split by the enormous Valles Marineris, a jagged rift that ran nearly halfway around the planet, like the open wound of a gigantic knife slash. Further west were the immense shield volcanoes, including mighty Olympus Mons, the biggest, tallest volcano in the solar system, nearly three times taller than Mt. Everest, on Earth.

Pointing to the video screen image of Olympus Mons and its yawning crater, Junior told Linda, "You could drop Mt. Everest down into that crater, it's so big."

Linda breathed, "Gosh!"

The camp that the Earth-born explorers had established was perched on the northern rim of the Valles Marineris, near its end. In a telescopic image of the camp, Junior could see a cluster of plastic domes linked by what looked like tubes and a maze of tractor tracks in the reddish ground surrounding everything. Home sweet home for the scientists.

"That's where we'll be living," Junior told Linda, "until we establish our own base."

"Where will that be?" she asked.

With a shrug, Junior replied, "Don't know yet. We haven't settled on a site."

===

"Definitely not!"

Junior's mouth dropped open. "But Dr. Cranston is in favor—"

"*Mister* Cranston is a deskbound bureaucrat back in Amsterdam. I'm the director of this operation and I say we're not going to have a goddamned museum here and tourists sashaying through our base, sticking their greedy fingers into the work my people are doing."

Jeremy Wexler was sitting behind his delicate little desk, frowning mightily. Director of the Mars exploration operations, Wexler was a smallish man, narrow shoulders, sunken chest, and deep brown eyes that glittered with enraged passion.

Sitting in front of Wexler's desk, Junior felt confused, totally surprised by Wexler's flat refusal to even consider his plan to build a museum somewhere on Mars.

"It won't interfere with your work," he objected.

"The hell it won't!" Wexler leaned forward in his skimpy little desk chair and jabbed an angry finger at Junior. "I'm not going to have you disrupting the work we're trying to do here, building a goddamned museum and bringing goddamned tourists up here to gawk at us."

"Mr. Cranston okayed the idea," Junior said. It sounded pitifully weak, even to himself.

"Cranston is a paper-shuffling bureaucrat who doesn't know his ass from his elbow," Wexler fulminated. "I will *not* have him or any other goofball in Amsterdam interfere with the work we're doing here on Mars. And that's final!"

Junior stared at the man. His face was red, his eyes blazing. His hostility was like a brick wall blocking everything Junior wanted to accomplish.

"But we won't interfere with the work you're doing," Junior pleaded. "We could site the museum on the other side of Mars, if you like. You and your people won't even know we're here."

"Like hell."

"But—"

"The answer is NO!" Wexler shouted, rising halfway up from his swivel chair. "Now get the hell out of here before I call security and have you thrown out!"

Slowly, with a growing anger simmering inside him, Junior got up from his chair and walked to the door. He opened it, hesitated, look back at the man.

"OUT!" Wexler yelled.

Junior stepped out of the narrow little office and softly shut its door. *The whole project is ruined*, he thought. *Worst of all, Linda will see me as a flop, a failure. She'll never get the chance to pose as Dejah Thoris and it'll be all my fault.*

He looked around Wexler's outer office. It wasn't much: just three tiny desks with two guys and a young woman sitting at them, their eyes intently focused on their desktop screens.

They could hear Wexler shouting at me, Junior realized. The three of them sat stiffly at their places, none of them willing to even glance in Junior's direction.

Alone, defeated, Junior left the outer office and headed down the empty corridor to the room that had been assigned to him.

═══════

Junior searched for Linda. Marsbase wasn't big enough for her to find many places to hide from him, yet he couldn't locate her anywhere, not in the little knot of laboratories at one end of the circular base, not in the empty cafeteria, the minuscule kitchen, not even in the warehouse-like supply section, where the base's scientific equipment and life-support provisions were housed.

Could she have gone outside? Alone? The cold hand of fear tightened Junior's innards. He rushed to the main airlock, feeling panic rising inside him.

"The woman you came here with?" asked the staffer who was sitting in front of the airlock's main hatch. "Yeah, she went out about half an hour ago—with three of the geologists."

"Where'd they go?"

The guy shrugged. *He can't be much older than I am*, Junior said to himself. *And he's a scientist or engineer, part of this Mars project. I'm just a showbiz clown.*

But Junior squared his shoulders and asked the young man to help him put on a spacesuit. With another shrug, the fellow got up from his chair and led Junior to a set of lockers where empty suits were hanging like sets of clothes in a haberdashery shop.

Junior wormed his legs and then his arms, into one of the nanofabric suits. As the young man handed him a transparent bubble helmet he warned, "You're not supposed to go beyond the yellow markers we've sprayed on the ground. The safety team up in the tower will be watching you."

Junior nodded, anxious to get outside and find Linda.

He stepped into the airlock chamber and fidgeted impatiently while the pumps sucked out the air until the pressure in the chamber equaled that outside, on the surface of Mars. The telltale plate next to the outer hatch went from green through amber and finally to red. Junior banged his gloved fist on the control stud that opened the hatch.

And stepped out onto the surface of Mars.

It took him a moment to realize it, but when it hit him it struck like a physical blow.

I'm standing on Mars! Junior whispered to himself. He could feel his innards quaking.

The land was bare, not a twig or a leaf anywhere, all the way out to the horizon. Reddish sand, gently rising in little hillocks. Craters dotted here and there. The sky was a deep blue, almost violet, along the horizon. High overhead it was black, and a few stars twinkled, even in the midday sunshine.

He shook his head, inside his bubble helmet. "Mars," he repeated to himself out loud, almost like a prayer.

Enough gawking, he told himself. *Where's Linda?*

He saw that there were teams of spacesuited people clustered here and there around the base's domes. Most of them seemed to be working on the digging equipment, although a few were fussing with one of the telescopes that angled upward, toward the stars. Everyone was in a nanofabric spacesuit, which made it impossible to tell which one—if any of them—was Linda.

Junior lifted a hand to scratch his head but bumped into his helmet instead. Annoyed, frustrated, he looked at the control pad on his left wrist. One of its buttons was labeled INTERCOM. He pressed it.

"Control," a woman's voice crackled in his helmet's earphones.

"I'm trying to find Linda Venture," said Junior.

The voice turned snappish. "Who is this?"

"I'm a visitor: Sam Gunn."

"I thought he died."

"That was my father. I'm Sam Gunn Junior."

"Oh."

"I'm trying to find Linda Venture," he repeated. "I was told she came outside with three men a short time ago."

The voice softened. "Let me check the logs."

It took a few minutes, but the woman's voice eventually directed Junior to a large pit, where a many-wheeled vehicle was busily digging into the Martian soil. It looked to Junior like a big metallic worm, with its head buried in the pit it was digging. A row of metal buckets was running along its back, hauling up mounds of dirt from belowground.

A gaggle of half a dozen spacesuited people stood at the edge of the pit. Junior tapped the intercom button again, then kept tapping on it until he heard a babble of voices chattering away. One of them was Linda's, he recognized.

"Linda!" he shouted into his helmet's microphone, and began racing in her direction, taking great soaring leaps in the light Martian gravity.

"Sam?" her voice asked.

Relieved beyond measure, Junior loped toward the group, edging around the cumbersome digging machine. One of the figures turned toward him.

"Sam!" she cried.

He sprinted up to her and clasped Linda in his arms. Clumsily. The nanosuits were not made for romance.

OUTSIDE

It took a while to get Linda away from the digging team. They were intent on showing her—and Sam, too, they reluctantly added—the wonders of their geological work.

"We've gone down nearly two kilometers," one of the geologists proudly explained.

Junior nodded inside his bubble helmet, even though to him one hole in the ground looked pretty much like all the others. But this one was on Mars, and the digging team was examining with patient intensity each bucketful of soil that the machine hauled up.

"There are microbes in this dirt," one of the men said, jabbing a gloved finger at the latest crumbly pile.

"Martian organisms," said the lone biologist in the group.

"We're comparing them with terrestrial biota to see where they're similar, and where they differ."

"The stuff of which Nobel Prizes are made," said another geologist.

Junior peered at the sample in the plastic container that the man was holding as if it contained a holy relic. All he saw was dirt.

"The organisms are microscopic. Too small to see with the naked eye."

"But they leave a trail. See this whitish stuff?"

Junior peered at the dirt, then nodded inside his helmet.

"Martian doo-doo!"

The others all laughed, even Linda. Junior tried to keep from frowning.

Turning to Linda, he said, "I've got to talk to you." And he gestured toward the main dome of the base.

Linda nodded inside her helmet, and Junior began to lead her back to the dome.

"Remember, Linda," one of the scientists called, "dinner tonight."

"Yeah. Dinner," added another voice.

"I'll remember," she said, turning and waving at the gaggle of men.

Grasping her wrist, Junior trudged back toward the dome.

"What's the matter, Sam?" she asked. "You look pretty grim."

"Wexler won't let us set up a base here."

"Wexler? Who's he?"

"The head of the whole operation here. The king of Mars. A hardheaded bastard."

"He won't let you set up the museum here?" she asked.

"Or anywhere on the whole damned planet," said Junior.

"Then how—"

"We can't," Junior snapped. "We can't do a mother-loving thing without his approval."

"But the guy back in Amsterdam said it was okay."

Nodding inside his helmet, Junior said bleakly, "And we've got all the materials we need for the museum on their way here: dome, exhibits, construction team, everything."

Linda went silent for several minutes, while Junior fumed irritably.

As they approached the dome's main airlock, Linda said, "Maybe if I talked to him . . ."

"You?"

"Not me, really," said Linda. "Dejah Thoris."

Junior stopped in his tracks and gaped at her.

====

They argued about it for the rest of the afternoon, in Junior's austere little cubicle. By the time they started for the base's tiny cafeteria, they had reached a brittle little truce: they agreed not to bring up the subject while they were eating with the scientists.

Linda was their center of attention, of course: the best-looking woman within more than sixty million kilometers. The base's other women—scientists, engineers, office workers—all paled into unhappy insignificance next to Linda's obvious charms.

She easily held the wide-eyed attention of the men at their table. Junior fumed inwardly as these scientists and engineers behaved like gawky teenagers near her. Men from other tables dragged up their chairs to join the throng centered on Linda, each of them vying for her attention. She wore a regulation set of jeans and a long-sleeved blouse, zipped to her collar. But the clothes clung to her generous figure temptingly.

The meal seemed to stretch on for hours. Linda smiled and laughed with her admirers, while Junior bunched his fists on his lap and thought about mayhem.

At last it was finished. The last scrap of dessert (faux apple pie) and the final bottle of fruit juice (no alcohol was allowed at the base) were consumed. Linda rose slowly from the table, smiling at the men who were obviously stripping her with their eyes.

"Thank you for a wonderful dinner," she told them. "I enjoyed every minute of it."

"So did we!" the men chorused.

As Junior led her back to their quarters, Linda teased, "You didn't have much to say, Sam."

He groused, "I couldn't get a word in edgewise with all those guys crowding around you."

"You're jealous!"

"No!" Junior snapped, then quickly added, "Yes, I guess I am."

"Good."

Without a word of discussion, Linda followed Junior into his privacy cubicle. As she closed the door quietly, she asked, with a smile on her lips, "You don't snore, do you?"

Still smiling, Linda began to pull open the Velcro fasteners of her blouse. Junior thought the noise was loud enough to wake up the entire base.

But he didn't care.

DAMN THE TORPEDOES!

Junior woke slowly the next morning. Linda was curled beside him, her lovely face relaxed, smiling.

Quietly he slipped out of the bed and padded barefoot to the microscopic alcove that housed the bathroom. As he showered in the lukewarm water coming from the spray nozzle, Junior pondered the situation he was in. The next supply rocket—due in two days—carried aboard it all the supplies for setting up the museum, and a crew to build it. But Wexler would have none of it. He wanted to send the supplies and the crew back to Earth, and Junior and Linda with them.

How to change the base director's mind? Junior asked himself, over and over. No answer came to him.

When Junior stepped back into the bedroom and began dressing, Linda was stirring deliciously beneath the sheet covering her. She opened her eyes and smiled at him.

"Good morning."

Junior smiled back. "It was a good evening too."

She giggled and opened her arms to him.

He almost stopped dressing. Almost. Instead, he muttered, "We've got to find some way to change Wexler's attitude."

"Let me try," Linda breathed.

With a firm shake of his head, Junior said, "No. That's out."

"Really?"

"Really."

"Then what are you going to do?"

Junior sank down onto the edge of the bed, next to her, and reached beneath the bed for his shoes. "I wish I knew."

"Maybe you should call Cranston, back in Amsterdam. He's Wexler's boss, isn't he?"

"He's more than sixty million kilometers from here. Wexler's in charge of this base. Master of all he surveys."

"Oh."

———

Leaving Linda to wash up and dress, Junior stepped out into the main, open area of the Mars team's dome. It was well past breakfast time, he saw. Most of the men and women were already at their desks or suiting up to go outside.

These people have made the grandest discovery in the history of human life, Junior said to himself, as he stood there watching them. *And Wexler's acting like it's his own personal property.*

And the answer to his problem suddenly popped into his mind: clear, complete . . . and maybe impossible.

Damn the torpedoes, Junior said to himself. *Full speed ahead!*

He went to one of the unoccupied consoles amid the scores of desks spread across the floor of the dome and put in a call to Pierre D'Argent, back on Earth, outlining his problem and suggesting a solution to it.

It took nearly an hour for his message to span the distance between the two worlds, and even more time before D'Argent replied. Junior did not move from the minuscule desk he sat at. He stared at the blank viewscreen as if he could make the Rockledge executive reply by sheer willpower.

As he waited he vaguely recalled a dream he had during the night before. With something of a shock, he remembered he had dreamed of Deborah. Not Linda, who was sleeping beside him. Deborah.

The memory of her haunted his consciousness. *Where is she? Why hasn't she answered my calls?*

He shook his head, almost angrily, and tried to forget about her.

Tried.

It was well past the lunch hour—Junior could tell by the way his stomach was pointedly reminding him that it was empty—before D'Argent's slickly handsome face appeared on the desktop screen.

Without preamble, the Rockledge CEO began, "I've received your message. You want to bring the president of the Astronautical Authority to Mars? Are you as insane as your father was? The president is a very busy man. He's not the type to go flying off to Mars—especially not to preside at the opening of your museum. That's nonsense!"

The distance between Mars and Earth made conversation impossibly tedious. It took more than an hour for a message to span that distance. So once D'Argent's carefully sculpted face stopped talking, Junior immediately began, "President LaBella is running for reelection next year, isn't he? What better way to show how well he's handled his job than for him to visit this outpost on Mars? It'll be sensational!"

Their haltingly awkward conversation took hours. Junior sat stubbornly at the console, using the time lag between messages to predict D'Argent's objections to his idea and create answers to him. Linda came to him several times—once with a tray of dinner—but Junior remained stubbornly at his post.

D'Argent visibly wilted as the long, awkward conversation trundled on. Sam was mopping up the last of his dessert (faux apple pie again), with Linda sitting beside him and a small crowd of Marsbase techies clustered around him, when D'Argent reluctantly threw in the towel.

"All right, all right," the Rockledge CEO finally agreed. "I'll talk to LaBella and see what he thinks of your idea."

Before Junior could reply, D'Argent added, "But he'll turn it down. I know he will."

Junior nodded, thinking, *If he says no, that'll be the end of the road.*

===

It took more than three days for the answer to reach Mars. Junior pictured in his mind how the question went from one office-bound flunky in Amsterdam to another, slowly, painfully climbing the bureaucratic ladder until it reached the president's desk.

Meanwhile, the resupply flight that carried the materials and manpower to build the museum arrived and unloaded: three men, six robots, and a small mountain of construction gear.

Wexler actually suited up and came out of the dome to grudgingly inspect the pile of materials and equipment. Junior had made certain that the stuff was deposited on the reddish Martian soil more than a kilometer from the main base. Still Wexler complained that it would interfere with his operation.

"Get it out of here right away," he snapped at Junior.

Standing beside him in a nanofabric spacesuit, Junior asked innocently, "Where do you want me to move it to?" He winced as he spoke, ending a sentence with a preposition. What would Miss McNiff say?

Wexler didn't hesitate for an instant. "I want this junk off this planet! All of it! Send it back to Earth, back where it came from!"

Junior nodded inside his helmet. "I'll have to set up a retrieval flight from Earth."

"You do that," Wexler barked. Then he turned on his booted heel and stamped back to the main dome.

Junior reluctantly started the process of setting up a retrieval flight, hoping—praying—that he'd hear from LaBella before he had to leave Mars.

BENNO LABELLA

Junior was standing out on the open Martian plain, beneath the utterly clear Martian sky, staring disconsolately at the pile of construction materials laying on the ground, gathering Martian dust. Three days had passed since his conversation with D'Argent and no word had come about his invitation to the president of the International Astronautical Authority.

Linda stood beside him, equally downcast. "Looks as if I'll never get to pose as Dejah Thoris," she said, bleakly.

He turned his head inside the fishbowl helmet of his pressure suit. With a weak little grin, Junior said, "You could always pose for me."

Also encased in a pressure suit, Linda tried to smile, but said, "It wouldn't be the same, would it?"

"No, I guess not."

The earphones in Junior's helmet gave off a warning hum. "Message incoming for you, Mr. Gunn," said the base communications system's computer.

"Message?" Junior asked. "From where?"

"Amsterdam."

Amsterdam! Headquarters of the International Astronautical Authority!

His voice trembling, "Who's it from?"

"Dr. Benno LaBella," the computer's flat, unemotional voice replied.

Junior felt a surge of elation rush through him. "Benno LaBella?" he shouted. "I'll come inside to hear what he has to say!"

Then he leaped about ten feet high in the thin, cold Martian air.

=====

Benno LaBella looked every inch the bureaucrat. Standing behind his handsomely ornate desk, he seemed too small, too shriveled for the elaborate furniture, despite his perfectly fitted midnight-blue suit. He was bald and slim—no, skinny—with narrow shoulders and a frail-looking chest. His eyes were narrow, dark, searching. His smile seemed pasted onto his pinched face.

"Mr. Gunn," he offered, with a politician's polite smile.

"Dr. LaBella," said Junior.

Then the IAA president's image froze on Junior's screen. *It'll be nearly two hours before his reply gets to me,* Junior told himself. *I ought to find something useful to do while I wait.* Instead, though, he sat at the desk staring into the desktop viewscreen's frozen image of LaBella, smiling, friendly, looking almost embalmed.

At last, as Junior was nodding off to sleep, LaBella's image came to life. "Mr. D'Argent tells me you've suggested I visit Mars."

"Yes!" Junior answered immediately. And for the next half-hour he explained about the museum he wanted to build on Mars.

Junior finished his spiel with, "We would name it in your honor, of course."

And then he waited and tried to keep himself from going insane.

It was a long, halting, maddening conversation. No, not a conversation, it was a pair of individual speeches shuttling back and forth over the more than sixty million kilometers separating Earth and Mars. Lunchtime came and went, then dinner time. Linda brought Junior a tray and he poked at it as he waited.

At one point, LaBella murmured, "You know, I'll be running for reelection next year."

Junior immediately replied, "A visit to Marsbase would show the Council how much you've accomplished."

More than two hours later, LaBella answered, "Yes, I suppose it would."

Later, the IAA president objected, "The trip would be awfully expensive. Our budget is stretched pretty tight already."

"Rockledge Industries would foot the bill," Junior replied immediately, keeping his fingers crossed. "Mr. D'Argent has assured me that he'd take care of all expenses."

"Really?" said LaBella, after a wait of some one hundred and fifty minutes.

The hours ground on, but LaBella continued talking with Junior. *As long as he doesn't say no*, Junior told himself, and he kept up the faltering, maddening semicommunication.

It was nearly midnight on Mars when LaBella finally smiled and agreed, "Young man, you've convinced me. I will go to Mars for the opening of your museum."

Junior nearly fainted from exhaustion.

JEREMY WEXLER

Junior grabbed a precious few hours of sleep, and as soon as he awoke he phoned Wexler's office.

The base director himself answered Junior's call: the Mars team was too small, too dedicated to afford secretaries.

Before Junior could speak a word, Wexler—his expression a hair's breadth away from a sour frown—said, "So you've gotten LaBella to agree to come visit us."

"And our musuem," Junior said, smiling at the desktop screen, relishing the chance to enjoy his victory.

Wexler sighed as if admitting defeat. "Very well, young man. You can build your silly little museum. But I warn you: it must not interfere with the work we're doing here. I don't care if Jesus Christ and all His apostles come to visit, I will not tolerate any interference with our work!"

With that, Wexler blanked the communications screen.

———

For good measure, Junior decided to build the museum a hefty five kilometers from the Mars team's cluster of domes. The construction went smoothly; within five days the museum was almost complete, a sizable dome set on the edge of the gigantic Valles Marineris rift.

And, in the one-room quarters that had been allotted to her back at the Mars team's base, Linda was sifting through the costumes that had been sent from Earth, preparing to pose as Dejah Thoris.

Junior was in the museum's dome, watching the construction team and its robots putting the final touches on an exhibit dedicated to the Orson Welles 1938 radio broadcast of *The War of the Worlds* that had panicked thousands of listeners who believed Martians were actually invading Earth.

His wrist phone buzzed. Junior lifted his left hand and saw that the phone screen was blanked.

"Hello," he said tentatively, wondering who was calling him.

"Would you like to see me?" Linda's voice asked.

"In costume?"

"What there is of it."

"Where are you?"

"In my quarters. Next to yours."

"I'll be right there!"

He hurried to the museum's main entrance, where the pressure suits for outside excursions were hanging, and hastily pulled on his own suit. It wasn't until he reached out to tap the airlock's control buttons that Junior realized he had forgotten to put on the suit's gloves.

You almost killed yourself, he snarled inwardly. Taking a deep, calming breath, he asked one of the construction workers to check him out in his suit.

Once outside, on the bare barren red Martian landscape, Junior clambered into one of the tractors standing idly near the dome's entrance and started the five-klick drive back to the Mars exploration team's base.

———

Rushing through the Mars base's main dome, Junior stopped at Linda's door and rapped gently upon it.

Linda's voice asked, "Who is it?"

"It's me!"

A moment's hesitation, then Junior heard the lock click. Linda's voice announced, "You may enter, Earthling."

He slid the door open and stepped inside. There, in the middle of the tiny room, stood Linda. She was wearing a few leather straps over her bare body, laden with various knives, swords, and a strangely shaped pistol.

Junior gasped, his eyes nearly popping out of his head.

"Dejah Thoris," he murmured.

"Do you like it?" Linda asked.

Junior swallowed hard, then nodded enthusiastically. He stepped to her and enfolded her in his arms. The various weapons she bore poked at him, but he hardly noticed the discomfort.

"You'd be worth fighting whole armies for," he whispered.

Twining her bare arms around Junior's neck, Linda—Dejah Thoris—whispered back, "I'd rather make love."

Junior swept her up in his arms and carried her to the bed.

DEJAH THORIS

One of the three men of the construction crew sent to erect the museum was also the team's animatronics specialist. He was a centimeter or so taller than Junior, handsome in a rugged, outdoorsy, blond way—and dedicatedly gay.

Junior spent the following morning with Linda and the specialist, observing them as the man directed Linda into various poses and snapped her picture with a hand-held tridimensional camera.

"Perfect," the specialist kept muttering as he clicked away. "You're so sexy, I'm thinking of taking the cure."

Junior did not crack a smile.

"That should do it," he said at last, well past lunchtime. "But it's going to take sheer genius to mold a robot as alluring as you are, Linda."

As the costumer left Linda's room, Junior uttered a long-held sigh of relief. Linda sank down onto the bed. "That was hard work," she breathed.

"Glad it's over," said Junior.

"Did you notice the way he kept glancing at you?" she asked. "I was getting jealous."

Junior shook his head. "You've got nothing to be jealous about."

Linda abruptly changed the subject with, "I wonder what the robot will look like."

"Nowhere near as beautiful as you."

They spent the afternoon together in bed.

═══════

After ten days of yelling, clanging, thumping construction work, at last the museum was finished, its dome—exactly five kilometers from Wexler's cluster of domes—standing near the lip of the immense Valles Marineris, waiting for President Benno LaBella to arrive on Mars and officially open it for visitors.

Weeks edged by. LaBella's office staffers in Amsterdam sent daily reports on the IAA president's agenda. The date for his trip to Mars came and went, then slipped again.

"President LaBella is a very busy man," one of his aides explained to Junior.

Sitting in his quarters in the museum's untouched dome, Junior bit his lip in frustration. And waited.

Pierre D'Argent seemed almost as worried as Junior. "At this rate," the Rockledge executive grumbled, "the blasted museum could crumble into dust before LaBella gets to dedicate it."

"Isn't there anything you could do to hurry him along?" Junior asked D'Argent's image on his desktop screen.

After the usual long wait, D'Argent shook his head woefully. "I've got a shipload of topflight people—entertainment stars, business leaders, politicians—all lined up to ride out to Mars with LaBella. But we can't get the man to nail down a definite launch date. It's maddening!"

Tell me about it, Junior said to himself.

The animatronic robot based on Linda's portrayal of Dejah Thoris was finished and standing at the museum's entrance in all its nearly naked splendor. In desperation, Junior sent a series of images of "Dejah Thoris" to LaBella's private phone number.

And was awakened in the middle of the Martian night by an urgent phone message from Amsterdam.

LaBella's round, bald face filled the screen of Junior's bedside phone.

His voice trembling slightly, the IAA president asked, "Those images you sent me . . . are they of a live human being or merely a roboticist's wet dream?"

Gazing at Linda, sleeping peacefully next to him, Junior whispered truthfully, "It's an animatronic robot, but it's based on a live human being." Then he sank back on his pillow and closed his eyes.

Nearly two hours later the phone's buzz woke Junior once more. LaBella's fleshy face was noticeably sheened with perspiration.

"This live human being," he asked, his voice trembling slightly, "she's with you, at the Mars base?"

Linda was stirring beneath the sheet covering her. Junior swiveled the phone console away from her. "Yes, sir," he said. "She's right here at Marsbase."

"Good," said LaBella, after the inevitable time lag. "Good." And he hung up.

Junior tried to get back to sleep but spent the rest of the night staring into the darkness of the bedroom.

The next morning a message arrived from Amsterdam: President LaBella would arrive at Mar-base within two weeks. Definitely.

It was a long two weeks. Junior spent much of his time going over every centimeter of the museum, making certain that each exhibit was in perfect shape—especially the animatronic version of Dejah Thoris.

Linda became strangely quiet while they waited for LaBella's arrival. D'Argent sent a list of the notables who would be traveling with the IAA president: Linda recognized most of the show business names but seemed unimpressed with the corporate and government people.

Junior kept tabs on the ship that LaBella was flying: it was a fusion-powered spacecraft, part of the IAA's private fleet. It took off from Earth orbit precisely on time and headed toward Mars without incident.

Two nights before LaBella's scheduled arrival, Junior asked Linda, "Are you nervous about all these A-list people coming here?"

Her gorgeous brown eyes went wide. "Nervous? Why should I be nervous?"

"LaBella must be fantasizing about you."

"So?" she said. "That's why he's coming here, isn't it? I'm the bait."

Sitting on the bed, looking up at her, Junior said, "The robot's the bait, actually."

She gave him a wintry smile. "He's not traveling all this way to screw a robot, Sam."

"He's not going to screw you," Junior snapped.

"Oh, isn't he?"

"No. Definitely not."

Linda's face became a rigid mask. "We'll see," she said.

TRUE LOVE

Despite Wexler's murderously unhappy frowns, all the Mars team's work was suspended on the day that LaBella arrived—accompanied by a phalanx of show business personalities and high-ranking executives of big business and government.

Junior stood beside Wexler as the shuttle rocket landed a kilometer or so from the site of the spanking new museum. The Marsbase director's resentful frown rearranged itself into an almost happy smile as LaBella appeared at the shuttle's hatch and waved to the assembled workers of the Mars team. Like everyone else, he was wearing a nanofabic pressure suit, complete with bubble helmet and life-support backpack.

Using the loudspeaker in his own helmet, Wexler bellowed, "Welcome to Mars!"

LaBella smiled broadly and continued waving as he came down the shuttle's wobbly ladder, nearly tripping on the next to the last rung. The man behind him—a handsome hunk of a Hollywood star—grabbed the IAA president's backpack and kept him from falling.

Junior couldn't help grinning. *That would have made a great publicity picture,* he thought, *LaBella landing on Mars flat on his face.*

Once he planted his booted feet on the Martian soil, LaBella read off a platitude-filled little speech that was spelled out on the inner surface of his helmet. The crowd of scientists and engineers applauded perfunctorily. And then an expectant hush fell over the crowd.

LaBella turned to Pierre D'Argent, standing beside him, and asked—in a loud voice—"So where is Dejah Thoris?"

Before D'Argent could answer, Junior stepped up to the IAA president and said in his most authoritative voice, "The Princess of Mars is waiting for you, sir, inside the museum."

"Let's go and meet her!" LaBella enthused.

The entire crowd—scientists, engineers, entertainment stars, business tycoons and government officials—swarmed toward the entrance of the museum, with Junior in the lead and LaBella trudging half a pace behind him.

They surged to the main entrance of the museum's dome. A significant traffic jam developed: the entrance could only accommodate half a dozen people at one time and *everyone* wanted to get inside to see Dejah Thoris. Most of the people—particularly the newly-arrived visitors—wanted to squirm out of their pressure suits before entering the museum proper.

Junior watched the wriggling, struggling pileup at the museum's entrance airlock, straining to keep from laughing at the traffic jam. *I should have realized that this would happen,* he told himself. *They each want to get inside and out of the damned suits.* He was barely able to keep a straight face.

The museum was staffed almost entirely by robots, squat little machines that stood by helplessly while the humans shrugged off their life-support backpacks and let them thunk to the floor, then began to pull open the suits' Velcro seals. The air in the oversized entry airlock was filled with thumps and screeches and increasingly impatient yowls.

Junior tried to impose some order on the growing chaos, but it was more and more impossible. It looked like a riot might break out at any moment.

Until an imperious female voice cried out, "Earthlings! Welcome to Mars!"

Everything stopped. Halfway out of their pressure suits, the visitors and Marsbase staff alike froze into immobility. And stared.

Standing at the hatch the led from the entryway into the museum proper, Linda—Dejah Thoris—gazed at the visitors with undisguised distaste.

The visitors gaped at her. Her lustrous dark hair falling to her bare shoulders, her beautiful figure almost fully revealed beneath her meager costume of straps and weapons, Dejah Thoris eyed the visitors from Earth with a tantalizing mixture of disdain and an amused smile.

"I am Dejah Thoris, Princess of Mars," she intoned. The crowd—overwhelmingly male—stood and ogled. "I welcome you to this temple of knowledge."

Pierre D'Argent, standing beside the floundering, fuddled LaBella, was the first to find his voice. "Thank you, oh fairest of all princesses. We bring you greetings from planet Earth."

Linda continued her masquerade, and while Junior watched, the visitors squirmed out of their pressure suits and entered the museum proper. It took more than an hour for the whole crew to get through the entranceway, and many of them didn't bother to take their pressure suits fully off themselves. But at last the entire troop was safely and contentedly inside the museum.

Linda—with D'Argent on one side of her and LaBella on the other—led the troop through the museum. They paraded past the Orson Welles exhibit and on to the Jules Verne display; past the lovingly recreated reconstructions of the primitive

NASA Viking landers and romantic presentations of the Martian visions of Cyrano de Bergerac, Percival Lowell, Ray Bradbury, and several others.

Junior worked his way to the head of the parade, pointing out the faithful representations of human imaginations about Mars, and keeping a wary eye on Linda and her two salivating companions.

INTERPLANETARY RELATIONS

It was a long, tiring, interesting day. Junior couldn't determine which segment of the crowd—the staff members of the Mars team or the newly arrived visitors—was the more interested in the museum exhibits.

But as he led the motley crew through the museum, he kept a close eye on Linda, striding purposefully in her skimpy costume, flanked on either side by LaBella and D'Argent. The Rockledge president's wife was not among the new arrivals, Junior noticed; she had stayed on Earth while D'Argent flew to Mars.

The scientists and engineers of the Mars team muttered and argued through much of the tour.

"That doesn't look much like the real landing site," Junior heard as they gathered around the *Viking I* exhibit.

Another voice grumbled, "They've got the wrong antenna on the lander."

"No, that's what was actually used."

"You're wrong."

"No, *you* are wrong."

"Hey," said a more charitable voice. "The birds landed on

Mars way back in the nineteen seventies. What difference does it make?"

A quiet but intense argument ensued. The rest of the crowd left the scientists muttering and disagreeing with each other and moved on to the next exhibit.

At last the tour of the museum ended and the visitors filed back to the main entrance—reluctantly, Junior noticed with some satisfaction. Some of them were still arguing, though.

LaBella had been silent for most of the tour. But as he tugged on his pressure suit before stepping out onto the frozen Martian landscape he said to Linda, in a slightly trembling voice, "Will the Princess of Mars deign to have dinner with a mere Earthling?"

Linda glanced not at Junior, but at D'Argent, before answering, "Yes, certainly. In the interest of interplanetary relations."

"Well spoken," said D'Argent, with a leering smile.

Looking past Junior to Wexler, Linda asked, "Can you kindly arrange for a dinner for the four of us?"

Before Wexler could reply, Junior snapped out, "Five of us, please."

Linda smiled at him. "Yes, of course. Dinner for five."

———

It was a painfully tense dinner.

The Marsbase's smallish dining room had been set up with a table for five in its center, surrounded by tables for six or more spread around it. The visiting VIPs took up those tables; the Mars team's staff—all except Wexler—had to wait for their dinners until the visitors were through.

Linda sat at the head of the central table, keeping up her impersonation of the haughty Princess of Mars. Junior seethed inwardly as he watched LaBella and D'Argent—seated on either side of Deja Thoris—both palpitating all through the meal.

At one point—just before dessert was served by the busy little robots—LaBella said to Linda, "You must come to Earth." Then he added, with a leer, "In the interests of interplanetary relations."

Linda smiled, nodded, and kept from looking Junior's way.

D'Argent chimed in, "I'm sure we could find a spot for you somewhere in Rockledge Industry's management structure."

Linda's eyes widened, Junior saw. She said, "I'm a trained physical therapist."

"Not an actress?"

"Oh no! I'm only posing as Dejah Thoris to help Sam," she dipped her chin in Junior's direction, "to get this museum underway properly."

LaBella grinned broadly. "There's no business like show business!"

D'Argent—smoother but not subtler—added, "And you show up very nicely indeed."

Junior clenched his teeth so hard he could feel them grinding painfully against one another.

———

At last dinner was finished. Junior was starting to push his chair away from the table when D'Argent announced, "Now let us drink to friendship between Earth and Mars." He summoned the nearest robot waiter with a wave of his hand.

"Champagne for everyone!" D'Argent called grandly. Within minutes a small armada of robots was pouring bubbly into long-stemmed glasses. Junior was surprised to see champagne on Mars, but a glance at D'Argent's smug smile told him that the Rockledge president had toted the liquor with him all the way from Earth.

As D'Argent grandly offered a toast to Dejah Thoris, Junior lifted his glass to his lips but didn't take a sip. He noticed that Linda did the same.

Not LaBella. The IAA president sloshed down half his glassful in one gulp, then smiled crookedly at Linda and muttered, "Must be some slot on my staff for interplanetary relations."

Toast after toast was gulped down, until at last Junior got to his feet and helped Linda out of her chair.

"Good night to you all," she said sweetly to LaBella, D'Argent, and the others. Then she took Junior's proffered arm and paraded out of the dining room, leaving the IAA president and the head of Rockledge Industries looking terribly disappointed. And angry.

JOB OFFER

At the exhibit dome's airlock, Junior and Linda pulled on their pressure suits and stepped out onto the Martian landscape. It was fully dark, and the stars hung above them, gleaming brightly.

"It's so beautiful!" Linda gasped.

Junior saw his own reflection in the tinted visor of her helmet, but he pictured in his mind how she looked.

"Not as beautiful as you," he whispered.

Linda said nothing, but he could imagine the smile on her lips.

Junior helped her up onto one of the tractors parked outside the airlock and drove her swiftly through the darkness to the main dome of the Marsbase. No one was at the airlock hatch, but Junior knew a Mars team member was on watch from inside the dome.

The two of them got through the airlock, wriggled out of their pressure suits, and headed for their quarters. Linda walked past the door to Junior's room, then turned when they reached her door.

"Goodnight, Sam," she said, then yawned. "It's been a long day."

Junior nodded. "You're tired?"

"Exhausted."

"Okay . . . Well, goodnight, then."

"See you tomorrow," Linda said, with a weary smile.

"Tomorrow." Junior kissed her lightly, then stood there as Linda opened her door, stepped into her quarters, and closed the door quietly.

Just in time. D'Argent and LaBella came tottering through the airlock hatch, followed by a half-dozen of the visitors.

"Where's the princess?" LaBella called as he wobbled past the desks, toward the sleeping quarters.

Putting a finger to his lips, Junior said softly, "Sleeping. She's had a long day."

D'Argent took Junior's hint. "So have we all. I think I'll turn in."

LaBella's high forehead puckered into a frown. "I thought we'd have a goodnight drink together."

Forcing himself to smile at the IAA president, Junior said, "Not tonight. She's really tired."

"But I thought . . ."

D'Argent smiled his oiliest and clutched LaBella's shoulder. "It's been a long day, Benno."

"But—"

"Come on," D'Argent coaxed. "I'll have a drink with you."

"It's not the same," LaBella grumbled.

As he led LaBella back toward the dome's dining area, D'Argent flicked a quick glance at Junior. It said, *You owe me one, kid.*

━━━━

Junior awoke the next morning to the sound of tapping on the door of his compartment. He sat up in the bed, swung his legs to the floor, and reached for his robe.

It was Linda at the door. No longer costumed as Dejah Thoris, she wore ordinary coveralls. Still her curvaceous figure widened Junior's eyes. He ushered her into his narrow cubicle, kissed her lightly, then padded into the minuscule bathroom for a quick shower.

Once he was dressed, Junior led Linda out to the dome's little dining section. Only a few of the Mars team's people were sitting at the tables, spooning up cereal and sipping coffee.

"Everything went well yesterday," Junior said, as they started on their breakfasts. He quickly added, "Mainly thanks to you."

She smiled modestly. "It was all your doing, Sam. You planned the whole thing: the exhibits, the costuming, the . . ."

Her voice faded into silence.

Junior changed the subject. "Did you sleep well?"

Her smile morphed into a smirk. "Someone knocked on my door after I was in bed."

"Who . . . ?"

With a shake of her long-tressed hair, she replied, "I don't know. I didn't get up to answer."

Junior frowned. "Must've been LaBella."

"Maybe."

Junior's frown deepened.

"Then my phone rang. It was Mr. D'Argent."

"Did you answer?"

"No."

"Good."

"But he left a message. Said he wanted to meet with me."

Junior said nothing.

"To discuss a position on Rockledge's personnel department," Linda went on. "He said they could use a qualified physical therapist."

"I'll bet," Junior growled.

"This could be a big chance for me, Sam. Rockledge Industries!"

"Harem girl."

SHANGHAIED

For nearly a week, Junior and Linda stayed a frosty arm's length from one another. She had several dinners with LaBella and Pierre D'Argent, and eventually announced to Junior with rapturous joy that she had been hired by Rockledge Industry's personnel department.

"Harem girl," Junior repeated sourly.

"Oh Sam," Linda said, looking genuinely distressed, "It's a big opportunity for me."

"Yeah."

She didn't try to comfort him. She didn't come to his bed. It was as if their earlier intimacies had never happened. Linda became cool, distant, aloof. Yet she was always near Junior, a former lover who had progressed beyond him.

Junior spent his days mostly in the museum, numbly showing the squad of big-name visitors that D'Argent had bought with him the details of the exhibits. Linda stayed close by, but out of his reach. The animatronic robotic presence of Dejah Thoris tore at Junior's heart every time they passed it.

After several days—and nights—of this painfully unhappy

situation, Linda came to Junior one morning, all smiles and happiness.

Junior was eating breakfast in the Marsbase cafeteria when Linda sat down next to him as if nothing had happened to separate them.

"I'm sorry I've been so . . . so distant," she said, in a soft, almost pleading tone.

Junior fumbled with the spoonful of milk-soaked cereal he was eating, his hands suddenly shaking. She was wearing ordinary coveralls, but on her they looked undeniably sexy.

"I've treated you terribly, haven't I?" she asked, repentance written on her gorgeous face.

Junior heard himself mumble, "No, I guess it's my own fault."

"A Rockledge vessel just arrived in orbit," she said, her tone subdued, wistful. "I thought . . ." Her voice died away.

Junior had to swallow trice before he could say, "You thought what?"

"Maybe you'd like to see it with me. Pierre told me it's got a private cabin for me."

"Now?"

"Now," she breathed.

Junior knew he should hesitate, he should let her wait for him to make up his mind, he should be distant, aloof . . .

But he heard himself gulp, "Okay."

So the two of them left the cafeteria, marched to the dome's main airlock, and wormed their bodies into a pair of nanofabric suits. As Junior lowered the suit's helmet over his head, he saw that his breath clouded the curving transparent bubble.

The Glassteel cleared once they went through the airlock and out onto the rust-red Martian plain. Hand in hand, like two children scampering across a playground, Junior and Linda trotted out to the squat shuttle rocket standing on the concrete pad a few hundred meters from the Mars team's cluster of domes.

A crewman was waiting for them at the base of the ladder leading up to the shuttle's hatch. Junior let Linda climb its rungs ahead of him, then followed her curvaceous figure into the shuttle's interior.

This is crazy! a part of his mind was warning him. But Junior realized that in a dispute between his mind and his gonads, his mind seldom won.

Another crewman, wearing coveralls emblazoned with a stylish Rockledge Industries logo on his chest, helped them to their seats and watched them strap in. The two of them were the ship's only passengers.

"Liftoff in five minutes," the crewman said, grinning down at them.

Junior reached out and clasped Linda's hand. Somehow his mind was asking itself where Deborah might be, how she was doing, but Linda was real and warm and smiling happily at him. That was all that really mattered, he told himself.

Liftoff pushed Junior down into his seat, but in a few minutes the rocket engines shut down and they were coasting up to a rendezvous with the Rockledge ship in orbit.

It was a little tricky getting up from his seat in zero-gravity, but Junior managed it without mishap. As did Linda, still beaming at him prettily. They went to the shuttle's hatch and through a claustrophobic access tunnel into the Rockledge vessel. A pair of hunky Rockledge crewmen helped them through the hatch and past a totally empty passenger compartment to an unmarked door.

One of the crewmen opened the door and gestured to Junior. "Step right in, sir."

The compartment was a bedroom, Junior saw. Snug, but comfortable, he thought.

Linda hesitated at the doorway. Junior extended his hand to her.

Her smile disappeared. "I'm afraid I'm not coming with you, Sam," she said—a trifle sadly.

"Not . . ." Junior felt his brow furrowing. "But I thought . . ."

"I know," said Linda. "I'm sorry."

The crewman stepped to Junior's side and he suddenly felt something cold and metallically hard press against his neck. An instant of pain, a sharp hiss, and his eyes fluttered closed.

The last thing Junior heard was Linda's voice, sounding almost sad. "Well, that's that."

BOOK FIVE: CERES

DEPARTURE

When Junior woke up, he was sprawled on the tiny compartment's bed. Alone.

Still groggy, his eyelids gummy, Junior sat up and looked around the telephone-booth-sized compartment. Alone. His legs rubbery, he slowly got to his feet and went to the door. Locked.

The speaker over the door announced, "Orbital separation in five minutes."

Orbital separation? Junior wondered. *We're leaving Mars?*

"Hey!" he shouted. "I'm not going with you! Let me out of here!"

No answer. No response at all.

Junior began to pound on the flimsy door with both his fists. "Wait up! I've got to get back to Marsbase!"

It was as if he were alone. No one replied to his shouts.

Then he heard, "Separation burn in thirty seconds . . . twenty-nine . . . twenty-eight . . ."

Junior's knees gave way. He folded down to a kneeling position as the countdown continued remorselessly.

". . . three . . . two . . . one . . . *ignition!*"

He heard the thunderous roar of the vessel's rocket engines

and felt an invisible hand push him across the pocket-size compartment. He slid into the bed feet first.

Then, as suddenly as it had started, the noise and pressure disappeared. Junior climbed to his feet, shakily, and staggered back to the locked door. Before he could touch it, though, the lock clicked and the door slid open.

One of the Rockledge crewmen glided into the compartment: an older man, gray-haired, thickset, a thin grayish beard hiding his chin. He wore faded gray coveralls, with an elegant Rockledge logo over his heart.

Eying Junior guardedly, he asked, "You okay?"

Scowling at him, Junior answered, "I'm not hurt."

"Good." The man turned back toward the door.

Junior scrambled to his feet and grabbed the man's arm. "Wait!"

He shrugged off Junior's hand with an annoyed frown. "Wait for what?"

"I'm supposed to be at Marsbase—"

With a snide little grin, the man said, "No you're not. You're supposed to be going out to Ceres. And that's where you're going."

Junior felt it like a blow to his solar plexus. "Ceres?"

"Yep. In the Asteroid Belt."

"But—"

"You're going to Ceres, kid. No two ways about it."

ON TO CERES

It was like being held in solitary confinement. Junior paced across the compartment he was locked in: one, two, three paces, then turn and go back to where he'd started from. The ship's acceleration was minimal: effective gravity felt less than he remembered from the Moon.

A burly crewman came in regularly with a pitifully skimpy meal on a tray, then reappeared half an hour later to remove it, whether Junior was finished with the food or not.

The wall screen mounted across from the foot of his bed remained blank. Junior scoured the bare little compartment but found no control wand for it. He counted the days by the lighting in the compartment. He awoke when the lights went on, slept when they turned off.

He spent his days trying to understand what was happening to him. Linda had betrayed him, that seemed pretty clear. She'd brought him up in this spacecraft and left him there, marooned, shanghaied, a prisoner on a one-way trip to Ceres. Who was behind this? LaBella? No, Junior couldn't believe that the president of the IAA could stoop to kidnapping.

D'Argent! The smiling, scheming head of Rockledge

Industries. He was behind all this. Had to be. He had the power and the cold-blooded merciless drive. Probably sitting at his desk, laughing his head off about how he snookered Sam Gunn's son.

Pierre D'Argent. His fists clenching every time he thought of the man, Junior swore that somehow, some way, he would return to Earth and wreak vengeance on him.

Then he looked around at the narrow compartment he was confined in. "Yeah," he muttered to himself. "Vengeance. Big talk for a guy who walked himself into this mess."

On the fifth day of his captivity, his door unlocked while Junior was nibbling at his meager breakfast and the thickset, gray-haired man he'd seen before stepped in, wearing the same coveralls with the Rockledge logo on his chest. The door slid shut behind him.

Junior was sitting on the bed, his breakfast tray on his lap. He looked up at the man's dark brown eyes.

"How're you doing, kid?" the man asked. His voice was flat, emotionless, like a doctor talking to a patient.

Suppressing a frown, Junior replied evenly, "I'm going slowly insane, thanks."

Without moving from the doorway, the man said, "Guess I would be too."

Junior asked, "How long are you going to keep me in this prison?"

The man made a snorting laugh. "You must be a mind reader."

Junior's brows hiked up.

Stepping to the desk chair—the room's only chair—the man sat down calmly and crossed one leg over the other. "I'm keeping you buttoned up in here because there are a few really bad apples out in the passenger compartment."

"Bad apples?"

"A couple of convicted thieves, one guy who murdered his girlfriend, another one tried to torch one of the Marsbase domes."

"That's your crew?"

"That's our passengers. They're all going to Ceres, where the Rock Rats'll sort 'em out."

Junior felt his brows knitting. "This is a prison ship?"

"It is on this run. I thought you'd be safer locked in here until we go into orbit around Ceres."

"But I'm not a criminal!" Junior snapped. "I'm a citizen of the United—"

The man raised a weary hand. "Whoever you are, whatever you are, you've got somebody pretty high up in the Rockledge pecking order pissed with you. That's why you're here."

"You can't do this! I have my rights!"

"Sure you do. But the farther from Earth you go, the less your rights count. You're going to Ceres and the Rock Rats will handle you."

"But that's not legal! You're breaking the law!"

"And getting paid damned well for it," said the older man, quite calmly.

"But—"

"Listen to me, kid. I'm the captain of this vessel. Out here, way past Mars, I'm the law. I want you to understand that, to accept it. I'm the law on this vessel and you'll do as I tell you. Period. End of discussion."

Biting back the reply he wanted to make, Junior stared at the captain for long, silent moments, his mind filled with a thousand unanswered questions.

At last he lifted the breakfast tray off his lap and put it down on the unmade bed, then got to his feet, thinking, *D'Argent. Pierre goddamned D'Argent. He's done this to me.*

Barely holding his emotions in check, Junior extended his hand toward the captain. "Thanks for letting me know where I stand."

The captain looked a little uncertain, but he stood up slowly in the light gravity and took Junior's hand. "I hope you'll find a place for yourself among the Rock Rats," he said.

Junior nodded. "Me too." But he was thinking, *I'll get back to Earth. Somehow, some way, I'll get back to Earth and make D'Argent pay for this.*

The captain turned and rapped once on the compartment's door. It slid open immediately and Junior saw two husky crewmen out in the passageway. *He's not taking any chances*, Junior thought.

The captain glided through the open doorway, then turned back to Junior. "By the way, we reach Ceres in two more days. We'll turn you over to the Rock Rats then."

Junior nodded. It wasn't until the compartment door slid shut again and he heard its lock click that Junior realized that the captain hadn't bothered to tell him his name.

THE ROCK RATS

Sure enough, two days after the captain's visit, the ship's acceleration stopped and it took up an orbit—around Ceres, Junior figured.

In his claustrophobically small compartment, Junior felt all sense of weight dwindle to nothing. Zero-g, he told himself as he floated off the floor panels. Putting up a hand to keep from bouncing off the overhead, Junior realized they must be in orbit.

Ceres was the largest body among the myriads of asteroids in the belt between Mars and Jupiter, he knew, nearly a thousand kilometers in diameter. The Rock Rats had made it their headquarters and even built a ramshackle space station orbiting the rock by connecting a string of old, discarded, unwanted spacecraft. It was better living in their makeshift habitat than down in the dusty, dreary tunnels that honeycombed Ceres itself.

Floating in his makeshift prison cell was almost fun, Junior thought, although the novelty quickly wore away. He was hovering between his bed and the compartment's desk when the door slid open once again and the captain floated in.

"Come on, we're offloading you," said the gray-haired captain.

Junior pushed himself off the nearest wall and drifted to the doorway.

The captain grabbed Junior's shoulder and pointed him down the passageway. "Took off all the prisoners first," he said, in a low murmur. "Had to trank most of 'em. No trouble that way."

Junior nodded as he followed the captain along the passageway. No other crewman was in sight.

"Everybody else is off the ship?" he asked.

"Yep. We hand you over to the Rock Rats, then we get the hell back to Mars and eventually Earth. That's where we get paid for this trip."

As he nudged himself along the passageway with fingertip taps on the walls, Junior asked, "Who pays you, Rockledge?"

"Nope. The IAA. You're the only one Rockledge is paying for."

Ahah! thought Junior. *D'Argent. And Linda's probably warming his bed.* He felt his teeth clenching.

They came to a hatch at last, standing open with a pair of crewmen on either side of it. The captain gestured Junior through it. Junior found himself in a slightly springy access tunnel.

"So long, kid," said the captain. Then, with a slight wave of his hand, he added, "Good luck."

Junior heard himself reply, "Thank you, sir."

The captain blinked with surprise, but quickly turned to his crewmen and ordered, "Close our hatch. Let's get the hell out of here."

Junior hurried to the other end of the tunnel, propelling himself with nudges against the slightly yielding walls. He soared headfirst through another open hatch and found himself in what appeared to be a reception area: desks and examination arches. But no people.

Instead of being wide and high-ceilinged, this area was long and rather narrow. *Like the inside of a spacecraft,* Junior said to himself. *But it's been gutted and then outfitted as a reception center.*

"Welcome to Ceres," said a voice. It came from the desk immediately to Junior's right. No one was sitting at it, Junior saw.

"Please step into the inspection arch," said the slightly tinny voice. "Wait there until ordered to move ahead."

Only slightly puzzled, Junior strode to the arch and stopped beneath it. He realized he was no longer in zero-g; this area had gravity—not a full Earthly gravity, it felt more like the Moon's one-sixth-g. Still, Junior felt grateful. Zero-g was fun for the first few minutes, but after that it was more trouble than it was worth.

Still alone, Junior stepped out of the inspection arch when the automated voice told him to. It felt eerie, with no one else in the entire length of the tubular area. He reasoned that this must be one of the old, abandoned spacecraft that the Rock Rats had used to build their orbiting habitat.

"What do I do now?" he asked the thin air.

The tinny voice answered, "Please present your travel papers at the next desk."

Junior walked three paces and stopped at an empty desk. The same flat, emotionless voice said, "Your papers, please."

"I don't have any papers."

"Your papers, please."

"I don't have any papers."

For several moments there was nothing but silence. Then a different voice, low, almost grumbling, said, "Hold it there. I'll be out in a sec."

It took considerably longer than a second, but at last a human figure squeezed through the hatch at the far end of the tubular inspection station. Junior watched as a very large man, with flaming red hair and beard to match, strode down the central aisle that separated the desks and archways of the area where Junior stood, gaping at him.

The huge redhead stuck out a meaty hand. "Hello, mate. I'm George Ambrose—Big George, they call me. I'm th' mayor of this fookin' outfit, God help us."

BIG GEORGE

He was really big, many centimeters taller than Junior and huge all around, with arms almost as thick as Junior's torso and a wide, expansive body that strained the seals on the faded, tatty coveralls he was wearing.

Wrapping a massive arm around Junior's shoulders, Big George marched Junior to the end of the module they were in, through a pair of airlock-type hatches, and into what looked like an office area: desks with live people working at them, arrayed in precise rows all along the lengthy, tubular area.

"I knew your father," George was saying. "Helluva bloke. Absolutely fearless, you know. Just a little chap, but 'e had the guts of a burglar, 'e did."

Junior didn't say anything. He never got the chance. Big George blathered away nonstop as he hauled Junior past the desks and to a doorway marked simply GEORGE, that slid open automatically as they approached it.

Inside was a modest office, just a desk that looked tiny with George standing next to it and a pair of straightbacked chairs in front of it. One wall was a bookcase, filled with audiovisual desks, Junior saw. The opposite wall was a viewscreen, blankly gray.

Gesturing to the chairs, George said, "Take a load off, mate."

Junior sat.

George sank onto his desk chair like an elephant being lowered by a crane. Leaning his beefy arms on the desktop, he stared at Junior for several long, silent moments.

At last, "You don't look much like 'im. 'Cept for the red hair, o'course. You're considerably taller than Sam was, and better lookin'."

"My mother's genes, I guess," said Junior.

Big George nodded ponderously. "Guess so. Sam had a kinda squidgy face. You look more like a Roman god."

Junior felt his brows hike.

"He was a good man, Sam was. No matter what they say about 'im. He was a good man."

Then why did he run away from my mother? Junior asked himself.

"Well then," said George. "What's past is past. The question now is, what're we goin' t'do with you?"

"Send me back Earthside," Junior replied immediately.

George's face contorted into a frown. At least it looked like a frown to Junior. Hard to tell, with all that thick thatch of hair and beard.

"'Fraid we can't do that, kid."

'Kid' again, Junior groused inwardly. Aloud, he asked, "Why not?"

"Somebody pretty high up in th' Rockledge peckin' order paid good money to have you sent here. So we'll have to keep you here for a while."

"How long?"

George shrugged his massive shoulders. "Depends."

"Depends on what?"

Strangely, Big George grinned at Junior. "You got your father's guts. I'll give you that."

"I want to get back to Earth."

"Yeah, I s'pose you do. But I think you'll be safer here, with us Rock Rats. At least for th' time being."

Junior started to snap out a reply but hesitated. *This man isn't an enemy. Don't turn him into one.*

"Okay," Junior said. "So I'm here for a while, is that it?"

"Part of it," George said, relaxing visibly. "Question is, what're we gonna do with you? What skills d'you have?"

Junior shrugged. "Nothing much."

"Hm," George rumbled.

"I worked on the family farm . . . until my mother died."

"Sorry to hear that."

His whole body tensing, Junior added, "And a flock of lawyers took the farm from me."

Obviously suppressing a grin, George said, "Your dad di'n't think much of lawyers, either."

"I'm pretty good with computers."

"Oh? Can you manipulate files? Insert orders into 'em? Orders that the originators di'n't put in themselves?"

That sounds illegal, Junior thought. But he shrugged and replied, "Depends on the security features in the files, I guess."

For several moments George remained silent, staring at Junior, obviously trying to assess him.

At last, "Okay . . . you'll be my assistant, pro tem. We'll try to figure out what you're good at."

Junior said, "I'd like to find a way to access my bank accounts, back Earthside."

George's shaggy brows rose. "Bank accounts?"

"My father left a fair amount of money scattered around in

banks all across the USA. I've been taking them over, proving I'm his son and heir."

With a heavy shake of his head, George muttered, "That won't do you much good out here."

"Too bad."

"Yep. Too fookin' bad." Sitting up straighter in his swivel chair, George said, "For the time bein', we'll try to figure out what you're good at."

"I don't really have much background in anything," Junior admitted.

Big George nodded heavily. "Neither did your old man, but he managed to work his way past that."

MAROONED OFF CERES

For the next few weeks, Junior worked as Big George's assistant. He quickly learned that this makeshift space station orbiting Ceres was the headquarters for the hundreds—maybe thousands—of independent miners and explorers roaming through the Asteroid Belt. Most of them were prospecting through the Belt, seeking out asteroids rich in metals or minerals that were in demand back at Earth—and the ever-growing number of space habitats hovering between Earth and its moon.

Junior had pictured in his mind the men who explored and exploited the riches of the Belt. He quickly found that his picture was almost totally wrong. Instead of rugged, pioneering individuals scouting through the asteroids like the miners he had read about in his history books, the Rock Rats were mostly college-educated mineralogists or other types of trained engineers, using the latest, most modern technological tools to seek out and develop valuable chunks of rock that floated through the vacuum of space more than four times farther from the Sun than Earth's orbit.

Many of the Rock Rats had even brought their families with them out to the Belt, men, women, and children living together in their spacecraft, searching for a big, mineral-laden rock that could make them wealthy for the rest of their lives.

Such dreams of riches were rarely fulfilled, but discoveries of iron-rich asteroids (with a few dozen tons of gold and other precious metals in them as impurities) happened often enough to keep the dreams alive.

The fundamental problem, Junior discovered, was that by the time a prospector found a profitable asteroid he had almost always run up enough bills to soak up most of the profits. The real money was being made right here at Ceres, by the clerks and shopkeepers and paper-shufflers. And by Rockledge and other Earth-based corporations.

Ceres was where the prospectors and miners came for supplies, for rest, and for relaxation. The Tinkertoy space station that Big George presided over offered supplies, comradeship, and entertainment.

Linda could have made a career for herself out here, Junior told himself. And then his mind wandered to Deborah. *Where is she? Why hasn't she returned my calls? What's happened to her?*

Gradually, Junior made new friends among the men and women who worked in the space station orbiting Ceres. Most of them weren't miners or explorers, but accountants, computer specialists, and office managers. They lived at the space station instead of roaming through the Belt in search of a fortune in minerals. And they made better livings, for the most part, than the miners and explorers.

What is it that the miners need and aren't getting? Junior asked himself. *What can I offer them that they don't have now?*

He realized that most of the people—and families—roving through the Belt seemed reasonably content with the lives they were leading. Oh, the parents worried about their children, and many of them sent their kids back Earthside for education.

But the parents remained in the Belt, or at least most of the fathers did, and continued searching, seeking, hoping for the big strike that would allow them to retire Earthside to lives of wealth and ease.

After many weeks of pondering the question, Junior finally grasped what the Rock Rats needed, what they wanted:

Security.

"A what?" Big George growled.

"An insurance system," said Junior. "Insurance for the Rock Rats, against accidents or injuries."

George's normally pleasant expression flashed into a dark scowl. "Most of the Rats have insurance policies. But th' bloody companies won't pay off when they file a claim. 'Acts of god,' they say, and then they point to the clause in the policy that lets 'em off the hook."

Sitting in front of George's undersized desk, Junior countered, "Then we can offer policies that don't have such clauses buried in their fine print."

George h'mmphed. "And go broke pretty damned quick."

"No, we demand to see God and get him personally to deny the claim. When they can't produce God—"

George broke into a laugh. "Your dad tried that once. Sued th' bloody Pope, he did."

"He did?"

"He surely did."

"And?"

George scratched at his beard as he replied, "If I remember right, they settled out of court."

"See! It can be done."

"If you've got the guts of a burglar, like Sam did."

"We sue God's representative on Earth."

"Won't work," George said. "Damned insurance companies replaced their 'acts of god' clause with something that indem-nifies His representatives on Earth."

"Indemnifies."

"That's right. Those insurance companies have whole battal-ions of lawyers workin' for 'em. Sam scared 'em good, so now they've protected themselves."

Junior raced through the possibilities in his mind. And ended up muttering, "Shit."

"WE'RE NOT ON EARTH!"

Junior toiled away as Big George's assistant, shuffling papers (computer files, actually) and trying to figure out a way to make his idea about insurance for the Rock Rats into an actual, moneymaking operation.

You need money to make money, he quickly discovered. To offer reasonable insurance policies to the Rock Rats, he needed a deep well of cash that could pay off the claims that he would quickly be faced with.

Days he worked at the stultifying, monotonous chores that Big George handed him. Nights he scoured every scrap of information he could find about funding an insurance agency.

In vain. No matter how he pored over the situation, Junior found that he needed a large pocketful of money to make an insurance operation work, much larger than the funds he had already accumulated from his father's scattered bank accounts.

Until, after a couple of months of research, he hit upon an idea that offered a faint ray of hope.

A cooperative.

"Cooperative?" George asked, frowning, when Junior bounced the idea off him.

Nodding as he sat before George's desk, Junior said, "Yes! Everybody throws in a little cash, so we can build up a reserve that's large enough to cover the claims the Rats eventually make."

George shook his head ponderously. "How on Earth are you going to get the Rats to hand you their money?"

"We're not on Earth!" Junior retorted. "We're out in the Asteroid Belt, hundreds of millions of kilometers from Earth, where the Rock Rats risk their lives every day. And their families' lives too!"

George continued his negative head-shaking. "They're not gonna pony up money for something that may never happen to 'em."

"No," said Junior. "They'll put up a little bit of money so that if—and when—something happens to them they'll be covered by our insurance fund."

"Won't work."

"Yes, it will. I'll make it work."

George fell silent and glared at Junior.

After several wordless moments, Junior pleaded, "Let me try it, George. It's worth a shot."

"Waste of time."

"Let me try."

George began to drum his fingers on his desktop. "Sounds like something your father would come up with."

Junior broke into a smile. "What better backing could I ask for?"

═══════

With George's reluctant approval, Junior went to the owner of the New Pelican Bar and asked for a job as a bartender.

The owner looked familiar to Junior. He was a roundish

fellow: round ruddy face, thinning soft auburn hair, rotund bulging belly, wide staring deep brown eyes. Then George told him that his father owned the original Pelican Bar, at Selene, on the Moon.

But that didn't make him receptive to Junior's request for a job.

"Don't need a bartender," he told Junior, with a pleasant smile. "The robots do fine."

They were sitting at one of the Pelican's tables, alone this early in the afternoon. The two robots stood behind the bar, inert, staring blankly at the nearly empty room and its clutter of images of pelicans.

Like his father's place, this bar was also decorated with images of big, ungainly pelicans—photos, paintings, statuettes, even a video of a trio of pelicans gliding over the ocean, across the beachfront hotels of Miami Beach—all drowned now in the greenhouse warming that had covered most of Florida.

"The robots are efficient," Junior granted, "but they're not much on conversation."

"Don't need conversation."

Junior stared at the man, who was still smiling in his usual pleasant, non-confrontational way.

"People come to a bar to talk, to tell their troubles, to brag about their successes—"

"They talk to each other," said the owner. "And to me. If you knew the stories I've heard over the years . . ."

"But there's only one of you."

"And you want to make it two."

"I do. I think it would be good for your business. You can't tell your troubles to a robot. You get no sympathy, no reaction."

"The robots work for free. No cost at all, except for maintenance."

Forcing himself to grin at the man, Junior said, "I'm maintenance free."

"Hmm."

"Tell you what," Junior offered. "Let me work with the robots for a week. Without pay. Then tote up how much the bar bills have come to, and I'll split the amount we've gone above the previous week's take."

The owner's face took on a crafty look. "Will you split the loss if we don't take in as much as last week?"

Without an instant's hesitation, Junior said, "Sure!"

"Okay," said the owner. "You can start tonight."

BARTENDER

The mechanics were simple. Junior went to work behind the bar, amidst the two robots and the myriad images of pelicans that festooned the establishment.

His first night no one seemed to notice him, until one of the patrons—a horny-handed, dour-faced miner—came up to the nearly empty bar and said, "You're new here, aint'cha."

Nodding and smiling, Junior answered, "This is my first night."

The miner's face twitched into a guarded smile. "How do the robots feel about you?"

"No complaints . . . so far."

The miner laughed and ordered a Daiquiri. Junior went to the bar's computer and entered "Daiquiri." Nearly a dozen different versions of the drink scrolled out on the screen.

Junior called back to the miner, "You want a—"

"I want a plain old Daiquiri," the miner shouted back. "Not one of those fancy-pants mojitos or whatever they call 'em."

Junior nodded, squinted at the recipe at the top of the computer screen, and clicked on the indicated key. The elaborate drink mixer standing next to the computer whirred and

176 | BEN BOVA

chugged for a few moments, then a frosted Martini glass filled to the brim with a pale liquid slid out of its innards.

Junior took it in his hands carefully, turned back to the bar, and deposited it in front of the miner.

The man took a sip, smacked his lips appreciatively, and said, "Not bad!"

Within less than ten minutes the bar was crowded with customers, most of them ordering elaborate drinks, testing whether Junior (and the bar's computer) could produce what they asked for.

Junior worked with a smile and handed his customers the drinks they ordered, thankful that the computer had a wider range of knowledge than the mostly male customers did.

The two robots that had been working the bar hung back, silent and unmoving, as Junior placed a motley assortment of potables before his newfound customers. In Junior's eyes somehow the automatons seemed resentful, unhappy.

But the bar's owner, watching Junior and the crowd at the bar from across the crowded room, was smiling joyfully.

═══════

It took a bit less than a week for Junior to establish himself as the Pelican Bar's favorite bartender. The customers were mostly male, although as the crowd at the bar thickened, some women inevitably joined in the conversations, the confessions, the chat.

Junior listened to their stories intently. Most of the drinkers were not miners, but residents of the Ceres-orbiting ramshackle space station. Big George Ambrose himself was a regular customer, often filling both his ham-sized fists with pitchers of beer. Laughter and good spirits echoed 'round the bar, especially when a miner who had just claimed a rich asteroid joined the crowd.

The throng swarming around the bar grew to such a size that even the two robots became busy again. Junior felt good about that; he had hated to see the man-sized automatons standing idle behind the bar. Somehow they looked sad, he thought.

Be happy in your work, Junior told himself every evening as he headed toward the Pelican Bar. Little by little the clerks and administrators and miners began unburdening their souls to Junior. He heard tales of marital betrayals, corporate chicanery, rivalries (mostly over women), and even bloody confrontations.

There was never any violence in the Pelican Bar, though. The owner usually caught the warning signs of carnage long before fists started flying and used the bartending robots to escort the belligerents outside the establishment.

"The Pelican is a place for good fellowship," he would announce to the crowd. "No fisticuffs in here."

Then one evening a slim, slight slip of a young woman showed up at the bar. She was obviously Asian, with her almond-shaped eyes as dark as space, pale-brown complexion, black hair cropped short. Junior saw that she looked—not sad, really, but downcast, serious, lost in her thoughts.

With a grin, Junior told her, "Haven't seen you in here before."

She smiled faintly. It seemed to Junior that it took her a conscious effort to go that far. "I haven't been here for a while. Been out searching for a rich strike."

He smiled back at her and introduced himself. "My name's Sam."

Her eyes widened. "Sam what?"

"Sam Gunn . . . Junior."

"You're Sam's son?"

With a happy nod, Junior acknowledged, "That's right."

Her face flashed through a dozen expressions in less than a second. "I knew your father!"

"You did?"

"Yes! I fell in love with him."

You're not the only one, Junior thought. But he said, so softly that she barely heard him over the noise of the clustering crowd, "He was a romantic guy, from what my mother told me."

"Very romantic," she acknowledged, with a sad little nod.

Junior told her, "I never knew him. My mother told me about him on her death bed."

"Oh . . . I'm sorry about that."

Junior shrugged and tried to lighten the scene. "The owner of this bar knew him."

She nodded faintly. "Sam had an army of friends . . . and enemies."

Not knowing how to react to that one, Junior asked, "What's your name?"

"Song-li Chunxi."

"That's a pretty name."

"You're a flatterer. Like your father."

Junior shook his head. "I'm not much like him. My mother raised me pretty strictly."

Her tentative smile ghosted back to her lips. She asked, "So what are you doing out here?"

Junior shrugged. "Trying to get rich."

Song-li's smile widened. "Welcome to the club."

The slim, nervous-looking guy standing at the bar next to Song-li shouted over the crowd's noise, "Hey, how do I get drink, huh?"

Junior flashed a smile at Song-li, then turned to the man. "What would you like, sir?"

"Dirty Margarita."

"On its way," said Junior. And he turned to the drink machine.

THE RRL&C
INSURANCE COMPANY

Night after night Junior listened to the customers crowding the
bar, their hopes, their plans, their ambitions, their problems.
Subtly as he could, he began to plant the idea of an insurance
fund among the (mostly) men who poured out their troubles
while Junior poured drinks for them.

"Insurance?" was their all-too-common response to Junior's
suggestions. "I got insurance from Rockwell. What do I need
with more of it?"

"Have you made a claim?" Junior would ask.

"Not since last year."

"How'd it go?"

"Bastards are still studying it."

"They haven't paid you anything?"

"Not one centavo."

Junior would shake his head sadly. "They take your money,
but they don't pay your claim."

"Yeah. So what else is new?"

Junior would hesitate, then lean closer to his customer and
offer, "We ought to set up our own insurance system. Leave
Rockledge and the other corporations out of it."

Over several weeks, Junior planted that suggestion with dozens of the bar's steadiest customers. Until . . .

"How we gonna pay for your insurance policy?" came the inevitable question.

"Chip in a small contribution," Junior would reply. "If we got enough people pooling their inputs, we could fund an insurance operation that would pay on the claims you guys make."

One of the bar's best customers—a hefty, overweight certified public accountant from Boston—became Junior's first customer.

It was late at night, well past midnight, when the CPA reached unsteadily into his pants pocket and pulled out a fistful of bills. "Here," he announced, in an overly loud voice that stilled conversations up and down the bar. "Here's my money. Sign me up."

Junior scooped up the bills and swiftly wrote the man a receipt. Smiling broadly as he handed the scrap of paper to the CPA, Junior announced, "Congratulations! You're the first customer of the Rock Rats Life and Casualty Insurance Company."

The other customers clustered around the bar sent up a thunderous cheer.

Junior became a stranger to sleep. Evenings—well into the early hours of the next day—he worked at the bar and signed up more customers for the RRL&C Insurance Company. After a few hours of sleep, he conversed with lawyers back Earthside to create an actual corporate entity, with himself as president and chief operating officer.

It was a ramshackle organization, with Big George Ambrose

as vice president and Frederick Mohammed Malone (still at
Selene, on the Moon) as treasurer. Junior trusted them both,
and figured that Malone was far enough from Ceres to avoid
becoming entangled in petty complications.

Junior's scheme almost worked.

The Earthside lawyers produced an official-looking document,
which Junior dutifully registered with the proper government
office in Amsterdam. The Rock Rats—from office workers at
Ceres to explorers and actual miners scattered through the Asteroid Belt—put up their pittances of money and received finely
printed policies. A few claims were made, mostly for minor
injuries (including a clerk's claim of eyestrain) and cheerfully
paid for.

The important thing, in Junior's estimation, was that
the RRL&C was solidly in the black. Maybe *solidly* was an
exaggeration, Junior thought, but the company was steadily
accumulating money.

Junior was becoming a popular guy: not merely the Pelican Bar's friendly bartender, but a young captain of industry.
He enjoyed the recognition; for the first time in his life, people
were admiring him.

One of his admirers was Song-li Chunxi. Junior took her to
dinner several times—very early in the evening before business
at the Pelican Bar became too demanding. Their relationship
was more friendly than romantic; Junior felt somewhat uneasy
dating a woman his father had slept with.

But all was going surprisingly well for Junior. Until Rex
Klamath showed up at the Pelican Bar one evening.

"Hey! How does a guy get a drink around here?"

Junior heard the rasping, unhappy voice. But he couldn't see who it had come from.

One of the miners looked down toward his left, then—with a lopsided grin—reached down and hauled up a dwarf and sat him on the bar's surface. He was not quite four feet tall, with a thick-looking body and stubby little arms and legs. Hair the color of a copper penny and bloodshot angry eyes.

"There ya go, little guy," said the miner.

The dwarf's squashed-in face contorted into a savage frown. "I'll let the 'little' pass this time, buddy. But don't use it again."

The miner—who looked like a fugitive from an Ivy League university back Earthside—grinned at the dwarf and raised both his hands in mock surrender.

"Well pardon me, pal. I was just trying to help you."

The dwarf's combative expression smoothed a little. "Okay. Apology accepted."

Junior put down the old-fashioned glass he had been polishing and said, "You're new here."

Almost in a snarl, the dwarf snapped, "Well ain't you a frickin' detective."

Forcing a smile, Junior said, "Welcome to the Pelican Bar. Your first drink is on the house."

"Big frickin' deal."

Leaning both his hands on the bar, Junior said, "I'm trying to be pleasant. Why are you such a grouch?"

The dwarf's unhappy expression morphed into a downright combative snarl. "Why not?" he snapped.

"You tell me," said Junior.

"So I tell you all my troubles and you make them all blow away, huh?"

Junior hesitated, forcing himself to smile instead of telling the pugnacious little man what actually sprang into his mind.

"Share the load, buddy. It helps."

"Bullshit."

Time to change the direction of this conversation, Junior said to himself. "What would you like to drink?" he asked.

"It's free, like you said?"

Junior nodded.

"Then I'll take a barrel of beer. Your best beer, not the slop you palm off on these dumbbells," he said as he gestured toward the other men lining the bar.

Junior stared at the pugnacious little person, then made himself smile. "One barrel of our finest brew, coming up." And he turned to the back of the bar, where a display of miniature beer barrels stood in a triangular pile beside the drink mixer. Junior pulled the topmost barrel from the stack of miniatures, found a funnel from the nearby drawer, and filled the little barrel to overflowing from one of the taps nearby.

"There you are," said Junior, with a smile, as he presented the minuscule barrel to the dwarf. "Do you want a glass, or will you chug it down straight from the barrel?"

All the conversations up and down the bar stilled. Everybody was staring at the dwarf, who was still sitting on the bar, looking puzzled.

Junior had never heard the place so still. *You could hear a pin drop*, he thought.

The dwarf stared at the miniature barrel for a long, silent moment. The bar's owner got up from the table where he'd been sitting, ready to order the robots to stop a brawl.

Suddenly the dwarf grabbed the tiny barrel in both his little hands, raised it over his head, and poured the beer from it. Some of it actually got down his throat, but most of it splashed over his face and shoulders.

REX KLAMATH III

The dwarf sat atop the bar drenched in beer. The crowd stood as if paralyzed, waiting for the next move.

Shaking the miniature barrel to get the last drops out of it, the dwarf broke into a big grin and handed the barrel back to Junior.

His face and shoulders soaking wet, he shouted, "Now I'll have a *dry* martini!"

The place erupted in roars of laughter. Junior took the little barrel from the dwarf's hand and shouted over the noise, "One martini coming up. Extra dry!"

One of the robots trundled up to Junior with a colorful towel in its mechanical hand and began soaking up the puddles of beer on the bar. The other robot brought a similar towel to the dwarf, who took it and mopped his face. The customers at the bar and across the saloon's scattered tables laughed heartily and began ordering fresh drinks for themselves.

Junior stuck out a hand to the dwarf. "My name's Sam. What's yours?"

Still wiping beer off his face, the dwarf extended a stumpy arm and replied, "Rex Klamath. The Third."

"I never met a Third before," said Junior.

"It's no big deal," the dwarf replied. "My father had a fantasy about being royalty or something."

Junior asked, "You're a miner?"

"Yeah."

Little by little, as he handled drink orders from the customers crowding the bar, Junior unraveled Rex Klamath's story.

He had been born into a sheep rancher's family in Australia, the youngest of four sons. His brothers were burly, strapping men. Rex was a disappointment to his father, a heartbreak to his mother. He learned very early in life to make his own way, alone, neither asking nor expecting help from anyone. His parents spent much of their meager income on his education, sending him (with one of his brothers as protector and guide) to a succession of quietly conservative private schools.

Rex did well in school and managed to face down the inevitable bullies and wiseguys who saw him as a butt for their pranks. He never let one of his schoolmates get away with the bullying. Little though he was physically, Rex Klamath earned a reputation for ferocious reaction to anyone who threatened him. Twice, he was thrown out of school for his unrelenting reaction to bullying by the bigger boys. On more than one occasion, he was hospitalized by brutal hazing. But so was the bigger schoolboy who had tried to haze him.

He left school for good when his mother died and made his way to the Asteroid Belt, dreaming of finding riches out in the dark emptiness of space. He crewed in other people's spacecraft until his father's death sent a fair inheritance to him. Rex used the money to rent a spacecraft and used the craft to search for profitable asteroids.

"Have you found any?" Junior asked.

It was late at the Pelican Bar. Merely a handful of customers were left slouching at the bar; the only table still occupied was the one where the bar's owner sat alone, nursing a vile-looking nonalcoholic drink.

"Would I still be here if I had?" Rex Klamath answered sadly.

It was an old story, Junior knew. People—mostly men—came out to the Belt to find a rich rock, get wealthy, and then head back to where they'd come from with their pockets stuffed with money. It actually happened often enough to keep the dream alive in the minds of the myriads of searchers who plied the dark emptiness year after year, making minor claims that barely kept them out of bankruptcy.

"It's that damned Rockledge and the other corporations," Klamath muttered bitterly as he sat atop the bar holding a mug of beer in both his tiny hands. "They've got everything tied up just the way they want it."

Junior nodded sympathetically. He knew what the sad little dwarf meant. The big corporations rented spacecraft and equipment to the miners, making them dependent on the corporation's generosity for their supplies, for the very air they breathed and the food they ate. When a Rock Rat laid claim to a reasonably rich asteroid, corporate lawyers swooped in and filched it from the discoverer's hands. Another asset for the corporation, while the actual discoverer hovered on the edge of bankruptcy and ruin.

Rex Klamath shook his head disconsolately. "They've got it all sewed up," he moaned. "You gotta be damned lucky to catch a break."

"Or damned smart," said Junior.

"NOW HERE'S MY PLAN . . ."

The Pelican Bar was nearly empty. Rex Klamath sat on the bar, his stumpy little legs sticking out, his tiny hands clutching the drink Junior had made for him, his oddly deformed face looking utterly gloomy.

"Damned smart? Whattaya mean?" he asked Junior.

Leaning on the other side of the nearly empty bar beside the dwarf, Junior said—very softly—"Maybe there's a way we can euchre Rockledge out of a few of the rocks."

"What the hell does 'yooker' mean?"

Trying not to frown, Junior replied, "Sort of like 'swindle.'"

Klamath grinned evilly. "Tell me more."

Junior hesitated, but a voice in his head told him, *It's now or never.*

Leaning closer to Klamath's stunted ear, Junior whispered, "We sneak the rights to the asteroids you claim."

Klamath looked up at Junior, his normal pugnacious expression replaced by a look of longing, and curiosity. For a long moment, he said nothing, but at last he whispered back, "Tell me more."

Junior looked around the nearly empty saloon. "Later. After we close."

188 | BEN BOVA

The dwarf nodded once, then turned his attention back to his drink.

═════

The Pelican Bar closed at last. Junior shooed the three remaining customers out of the front door while the owner turned off the lighted sign outside and began shutting down the interior lights.

Junior said goodnight to the owner and walked with Rex Klamath out into the central passageway of the one-time spaceship in which the bar was located.

As the two of them walked slowly toward their living quarters, Klamath asked impatiently, "So how do you figure to yooker Rockledge out of the rocks I find?"

Suppressing a smile at the dwarf's pronunciation of *euchre*, Junior asked, "How long does it take a message to get from your ship out here in the Belt to the bookkeepers on Earth?"

The dwarf pondered the question for the better part of a minute, then answered, "Depends on where in the Belt I am. Anywhere from about twenty minutes to an hour or more."

"Okay," said Junior. "Suppose you send your message about finding a new rock to me, here at Ceres, instead of to Earth."

"That'd be . . ." Klamath hesitated. Then, his face lighting up, he exclaimed, "And you send it on to Earth, claiming the rock!"

Nodding, Junior said, "And you send your claim to Rockledge ten or twenty minutes later."

"Your claim gets there first!"

"And we get the rights to auction off the rights to the rock, instead of Rockledge."

"And we get rich!"

"Instead of Rockledge."

Klamath chortled happily. But then, "The Rockledge people ain't gonna like it."

"It'll take them a while to figure it out. The bigger the organization, the longer it takes them to figure out what we're doing."

"But when they do . . . those bastards can get pretty rough."

"We'll have the law on our side," Junior said.

"Maybe. But they'll have the muscle on their side."

Cocking a brow at the dwarf, Junior challenged, "Scared?"

"Yeah. A little."

"We'll only need three or four fair-sized asteroids. Then we can retire."

Klamath went silent. Junior thought he could smell wood burning as the little man pondered the possibilities.

L'audace, toujours l'audace, Junior reminded himself.

He urged, "By the time Rockledge realizes what we've done, we'll have retired and gone back home to Earth."

"Where they can grab us more easily," Klamath muttered.

"Where there are courts of law to protect us."

With a sigh that was part reluctance and part longing for wealth, Klamath said, "Okay. What the hell. Let's see how far we can get."

Not a heroic declaration, Junior thought. *But good enough. 'Twill do.*

EUCHERING

The next three months went peacefully. Junior worked at the Pelican Bar, signing up more miners and clerks for the RRL&C Insurance Agency. Feisty little Rex Klamath took off in his rented spacecraft to search for rich asteroids to claim. Junior had occasional dinners with Song-li, but nothing deeper developed.

Then, late one night, as Junior returned to his room after closing the bar, he saw that his phone screen was blinking. "Phone answer," he called out, his usual tiredness suddenly dissolving when he saw that the call was from Rex Klamath.

The dwarf's oddly distorted face was smiling happily. "Found a good rock," he announced, with no preface. "Ought to be worth at least three or four billion."

"Have you put in a claim for it?" Junior asked.

"Not yet. Got the paperwork all set to go, though."

"Send it to me. I'll shoot it off to the authorities on Earth for official registration."

"Right!"

"Give me half an hour, then you can squirt it to Rockledge."

"Will do," said Klamath.

Junior's fingers were trembling as he sent Klamath's claim Earthward. Then he sat on the edge of his bed, unable to even think of sleeping, until the acknowledgment from Earth appeared on his computer screen.

CLAIM ACKNOWLEDGED.

We've done it! Junior said to himself. *The rock is officially ours!*

It wasn't until he was in bed, half asleep, that a voice in his head asked, *What's Rockledge's reaction going to be?*

═══

There was no reaction from Rockledge. Nothing at all. *They're not worried about one lousy asteroid,* Junior told himself. *It's small potatoes for them. Rex and I are like mice nibbling in the pantry compared to Rockledge's interplanetary operations.*

Yet still he waited for Rockledge's eventual reaction. In fear.

═══

Two asteroids they claimed with no reaction from Rockledge. Then three. Junior felt that was enough. They auctioned the mining rights to the rocks in the Astronautical Authority's interplanetary market center, in Amsterdam, without any problem. Suddenly Junior was a wealthy man, and so was Rex Klamath. The dwarf was happily coasting back to Ceres, ready to retire and return to Earth.

Junior was ready to quit his job as bartender at the Pelican. Who needed it? He was a millionaire!

But a question arose in his mind: What's next?

Suddenly Junior realized what his father's life had been like. What's next? When you don't have to worry about where your next meal is coming from, when you have the whole blinking solar system out there—filled with opportunity and adventure—where do you go? What's your next move?

Junior thought he knew. He was heading back to Earth, to find Deborah. *True love,* he told himself. *That's my goal.* Deborah Salmon was the woman he longed for.

Until the next morning, when he received two videocall messages.

The first was from Pierre D'Argent, president of Rockledge Industries.

D'Argent's image on Junior's screen was smiling, as usual. But the smile seemed forced, artificial: "Hello, Samuel. How are you?"

The distance between Earth and Ceres made actual conversation impossibly tedious: at this point in their respective orbits, it took more than an hour for a message to go one-way, even moving at the speed of light.

So D'Argent continued without waiting for a response. "My people on Ceres tell me you're tending a bar now. I hope you find that to your liking. Sounds rather pedestrian to me, but to each his own."

The Rockledge president's smile faded as he went on, "The reason I'm calling is that it has been brought to my attention that three fairly rich asteroids have been claimed by a corporation that lists you as its president—S. Gunn and Company.

"The curious thing," D'Argent went on, "is that the claim was filed by one of the Rock Rats who is under contract to us, Rockledge.

"I hope you can straighten out this matter. From what my treasurer tells me, it looks as if S. Gunn and Company has stolen assets that rightfully belong to Rockledge.

"Do call me back right away."

D'Argent's counterfeit smile curled his lips again as his image faded from Junior's screen.

To be replaced by a new image, of a sad-faced IAA official announcing, "Tracking of the spacecraft *Idaho*, rented by one Rex Klamath III, has abruptly shut down. Apparently, the craft has been destroyed."

GETAWAY

"Destroyed?" Junior gasped at his computer screen—which had gone blank the instant the message from the IAA had ended.

For several eons-long moments, Junior simply stared at the blank screen, wondering what had happened, what to do.

Then the screen lit up again, showing Klamath's deformed face. "Got a ship heading my way. It's running silent. I'm going dark too and getting the hell out of this area as fast as I can."

End of message.

Junior sighed out a breath that he hadn't realized he'd been holding. *Rex is all right,* he told himself. *His ship hasn't been destroyed, he's gone silent and running like hell to avoid Rockledge's killers. Rockledge is moving a lot faster than I thought they would. Score one for D'Argent.*

Junior realized that Rockledge Industries must have several ships cruising through the Belt, ready to respond to orders from corporate headquarters with the speed of light. *I hope Rex can get away from whoever's coming after him.* He knew that spacecraft disappeared fairly often out in the dark and empty stretches of the Belt. Not all of those losses were accidents, he realized.

Two wars had been fought in the Asteroid Belt in bygone

years. Wars pitting the major corporations against each other. Ships had been destroyed. People had been killed. The Rock Rats' original base of operations at Ceres had been wiped out with more than a thousand killed.

There had been no outright hostilities in the Belt since the lunar nation of Selene had led a peace movement, nearly a decade earlier. But corporations like Rockledge could still play rough when they wanted to, Junior realized. And little Rex Klamath was in their sights.

What to do? Junior asked himself, over and again. *Will they be coming after me?*

And suddenly a raging anger boiled up inside of him. *I'll come after them*, he swore to himself. *I'll go Earthside and nail that sneaking Pierre D'Argent. So help me, I will.*

But the heat of his anger shriveled and disappeared almost as soon as it arose. *How can I nail D'Argent?* he asked himself. *More importantly, how can I keep D'Argent from nailing me?*

Looking around his narrow bedroom, Junior realized he had to get away from Ceres, and quickly. Before Rockledge's hired thugs could reach him.

But go where? And how?

═══════

Like his father before him, Junior always kept a travel bag packed with a set of clothes and the toiletries he would need for a quick getaway. Seemed like the prudent thing to do.

Now, hefting the little bag in one hand, he headed for the door of his compartment, ready to go . . . where?

Not toward Earth, he told himself. *That's Rockledge's home territory.* Mars was the center for scientific teams exploring its rust-red expanse: he would need approval from the IAA to land there. Venus and Mercury were desolate, off-limits to private visitors, scientific investigators only.

The only working habitation in the Asteroid Belt was this collection of discarded spacecraft that Big George and his fellow Rock Rats had hammered into a space station orbiting Ceres. *This is exactly where Rockledge's hired thugs will come looking for me*, Junior realized.

Where to go? Where to run to? He could think of only one possibility: the half-built space station in orbit around gigantic Jupiter, twice as far from the Sun as Ceres. Beyond that there were no human habitations.

But how to get there? And how could he get the scientists at the station to allow him refuge there?

Reluctantly, Junior put his travel bag back in the closet and headed for work at the Pelican Bar, knowing that sooner or later Rockledge's hired thugs would come there looking for him.

Probably sooner.

━━━━

For three nights in a row, Junior faithfully tended the Pelican Bar, keeping an eye out for newcomers. He knew almost all of the joint's steady customers by name and tried to keep up friendly conversations while eying the front door for the sight of strangers.

No word from Rex Klamath. If the little man had eluded the hit team that Rockledge had sent after him, he was keeping as silent and invisible as death itself.

Junior spent his off-hours studying every scrap of information he could find about the space station being built in orbit around Jupiter. Its ostensible purpose was to serve as a base for the highly automated scoop ships that skimmed the uppermost layers of Jupiter's thick, roiling atmosphere, skimming hydrogen and helium isotopes to feed Earth's growing accumulation of nuclear fusion power plants.

A scientific research station, he realized, out at the ass end of human settlement of the solar system. *What would they need, what do they want,* that I could provide for them? *Not a bartender,* Junior told himself. *Something that would increase their prestige, brighten their image in the eyes of the people they've left behind on Earth.*

After days of pondering the question—and nights of looking for strangers at the Pelican Bar—Junior decided that what those scientists would greet with open arms was a publicist who promised to tell their story to people back home on Earth.

His only problem, Junior realized, was convincing the scientific staff that he was a legitimate publicist.

It was the same night that Junior hit on that idea that the two men from Rockledge showed up at the Pelican Bar.

TWO GENTLEMEN FROM DETROIT

They didn't look like thugs. The two of them were dressed in ordinary-looking business suits, light gray. But they were strangers, newcomers to the Pelican Bar, still wearing heavy rented boots to help acclimatize them to the lunar-level gravity of the Ceres-orbiting space station.

They hesitated at the Pelican's entrance, glancing around at the crowd for a moment or two, then made their way to the crowded bar. Junior smiled pleasantly at them, despite the racing of his heart, and asked them what they wanted to drink.

Instead of ordering, the taller of the pair asked, "You're Sam Gunn, aren't you?"

"Sam Junior."

The shorter one said, "The president of S. Gunn and Company?"

Trying to keep his smile in place, Junior nodded.

"You're rather young to be heading a corporation."

Still smiling, Junior asked, "How old does a man have to be?"

The taller one said, "Never mind that. Your company recently claimed three asteroids that rightfully belong to Rockledge Industries."

Junior hiked his eyebrows as if surprised. "The IAA says they belong to us. We filed claims for them, and Copenhagen approved all three of them."

"Copenhagen wasn't informed that all three of the asteroids were claimed by an employee of Rockledge Industries."

"A Mr. Rex Klamath."

"The third."

"Rex isn't a Rockledge employee," Junior objected. "He works freelance, like most of the miners out here."

By now, many of the men clustered at the bar were moving away from the two newcomers, although a few edged closer to them, listening intently to their conversation with Junior.

His innards trembling, Junior said as coolly as he could manage, "Most of the people who go scouting through the Belt have consulting agreements with one corporation or another."

"Klamath is a Rockledge employee," the taller man insisted. "I can show you the employee agreement he signed." And he reached for the inside pocket of his jacket.

Suppressing an instinct to duck behind the bar, Junior maintained, "Rex is a freelance miner. He's laid claim to dozens of asteroids—"

"For Rockledge."

"Well, his three most recent claims have been for S. Gunn and Company."

Shaking his head disappointedly, the taller man replied, "That won't hold up in a court of law, Mr. Gunn."

"That's for a judge to decide."

The shorter man puffed out a breath. "Look, Mr. Gunn, we're not here to argue with you. Those asteroids properly belong to Rockledge Industries, and Mr. D'Argent wants you to admit it."

It suddenly struck Junior that these two men were not hired assassins, but lawyers. Lawyers!

He drew himself up as tall as he could and replied, "Mr. D'Argent will have to prove his case in a court of law, then."

The two men looked at each other, disappointment and sorrow sculpting their faces. "You're making a mistake, Mr. Gunn."

"See you in court, gentlemen."

"I doubt that this matter ever will get to court."

Junior made a shrug. "We'll see."

"Yes, we will."

Forcing himself to smile, Junior asked, "Now then, what can I get you to drink?"

The two of them looked at each other, then turned back to Junior.

"A Manhattan," said the taller one.

"Do you have Jack Daniel's?" the other asked.

"Shipped in from Tennessee twice a year," said Junior.

"On the rocks, please."

"Coming right up."

But as Junior turned toward the drinks machine behind the bar, the taller man asked, "Are you really the son of Sam Gunn?"

Grinning, Junior replied, "I'm a son of a Gunn, alright."

They spent the night drinking and exchanging stories about the exploits of Junior's father.

Junior spun tales and laughed with them, but in the back of his mind, he knew that as soon as these two lawyers reported to Pierre D'Argent, an assassin would be sent to erase his claim and his life.

ESCAPE ROUTE

By the time he had helped the Pelican Bar's owner to close the place and made it back to his quarters, Junior had made up his mind. *On to Jupiter,* he told himself. *As fast as I can make it.*

But it wouldn't be Sam Gunn Jr. heading for Jupiter, he knew. He had to establish a new identity. He spent the early morning hours doing just that, inserting an invented personality into the personnel records in Amsterdam.

Glancing at his computer screen as he narrated a wholly fictitious biography into the IAA's personnel records, Junior grinned wickedly. *They've got safeguards against anybody trying to filch information out of their records,* he realized. *But inserting new information into the system is a lot easier.*

Fortunately, the IAA system did not compare the ID photos accompanying each biographical sketch against the myriads of other photos attached to earlier bios. Junior sighed out a puff of relief as his picture was accepted, together with his fictitious biographical description, without a hitch.

By the time the space station's lighting system turned up to its daytime mode, Junior had created a new persona in the IAA's personnel files: a young but brilliant recent graduate from the School of Journalism at Temple University, in Philadelphia, Pennsylvania:

Walter Cronkite IV.

━━━━

Sam Gunn Jr. quit his job at the Pelican Bar two days later. Walter Cronkite IV boarded the resupply rocket that was heading for the aptly named spacecraft *Zeus,* which stopped briefly at Ceres to pick up a load of refined metal paneling for the ongoing construction of the mammoth space station that was being built in orbit around the giant planet.

The crewman on duty at *Zeus*'s main hatch eyed Walter Cronkite's forged data briefly, then looked up at Junior warily.

"We got no info on pickin' up a passenger at Ceres."

Junior sighed mightily and shook his head. "Those blazing idiots Earthside! They screw up everything, don't they?"

The crewman's suspicious scowl eased into a guarded smile. "Your info looks okay. Funny we didn't get a heads-up from Amsterdam, though."

"Probably it'll come through after you're halfway to Jupiter."

The crewman grinned. "Yeah. That'd be just like those goddamned paper pushers."

He slid Junior's forged disc into the pocket-sized electronics box he held. It beeped satisfactorily, and Walter Cronkite IV entered the spacecraft.

━━━━

It took more than a week for the spacecraft to ply its way to Jupiter. Junior was the only passenger aboard, but he made friends easily enough with the six-person crew: one married couple, two veteran spacemen, and a single woman astrogator—largish, unfriendly, putting in time until she could retire and return to her native Zaire.

Then there was the captain, a smallish man from Guam with square shoulders, a slight limp, and a face that could freeze molten lava.

They all took their meals together, at the captain's insistence. "Builds morale," he insisted. "Share meals and share your troubles."

Junior had no intention of sharing anything with them. But sitting with them three times each day forced him to flesh out his Walter Cronkite persona.

"So you're a newsman, eh?" the captain probed.

"That's what I'm hoping to be," Junior replied modestly.

"In your family's blood, eh?"

Junior hesitated, thinking as quickly as he could before replying, "My great-great-grandfather was a very famous journalist back in the Twentieth Century USA."

"And you aim to follow in his footsteps, eh?"

"If I can."

"Is that why you're traveling to Jupiter?"

"Yes, sir. I believe that the work being done at Jupiter is vitally important to everyone on Earth."

"Scooping fuels for fusion power plants," said one of the crewmen.

"That's right," Junior replied honestly. "It's vital work. Crucial to our future."

"Work's done mostly by automated machinery," said the captain. "Hard to make heroes out of them."

Junior nodded in agreement, but said, "It's the people who make the machines work, they're the important ones."

"Engineers," scoffed the captain. "Trained seals."

"Not at all!" Junior objected. "They keep the automated machines working. It's not glamorous work, I grant you. But it's important. Vital."

"You're repeating yourself," the captain huffed. And he turned his attention to his soup.

BOOK SIX: JUPITER

APPROACHING
THE GIANT

Junior's quarters aboard *Zeus* were smallish, but relatively comfortable: a private compartment next to the captain's, not much bigger than a broom closet, but furnished with a reasonably restful bed and a sliver of a closet. He shared the crew's bathroom; at least the shower's water was warm enough, heated by the ship's nuclear reactor.

But after a week of cruising through the dark emptiness of interplanetary space, Junior felt he was going slowly insane. The same handful of crew at meals, the same inane chatter around the table, the same captain directing everyone's conversation. Maddening.

The only relief from the boredom was the sight of the planet Jupiter, a faint reddish dot among the stars which gradually grew larger as they got nearer and nearer. Junior spent more and more of his time in the ship's observation blister, alone, separated from the mind-numbing blather of the crew and the self-important pronouncements of the captain, gazing at the slowly brightening sphere of Jupiter.

So it was a surprise when, after more than a week of mind-numbing loneliness, Junior was awakened by a sharp thumping on his compartment's flimsy door. Wrapping his robe around himself, Junior pulled the door open and saw the captain standing there with a happy smile on his slightly chunky face.

"Starting to get detailed imagery of Jupiter, Mr. Cronkite," said the captain. "Thought you might like to see it."

Nodding, Junior replied, "Yes, certainly. Thank you."

He swiftly pulled on his coveralls and made his way up to the ship's bridge.

As he ducked through the hatch, Junior saw three of the crewpersons sitting at consoles whose desktop screens displayed the status of the ship's systems. The captain sat in a sculpted chair in front of them, with a huge deck-to-overhead viewscreen showing their destination: the planet Jupiter.

Without turning to face Junior, the captain proclaimed, "Welcome to the bridge, Mr. Cronkite."

Junior's eyes were riveted on the viewscreen image.

Jupiter looked like a multi-hued beach ball, slightly flattened at its poles, as if some invisible giant were sitting on it. The body of the planet was streaked with clouds, stripes of gray and reddish brown, for the most part, parading in parallel bands across the bright disc. Off near the edge of the disc was an oval red blotch hovering amongst the lighter-colored clouds that were racing past it.

Still without turning toward Junior, the captain said, "Magnificent, isn't it? The Great Red Spot, there, is twice the size of Earth! It's been there since Galileo's day, at least."

Unable to take his eyes off the planet's image, Junior edged between the crew's stations and stopped at the captain's commodious couch.

"It's . . . it's tremendous," he breathed.

"Big enough to swallow all the other planets, from Mercury

to Neptune, and then some," the captain enthused. "The giant of the solar system."

It was hypnotic, Junior realized. He stared at the image of the immense planet, visions of ancient myths and modern astronomical facts swimming through his consciousness.

Forcing himself to tear his eyes away from the big viewscreen, Junior looked down at the captain. The man seemed positively overjoyed.

Reaching out a pointing finger, the captain asked, "See that little dark dot just next to the Red Spot? That's our destination. That's station *Galileo*."

=====

His head swimming from the imagery of Jupiter, Junior stood rooted to the bridge's decking as the captain pushed himself up from his chair and grasped his arm in an almost fatherly way.

"Come on, Mr. Cronkite. We've got to prepare for entering Jupiter's magnetic field."

As the captain led Junior off the bridge, the ship's public address system blared, "JUPITER APPROACH. MOVE TO EMERGENCY SHELTER. ALL PERSONNEL DON PROTECTIVE ANTI-RADIATION GARMENTS."

Junior followed the captain forward along the ship's central passageway. They stopped at a heavy-looking hatch.

"This is the emergency shelter," the captain explained as he punched out a code of the keyboard mounted next to the hatch. "We stay in here until we've slipped beneath Jupiter's magnetic field."

"How long—"

"The better part of a day," said the captain, as he swung the hatch open and gestured Junior inside.

The shelter looked claustrophobic, Junior thought. It was a narrow compartment with ten seats, five on each side. At its front was a blank viewscreen and a console studded with buttons and switches.

"I can control the ship from here," the captain said as he slid into the command seat. "We'll be safe in here."

Junior nodded and took the seat next to the captain. Before he could say anything, the rest of the crew trooped in, with the big Zairian woman swinging the hatch shut and sealing it.

"Snug as bugs in a rug," the captain said cheerfully. But Junior thought he detected a hint of nervousness behind the man's toothy smile.

The captain tapped on a few of the buttons arrayed in front of his seat, and a view of Jupiter appeared on the viewscreen. They were close enough now for Junior to see eddies and swirls in the belts of clouds racing across the planet's face.

"Where's the space station?" he heard himself ask.

"*Galileo*'s swung around behind the limb of the planet," the captain replied. "We won't see it again until we've broken below the underside of the magnetic field—in about eight hours."

Eight hours, Junior thought. The captain opened a closet door, and each member of the crew pulled out one of the nanofabric suits that protected them from the sharp rise in radiation as they cruised through Jupiter's intense magnetic field. Junior did the same, worming his arms through the suit's sleeves and pulling the hood over his head and sealing it. Then they all sat in silence as the spacecraft hurtled closer and closer to Jupiter's colorful cloud deck. The time ticked by slowly. No one said a word. They all seemed to be sitting rigidly in their seats, stiff with tension.

At last the captain called out, "Systems check."

One by one the crew replied, "Propulsion ninety-five percent."

"Life support: ninety-eight percent."

"Observation instrumentation: ninety-six percent."

And so on, through all the ship's systems. The captain nodded silently at each report.

Junior's mouth felt dry. He made himself swallow once, twice before he could make his voice work.

He asked the captain, "How many times have you made this flight to Jupiter?"

The captain flicked him an annoyed glance. "We've run the simulation about twenty times."

"Eighteen," came the voice of one of the crewmen.

Simulation? thought Junior. *That means they've never done it for real!*

ARRIVAL

Jupiter loomed closer and closer. The unfinished space station, *Galileo*, swung around the curve of the giant planet's bulk and grew into a pair of linked side-by-side dark circles as *Zeus* edged nearer to it.

One of the station's sizeable rings looked incomplete. Junior could see the sparks of welding lasers flashing along its curving structure and, as they got nearer to it, clusters of smaller objects—many-armed construction vehicles, even one-man units—flitting back and forth, busily engaged in building the unfinished half of the space station.

Tubes big enough to accommodate work crews connected the finished circle of the *Galileo* station to the one still under assembly. *There must be at least a hundred people working on the job*, thought Junior. *More, maybe.*

At last the safety pod's automated speaker announced, "DOCKING COMPLETE. SHIP IS SECURE."

Junior blinked several times. He hadn't noticed even the slightest thump. Either the ship's command and control system was exquisitely precise, or he'd been so absorbed watching the construction work that he paid no attention to the ship's maneuvering.

Either way, it made no difference to the captain. "Up and at 'em!" he shouted. "Let's get out of these damned nano suits and into the station."

As one person, the crew rose to their feet and started peeling off their protective nanosuits.

In a line headed by the captain—with Junior right behind him—the crew filed out of the shielded cabin, down *Zeus*'s central passageway, and through a hatch that brought them into the space station *Galileo*.

Junior looked around as he stepped across the hatch's coaming. *Galileo*'s reception area was strictly utilitarian: small, cramped, with a single inspection station consisting of one examination arch and a tiny desk, where a bored-looking overweight, auburn-haired woman sat, her head propped on a fist. She looked half asleep.

But she seemed to snap awake as the captain stepped up to her desk and whisked out his identification diskette.

"Hi," she piped as she touched a button on the desk and a computer screen rose slowly from its top.

"Hello," said the captain.

"Have a good flight in?"

"Uneventful."

"That's the best kind."

She gestured to the inspection arch, and the captain stepped under it. Somewhere a hidden device whined and squeaked.

"Your diagnostics need maintenance," the captain said, with a slight smile.

"Not my department," said the woman.

Walking to Junior and placing an almost fatherly hand on his shoulder, the captain said, "This is Walter Cronkite the Fourth. A journalist from Earth."

The woman's eyes went wide. "Journalist?" She peered at her computer screen. "We've got nothing about a journalist."

"My paperwork got screwed up in Amsterdam," Junior lied.

"Huh." The woman stared at her screen more intently, then shook her head. "Nothing here about a journalist."

Junior started to say, "I've come all this way—"

"You go wait over there," the woman said, pointing. "I've got to call the director."

Junior nodded and walked away from her desk. The rest of the crew went through their registration with no problem. They all left the inspection station, heading deeper into the station, leaving Walter Cronkite IV alone with the heavyset woman.

Junior stood next to the little station's bulkhead, wondering what he could do to get past this tired-looking woman and into the station proper. After a wait that seemed hours long, at last the far door slid open and a dapper-looking, gray-haired man entered the inspection station.

He looked at Junior with slightly suspicious light brown eyes.

"Walter Cronkite?" he asked, in a soft, wary voice.

Junior straightened and answered, "Yes, sir."

"The Fourth?"

"Yes."

Extending his right hand, the man said, "I'm Harold Johannsen . . . the First. I'm the Director of station *Galileo*."

Junior grasped his hand. "Pleased to meet you, sir."

Johannsen smiled minimally. "We don't seem to have any paperwork on you."

With what he hoped was an annoyed shrug, Junior offered, "It's probably sitting in Amsterdam, under a pile of other paperwork."

Even as he spoke, Junior realized the term *paperwork* was a holdover from an earlier age, when records were actually printed on sheets of paper.

Johannsen peered at Junior. "Well, you're here. Follow me,

please." With that, the captain strode toward the hatch from which he had entered the inspection station.

Junior marched along behind him, through the hatch and along a short, blank-walled passageway that ended at a door marked, Harold Johannsen. Private.

Johannsen opened the door and, turning slightly, gestured Junior into his office.

It was a small but well-appointed compartment with a handsome faux mahogany desk and two comfortable leather chairs in front of it. The walls on either side were floor-to-ceiling bookshelves, empty for the most part. A viewscreen filled the entire wall behind the desk, showing Jupiter: massive, looming, with swirling clouds of various shades of red, white, gray streaming across its face. Junior could see a couple of moons hovering just over the curve of the planet's disc.

As he slid into his desk chair, Johannsen asked, "What brings you all the way out here, young man?"

Blinking as he turned away from the image of the giant planet, Junior replied, "I'm a journalist. I want to do an in-depth report on the work you're doing here."

"Do you?"

"Yessir, I do."

"Who are you working for?"

"I'm a freelancer at present. But I think that doing a good story on your work will get the major news organizations back Earthside to recognize my abilities."

Johannsen leaned back in his yielding desk chair. "So you want to use our work here at Jupiter to get yourself a steady job, is that it?"

GIVE AND TAKE

Junior felt his brows knitting. Forcing himself to remain calm, even pleasant, he said to the captain, "I suppose that's part of it. But—"

"No buts, Mr. Cronkite! I've got twelve hundred and some people here—scientists, engineers, technicians, cooks, and pantry workers. Not to mention a phalanx of robots. We're farther away from Earth than any human team has gone. We're searching for extraterrestrial life down in that hellhole called Jupiter. And all you see is an opportunity to use our work to feather your own nest."

"That's not fair!" Junior snapped. "I'm trying to help you, to get the people Earthside to recognize the importance of the work you're doing."

"And feather your own nest," the captain repeated.

"What's wrong with that?" Junior demanded. "You're here to further your own career, aren't you?"

"We're talking about you, Cronkite, not me."

"But what brought you out here? Why did you come to this outpost? What are you looking for?"

"Advancing human knowledge," the captain answered.

"And feathering your own nest," Junior insisted.

The captain glared at him.

Junior continued, "Won't this operation you're heading bring you recognition and advancement, once you return to Earth? Isn't this mission a step upward in your career?"

Johannsen sat in stony silence for several agonizingly long moments, staring at Junior with unblinking eyes. Slowly his fierce expression faded, morphing into a broad, twinkle-eyed grin.

"By God, you've got guts, young man. And brains."

Junior felt his jaw sag open.

The captain leaned forward and extended his right arm across the desktop. Surprised and more than a little confused, Junior gripped his proffered hand.

"It's not many men that can stand up to me, Mr. Cronkite. You've passed my test with flying colors."

Forcing a smile, Junior asked, "This was a test?"

"That it was. And you passed it. Now how would you like to take a dip in Jupiter's fine, cold ocean?"

═══════

It all happened so fast Junior never got a chance to say no. Captain Johannsen marched Junior down the station's central passageway, to a double door marked "Extra Vehicular Operations." He tapped on the control pad set into the bulkhead and the doors slid quietly open.

Junior saw an enormous, cavernous workshop, with dozens of men and women—all in coveralls of various colors—clustered around a five-story-high spherical metallic object looming over them. It was resting on what looked like a giant sliding skid. A pair of metallic tracks extended from the skid to a huge airlock hatch. Tightly shut.

Workers were crawling over the sphere, others entering it through hatches that looked minuscule, compared to its height and girth.

"That's one of our probes," said Johannsen, a hint of pride in his voice. "Tomorrow you're going down into the Jovian ocean in it to meet the Leviathans."

"I am?" Junior gasped.

"If you want to write about what we're doing," the captain said cheerfully, "you've got to witness what we're doing."

"And just what is it that you're doing?"

The captain seemed to draw himself up a little taller, straighter. "We are attempting to establish communications with an intelligent extraterrestrial species."

═══════

Junior had hardly a moment to object or ask more questions. Johannsen led him from the hangar where the gigantic spherical vessel was being prepared for a dive into Jupiter's planet-wide ocean to a minuscule medical facility, where the same bored-looking hefty auburn-haired woman supervised a highly automated set of instruments that probed, poked, and thoroughly examined him.

All through the procedure, Johannsen nattered away. "They're huge creatures, the Leviathans. Kilometers in length, big as a minor city on Earth. They just cruise through the ocean, endlessly, feeding on the organic matter that drifts down from the ocean's upper levels."

Despite the medical probe stuck between his teeth, Junior managed to ask, "What makes you think they're intelligent?"

"That's what the psych people believe. The beasts flash images to one another, big pictures they display on their flanks."

"Really?"

"Really. The psych people are delirious over that. The Leviathans have a language, they believe. It's a visual language, but it shows a degree of intelligence."

Junior tried to ask another question, but the probe was pushing deeper into his mouth, nearly choking him.

THE SUBMERSIBLE

Once the medical examination was finished, Johannsen led Junior through the station's central passageway to an area that was lined with doors.

"Crew's quarters," he explained. "You'll sleep here." And he opened one of the doors.

Junior saw a neat little bedroom, not terribly large, but bigger than his cubicle aboard *Zeus* and apparently comfortable.

"Get a good night's sleep," Johannsen said, more like a command than a suggestion. "Tomorrow, bright and early, you go to meet the Leviathans."

And before Junior could nod his acquiescence or say anything, the Director closed the door and left him there, alone.

Slightly puzzled, Junior poked into the pocket-sized clothes closet that stood beside the bed. Several sets of coveralls hung there, light gray in color. The private bathroom seemed downright luxurious: sink, toilet, shower, and a medicine chest that held soap, shaving implements, and other toiletries. A single spindly chair stood on the far side of the bed.

Junior saw a clock on the tiny table next to the bed: it read

10:22 p.m. He realized that the station was running on the standard Greenwich Mean Time scheme.

Suddenly a feeling of tiredness came over him. *It's been a long day,* he thought as he undressed, pulled on one of the coveralls from the closet, and got into bed. But instead of trying to sleep, he fished his handheld computer from his pants, hanging on the back of the room's only chair, and looked up the information it held on Jupiter's Leviathans.

Not much more than the captain had told him. They were huge creatures, several kilometers in length, that swam placidly through Jupiter's planet-wide ocean, sweeping in the constant flow of organic materials that drifted down through the ocean's depths. They flashed pictures along their massive flanks, which might indicate language, intelligence. But all attempts to make meaningful contact with them had achieved no success so far.

A major problem in studying them, according to the computer's information, was communications between the exploratory submersibles and the orbiting station. Jupiter's highly acidic waters absorbed the wavelengths of radio waves and even laser beams within a few hundred meters. The submersibles that the scientists used had wire antennas that they could unreel while in the water, but they only ran a few dozen kilometers long, and the Leviathans swam far deeper than that.

So the submersibles were effectively out of touch with the space station and the relay satellites that the scientists had placed in low orbits around the planet. Down at the depths where the Leviathans dwelt, the visitors from Earth were quite effectively cut off from communications with their cohorts in the *Galileo* station until they rose to shallower waters.

Huh, Junior said to himself as he put away the computer and slipped under the bedcover for sleep. *We'll be on our own down there. Should be interesting.*

He realized that *interesting* was often a word used by explorers in place of *terrifying*.

═══════

Junior was awakened by the clock's tinny announcement, "Oh-six hundred hours! Breakfast is served until oh-seven-thirty!"

He showered quickly, then pulled on one of the gray coveralls from the closet; it felt tight across his shoulders, and the pants barely reached his ankles. *Good enough,* Junior told himself. *You're not here for a beauty contest.* He stepped into the passageway outside his door. A half-dozen crewmen were hurrying past, and Junior followed them to the canteen where breakfast was being served by a squad of stubby robots. He found an empty seat and wolfed down a trayful of eggs, meat, and fruit.

As he was mopping up the last of his meal, everyone suddenly snapped to their feet. Surprised, Junior stood up too. Director Johannsen strode into the canteen, smiling gently at his crew.

"As you were, people. Finish your meals. Then we go to meet the beasts once again."

═══════

Everyone gobbled down the remains of their breakfasts, then trooped down to the capacious hangar where the spherical submersible vehicle waited. The captain shook hands with each of the nine men and women who made up the probe's crew—plus Junior—and wished them all "good hunting."

Junior thought that his cheerful words were out of place, but he said nothing, just followed the rest of the crew through a hatch in the submersible's outer shell and into a long, tight, claustrophobic tunnel that sloped down into the heart of the submersible.

The crewman walking next to Junior explained, "The sub's built of five compressible layers surrounding our working deck. As we go deeper into the ocean, the outer layers squeeze together, take up the pressure, so we can get down to the levels where the big brutes live."

Junior nodded as they strode down the seemingly endless tunnel. He noticed a set of rail lines running along the tunnel, a meter or so lower than the platform that they were walking on.

"We've got a trolley that carries us down to our deck," the crewman continued, "but on our last mission it got itself stuck halfway down the tunnel. Pressure warped the tunnel a little and the safety system shut it down. We had to walk out, once we got to the surface."

"And now we walk all the way," Junior said.

"Yeah. The skipper didn't want to hold up the schedule, so we walk until the maintenance people can straighten out the trolley run."

At last they came to a massive hatch, which swung open automatically as they approached it. The crew filed in and took the chairs arranged before an array of blank viewscreens. Junior saw that there were three pull-down seats along the rear bulkhead, behind the crew's sculpted recliners. Before the crewman could tell him what to do, Junior yanked one of the seats down and squatted on it. It was hard and not very comfortable.

"Better strap in," said the crewman. "Splashing into the ocean can be kinda rough."

With that, the crewman turned and went to his place, two rows from Junior's thin-cushioned pad. Junior reached back to the safety belt control as he watched the crew check out their instruments. The viewscreens at the front of the compartment lit up, showing status reports on the vessel's various systems.

As Junior watched, the huge sphere of the ship slid toward a giant hatch, which opened to reveal the black, star-studded depths of space. *Jupiter is behind us, of course*, Junior said to himself.

No one had thought to give Junior a set of earphones, so he watched and waited in silence for the probe's ejection from the *Galileo* space station.

They're talking to each other, and to the command center aboard the station, he knew. But he heard nothing except their chatter—too low to be understandable to him—and the background hum of electrical equipment.

Then a sudden surge of thrust, and the vessel was literally shoved out of the space station.

INTO THE ENDLESS SEA

"Everybody strapped in?" asked the woman in the command seat, up front. One by one the crew acknowledged that their safety harnesses were buckled properly. Junior added his voice once the others had reported.

"Probe Alpha ready for immersion," he heard the commander report.

The central viewscreen showed the star-filled blackness of space sweeping past, then the bulk of Jupiter loomed ahead, growing swiftly bigger until it filled the screen.

"IMMERSION IN FIFTEEN MINUTES," the ship's public address system announced. Junior saw that each of the crew was hunched over their computer screens, monitoring the ship's systems.

One of the men got to his feet and came back to Junior, a set of headphones in one hand. "Here," he said, proffering the earphones, "you'll need these."

"Thanks," said Junior, reaching out to take them in his hands. Once he slipped them on, he could hear the crew's clipped, economical chatter. Somehow it made him feel better, almost a working member of the team.

The ship jounced and shuddered as they dove through

Jupiter's topmost cloud deck. After several such decks, the screens cleared again and Junior saw far below an endless vista of sea, waves marching along in unimpeded lockstep.

That ocean is more than ten times bigger than the whole Earth, he told himself. *And who knows how deep?*

He quickly recognized the team leader's voice. "Immersion in five minutes," she said. Junior thought he heard tension straining her words.

The central viewscreen showed nothing but the ocean, racing closer, closer. The PA system ticked off, "IMMERSION IN ONE MINUTE . . . FIFTY SECONDS . . . FORTY-FIVE SECONDS . . ."

Junior tensed as the ocean surface loomed closer, closer. The vessel shuddered as if struck by a gigantic hammer and the viewscreens showed nothing but bubbling, frothing water all around them.

"Immersion confirmed!" the team leader exclaimed, sounding excited. "Systems reports."

One by one the crew members reported:

"Hull integrity confirmed."

"Life support verified."

"Sensors active."

One by one, each of the vessel's systems were reported to be working as designed. Junior thought he heard satisfaction—and relief—in the crew's voices.

Once all systems were confirmed to be operating normally their leader reported to the space station, "Alpha One in the water with all systems *go.* Preparing to dive."

"You are cleared to dive," came the response.

Now we go hundreds of klicks below the surface, Junior knew. Maybe deeper. Down to where the Leviathans dwell.

The bridge became quite silent. No chatter among the crew; each of them hunched over their instruments as the submersible glided deeper and deeper into the endless Jovian ocean. From his uncomfortable seat at the rear of the bridge, with the safety harness straps pressing into his shoulders and lap, Junior kept his eyes on the viewscreens up front. Nothing much to see, except water bubbling past and—now and then—smallish sea creatures swimming by, some with flagella wriggling, others with fins and tails undulating, very much like fish on Earth.

They passed a huge tentacled creature, its long arms waving, saucer-sized eyes peering into the deepening gloom of the ocean's depths. It passed them apparently without taking any notice.

"We don't look good to eat," said one of the crewmen, his voice just slightly shaky.

"Thank goodness," the leader added.

Deeper and deeper they dove. The water seemed empty of life at this depth.

"It's a desert."

"Pretty wet for a desert."

"You know what I mean!"

"There's plenty of life hereabouts. Microscopic. Too small for us to see."

"But our sensors are recording it."

For hours they descended, while the crew chattered back and forth. Junior heard the tension in their voices. He himself felt the strain building inside him. Until . . .

"There they are!" the leader called out.

She flicked her fingers across her keyboard and the big central viewscreen switched to a view at some depth below them. A formation of shapes far below them, gliding along placidly through the murky depths of the ocean.

"Pretty damned deep," said one of the crewmen.

"Is it within our operational limits?" the commander asked.

Another voice, female, replied, "Close to our safety limit."

The skipper said, "But not beyond the limit."

"No, Ma'am. Near the edge, but not beyond it."

"Then let's go down and see them."

Junior felt conflicted. On the one hand, he badly wanted to see the Leviathans. On the other, he didn't want to die in the boundless depths of this alien sea. Realizing he had to go along with the commander's decision, he still felt that he would prefer to be home in Jackpot, Nevada. By far.

But—*damn the torpedoes*, Junior said to himself. *Full speed ahead!*

LEVIATHANS

Slowly, slowly the Leviathans took shape as the submersible sank deeper toward them. They were a herd, more than twenty of them, gliding peacefully through the murky depths of the ocean.

Bigger, bigger they grew as the strangers from Earth approached them.

Leviathans.

Junior couldn't take his eyes away from the screens at the front of the compartment. The Leviathans swam leisurely, calmly through the deep waters, seemingly paying no attention to the submersible's approach.

They were *huge*. Immense. Dwarfing the globular submersible, they made their way through the deep waters, mouths stretched wide to take in the nutrient-rich water. Feeding. Untroubled by the tiny visitor from another world. Uncaring.

Magnificent, Junior thought. *Tremendous. Lords of their domain.*

He stared at them, eyes goggling at their immensity. Bigger than football fields; bigger than whole stadiums. Hundreds of meters long, dozens of them. Their flanks were studded with eyes, row after row of eyes. Junior couldn't get over the feeling that they were watching him, staring at him, trying to determine who or what this strange visitor might be.

Suddenly the beast closest to their sub lit up its flank with a picture. Meticulously detailed, down to the last welded seal, the Leviathan showed an image of the visiting submersible.

"That's us!" someone yelped. And Junior realized it was he himself who shouted.

Within an instant the exquisitely comprehensive image appeared on the flanks of each Leviathan swimming in the formation.

"Are they saying hello?" the commander asked.

One of the crew replied, "Or maybe, 'Go away?'"

Junior just goggled at the immense beasts' imagery.

"They know we're strangers," said a woman's voice.

"But they don't seem upset."

"Or surprised."

The Leviathans simply plowed on through the deep, dark water, unworried by the strange new visitor.

"They have no concept of the universe beyond these waters," said one of the crew's scientists. "They've never seen anything beyond this ocean they swim in."

Another voice suggested, "Maybe we should blink our lights at them. Get some reaction, perhaps."

After a nerve-stretching moment of silence, the commander said, "Okay, try it. Two flashes."

"Aye, ma'am."

The compartment's lights dimmed once, twice. No reaction, Junior saw. But then . . .

The Leviathan nearest them blanked the image on its flank of the submersible. Once, twice. Then the beasts nearest it did the same. Within a few seconds, the entire herd of the creatures blinked the images on their flanks once, then twice.

"Contact!" shouted the captain.

"We've made communication with the Leviathans!" said the man who had suggested blinking the lights.

"Communication with an extraterrestrial species!" exulted another voice.

Junior thought that blinking their lights a couple of times wasn't such a tremendous accomplishment, but the crew apparently felt otherwise. They were thrilled.

Scientists, Junior said to himself. But inwardly he felt a surge of excitement. And he remembered from his school days the tales of how the earliest white explorers struggled to make meaningful communications with the native men they found on the strange treeless plains beyond the Mississippi River, the territory that no less than Zebulon Pike proclaimed as "the great American desert."

═══════

For hours Junior stared at the viewscreen images of the gigantic Leviathans, swimming placidly through Jupiter's deep, deep ocean.

"They don't do much, do they?" said one of the crew.

Another, a woman, rejoined, "They're feeding."

"Is that all they do? All the time?"

"Not a bad life," said a man's voice.

"You'd like it, wouldn't you? Chow time all the time."

Junior kept his eyes on the viewscreens. The Leviathans still showed their images of the submersible on their flanks. *What can we do to get them to change the imagery?* Junior asked himself.

For hours they cruised along on the outer edge of the Leviathans' formation. Chatter among the crew dwindled and then stopped altogether. The commander stared at the viewscreens as if hypnotized, her chubby fingers flicking impatiently across the control panels on the arms of her chair.

Come on, Junior urged the beasts silently. *Do something.*

But the gigantic creatures continued to swim placidly through the ocean's water as if they knew that the stranger among them was merely a visitor, a temporary phenomenon that offered them no threat.

"This is boring," said one of the crewmen.

And Junior recalled again his history lessons, from back in Nevada, the old Air Force maxim: *Flying for the Air Force means long hours of boredom—punctuated by moments of sheer terror.*

But there was no terror among the Leviathans. Nothing but serenity as they glided along, propelled by the huge flukes of their tails.

Then Junior noticed that one of the creatures was behaving strangely: shuddering, great throbs of pulsations racing along the length of its massive body.

The animal writhed and twisted as it quivered and turned away from its position among the other creatures, which broke the formation they had been holding and opened a path for the struggling brute.

It surged past the edge of its mates' assembly, heading toward the humans' submersible.

The captain pounded on her control panel and their little vessel dove out of the path of the bucking, thrashing, Leviathan.

Junior saw one of its myriad eyes detach itself from the beast and float off by itself. Then a tail fluke broke up into a dozen smaller, flailing, wriggling bits of flesh.

"It's falling apart!" someone yelled.

DARTERS

As Junior stared, open-mouthed, at the viewscreens, he saw the struggling Leviathan seemingly shake itself apart. Pieces flew from its body in all directions. It was separating, disassociating, its long bulk splitting open, its innards wriggling free.

"It's breaking up!" cried one of the crew.

The submersible's PA system, announced calmly, "UNIDENTIFIED CREATURES APPROACHING RAPIDLY."

Flicking his gaze to one of the screens on the far left of the compartment's array, Junior saw a compact group of smaller creatures—slim, fast, purposeful—dashing toward the struggling, disassembling Leviathan.

"Darters!" shouted the commander. "Carnivores."

Junior watched the swift-moving formation of darters swarm about the disassociating Leviathan. They snatched at the pieces that had floated free of the creature's body and even nosed their sharp-toothed snouts into the still-quivering remains of its body.

Not a sound from the submersible's crew. They all watched, horrified, as the darters chewed up the various parts of what was once a unified, living, giant animal.

At last the commander spoke up. "Huddleston and his crew identified the darters last year. He correctly assumed they were carnivores."

"But the Leviathan . . ." moaned one of the crew.

Another voice muttered, "It's like a pride of lions attacking a sheep."

Junior noticed that the troop of Leviathans, still nearby, did nothing to protect their fellow member from the murderous darters. *We should do something*, he thought. But then he asked himself, *Do what?*

━━━━━

The darters were having a feast. Junior saw one of the shark-like creatures nose into what was left of the body of the disintegrating Leviathan and yank out a long, ropey, purplish cylindrical shape, the Darter's teeth chewing on it visibly. *An intestine?* Junior asked himself.

The other darters were busily chasing after the parts of disassembling Leviathan across the bloody, teeming sea as they fled blindly from the slaughter.

"We should help the poor thing!" cried one of the crew.

"No interference," came the commander's stern voice. "We're here to observe and record."

"We don't have anything to fight with, anyway," said another crew member.

Junior knew what they were feeling. To simply sit here and passively watch this slaughter seemed totally wrong.

And then he noticed one of the darters speeding directly at the submersible.

"All strapped in?" the captain shouted. A chorus of ayes answered her.

Junior tugged on the safety straps fitted snugly against his shoulders. Just in time.

The Darter slammed into the submersible like a giant animated torpedo. The vessel jounced and shuddered.

"DEFORMATION, SECTION TWENTY-SIX C," announced the PA speaker, as calmly as a man saying, "Drat."

"Damage assessment!" the captain barked. The main screen in front of her showed a list of numbers that meant nothing to Junior, except that some of them were in glaring red.

The Darter, meanwhile, had bounced off the sub's round hull and twisted around to swim alongside their vessel.

"He's trying to figure out what we are," said one of the crew.

"Trying to figure out if we're edible," another voice replied, grimly.

After a few genuinely terrifying moments, the Darter raced off and joined its companions snatching up the various pieces of what had been a living Leviathan moments earlier.

"SECTION TWENTY-SIX C LEAKING AIR," announced the PA system.

The commander muttered, "Better get ourselves out of here." And her stubby fingers flicked across her control buttons.

The submersible began to rise above the carnage that had spread about them. Junior stared at the viewscreens as the images of the Leviathans and darters shrank smaller and smaller until they were lost in the ocean's blood-stained waters.

———

It took nearly three hours for the submersible to reach the ocean's surface. It bobbed in the everlasting waves while the commander analyzed the data on their outer surface's damage. The crew sat in tense silence as she reviewed the damage assessment.

"Could be worse," she said at last. "The automatic repair system has sealed the leak. We can get back to the station without any serious problems."

Junior felt the crew's relief like a wistful sigh gusting through the vessel's command center. But he found himself wondering about the commander's "serious."

He felt a lot better when the commander ignited the submersible's rocket engines and the vessel obediently leaped out of the ocean and raced toward the clouds, high overhead.

One of the crewmen broke their expectant silence, "That damned Darter might've ruined our ship."

"We need to arm ourselves," said a woman's voice. "Protect ourselves against them."

"No!" the commander snapped. "Standard orders forbid our interacting with the native life forms, except to try to communicate with them."

"Well, we did that."

"Yes, we did. The IAA will be happy to hear about it."

"I still think we need to protect ourselves."

"Strictly forbidden," the commander repeated.

"Then let's bring a couple of those fat-assed bureaucrats down into the ocean with us and see how they like being attacked!"

A chorus of chuckles showed the crew's agreement.

SHIPMATES

Under the commander's careful control their submersible reached orbit alongside the space station and rode to within a hundred meters or so next to *Galileo*. Beyond the paired circles of the station, the planet Jupiter loomed immense, its colorful clouds racing across its enormous, looming expanse.

Junior watched as the commander tapped her control buttons as delicately as a concert pianist playing a Bach sonata. The spherical submersible glided onto the landing platform that extended from *Galileo*'s mammoth airlock hatch, was secured automatically, and pulled into the station's cavernous housing.

Once they were docked safely inside the station's huge hangar-like enclosure and the mammoth hatch sealed shut the captain announced, "Pressure's equilibrated. We can get out now."

Slowly, like people who had been recovering from a grueling ordeal, the crew got to their feet and filed to the hatch, grumbling about the long walk they had ahead of them.

"Those damned clowns better have the trolley working by the time we go down again," growled one of the crewmen.

"And the dent in the outer hull repaired," added the woman trudging down the long passageway beside him.

Junior had no complaints. They had gone down into the ocean, established a communication (of sorts) with the Leviathans, and survived the impact of an inquisitive Darter. Not a bad day's work, he thought.

It was well past the station's regular dinner time. They had been down in the ocean for so long. Most of the crew went straight to the cafeteria anyway and punched up sandwiches and drinks from the automated machines lining its rear bulkhead. Junior followed them and did likewise.

He sat with the rest of the crew, saying little, listening to their chatter. Most of the other tables were already empty.

"So where'd the skipper go?" one of the women asked.

"Off to make her report to Johannsen," said the man seated next to her. "In person."

"She's pretty impressed with herself, huh?"

The guy sitting across the table said, "First reaction anyone's gotten from the Leviathans. That's impressive, don'tcha think?"

"Those damned darters are pretty impressive," said one of the men, sitting a few chairs down the table.

"We ought to have something to defend ourselves against those bastards."

"Strictly forbidden."

"By the fat cats sitting on their asses in Amsterdam."

"They'll change their rules—once one of us get killed by the darters."

"Or after a sub gets sunk."

Junior barely suppressed a smile. *These people have come close to death,* he thought, *and survived. Now they're letting off steam. Can't say I blame them.*

Gradually, in ones and twos, the crew got to their feet and left the cafeteria. Junior saw that several of them paired together as they headed for their sleeping quarters. Within a few minutes, he was sitting alone at the table they had shared.

But not for long. The heavyset, auburn-haired woman he had seen when he first came aboard the *Galileo* and again at the station's highly automated medical examination facility, entered the cafeteria, selected a bottle of something from one of the dispensers, walked directly to Junior's nearly empty table, and sank down onto the chair next to his.

No word of greeting. No asking if he minded having her sit next to him. She just plunked herself down and popped open the top of the drink she was carrying.

Junior started to slide his chair back from the table, but she stopped him by laying her hand on his forearm.

"Don't run away," she said, her voice a soft contralto. "I won't bite you."

All Junior could think of to say was, "I didn't think you would."

"Good," she said, with a bit of a smile.

For a few hours-long moments, Junior sat there, not knowing what to say, what to do.

"My name's Yolanda Nordquist," the woman said. "Everybody calls me Yola."

She might have been pretty if she weren't so fat, thought Junior. Hesitantly, he said, "My name's Walter Cron—"

"You're Sam Gunn Jr.," said Yola. "I looked it up."

Junior felt a pang of alarm. *There goes my Walter Cronkite disguise*, he told himself.

Patting his arm almost tenderly, Yola said, "Don't worry. I won't tell Old Fusspot about your little deception."

Junior blinked. Several times. He didn't know what to say. Nothing came into his mind. He felt like a tiny animal caught in the claws of some monstrous carnivore.

Yola broke into a low chuckle. "Old Fusspot thinks he runs this station. I allow him to think so. As long as he doesn't get in my way."

"So you actually run things here?"

She nodded heavily enough to make her cheeks quiver. Jabbing a stubby forefinger toward Junior's chest, she said darkly, "And don't you forget it. You want something—anything—you come see me."

"Not Director Johannsen?"

"That fluffball," Yola sneered. "He couldn't find his way to the men's room if I didn't show him where it was."

Junior saw fire flashing in the woman's pale-blue eyes.

"Really?" he asked. Squeaked, actually.

"Really," said Yolanda Nordquist. Firmly.

YOLANDA NORDQUIST

Junior sat there, wondering what he should do, what he should say, as Yolanda Nordquist gulped a pale-blue liquid from the bottle she was holding.

Say something! Junior commanded himself. Silently. Nothing came to his mind. He sat there, watching Nordquist guzzling her drink.

At last she put the bottle down on the tabletop and asked him, "So how'd it go down there?"

Relieved, Junior began to tell her about the darters.

Nordquist interrupted with, "I told Old Fusspot we should put a couple of lasers on the submersibles. But you know him, he can't—"

With a small shake of his head, Junior said, "I don't know him. Hardly at all."

She gave him a cold stare. "I told Johannsen weeks ago that we should give the subs some defensive weaponry. But not him! Strictly by the book, that's Old Fusspot. We ought to send *him* down there. That'll change his mind fast enough!"

Junior glanced around the nearly empty cafeteria. A pair of men—paper-pushers from the looks of their perfectly creased trousers and loose, hip-hugging overshirts—were the only other people sitting in the place. From the grins on their faces, it looked as if they'd heard this kind of gripe from Nordquist before.

"He *is* in command of this operation," Junior said. Quietly. Softly.

Nordquist inched closer to him. In a slightly lower voice, she countered, "He *thinks* he's in command. Actually, I am. In all but name."

"But still—"

"But still, he has top position in the organization chart. Big deal! *I* run this operation. Me. You want anything, you need anything, you come to me. Got it?"

"Anything?" Junior heard himself ask. His voice sounded low, weak, even to himself.

"Anything," Nordquist confirmed. "Except sex. I refuse to pollute my God-given body."

That's when Junior recognized the little silver medallion hanging on a thin chain around her neck, nearly hidden by wads of fat. A crucifix standing within a flaming circle: the symbol of some religious order.

"You're a believer," he said.

Nordquist fingered the medallion. "The New Morality saved my life," she said, in a reverential near whisper. "More important, they saved my soul."

For the next three-quarters of an hour, Junior sat in silence while Yolanda Nordquist unrolled the story of her life.

She'd been born in Uppsala, Sweden, not far from Stockholm, the nation's capital. She didn't remember much about her father, who left the little family while she was still in diapers. Her mother was a household servant, who lost her job to a robot.

"Instead of turning to God," Yolanda said, her voice bitter as acid, "she became a prostitute, a whore. She died when I was five years old. On my birthday. Beaten to death by a drunken Armenian sailor."

Yolanda was picked off the streets by a team of New Morality volunteers who brought her to their church, where she was sheltered and fed. And educated.

"Thank God they found me before one of the thugs living in the neighborhood took my virginity," Yolanda said, crossing herself solemnly.

Eventually, the New Morality sent her to one of their universities and got her a clerical position in the Swedish space program.

"One thing led to another," Yolanda said, drawing her tale to an end at last, "and here I am, running this bunch of godless scientists. Strange world, isn't it?"

Junior had sagged back in his chair as he listened to her numbing autobiography. He nodded silently, unable to get up from the chair while Nordquist still had her hand resting heavily on his forearm.

Abruptly, she demanded, "So what's this Walter Cronkite sham all about?"

His mind spinning desperately, Junior heard himself telling Nordquist something close to the truth. He couldn't think of anything else.

"I'm hiding out from Rocklege Industries. They want to kill me."

Nordquist stared at him. "Kill you? What for?"

Slowly, hesitantly, Junior unreeled the whole story of the asteroids he and Rex Klamath had claimed.

"I don't blame them," Nordquist said as Junior's tale wound haltingly to its end. "Those rocks must be worth a few billion."

Nodding, Junior muttered, "If you live long enough to spend the money."

She patted Junior's arm again. "Your secret's safe with me, Sammy. Don't give it another thought." And she smiled—*like a snake gliding up to its prey*, Junior thought.

ASSASSINS

Junior slept uneasily that night. Nordquist had promised to scan the dossiers of anyone visiting *Galileo*, looking for potential assassins. But her assurances didn't make Junior feel any safer. Assassins don't advertise their business, he knew. Whoever Rockledge—D'Argent, really—would send looking for him wouldn't put down their true intentions on a visitor's entry form.

On the other hand, he had to keep up his disguise as Walter Cronkite IV, aspiring newsman. And that meant going through the motions of gathering information for his news story. With one eye searching for a potential assassin.

Dr. Johannsen was happily leading Junior through every nook and cranny of the *Galileo* station, with special emphasis on his own role as leader and director of the study of the Leviathans.

"We have to learn how to communicate through pictures," he told Junior, as the two of them stood in the huge, clattering hangar watching the maintenance team repairing the damaged submersible.

"We only have two of these vessels," Johannsen explained over the noise and clamor the repair work. "I've asked Amsterdam for a third vessel, but you know how long it takes bureaucrats to decide on anything."

Junior fought down his instinct to point out to Johannsen that he himself was a bureaucrat, sitting at a desk while sending out crews to dive into the deep and dangerous Jovian ocean. But he kept the instinct to himself. Barely.

Several days passed. Johannsen seemed quite content to spend most of his time with Walter Cronkite IV, even offering to look over the material he had written so far. Junior politely demurred, and Johannsen didn't insist.

Nordquist was always in sight, though. Wherever Junior went, usually with Johannsen, the woman seemed to be hovering in the background, watching, listening, waiting—for what? Junior wondered.

There were other women among *Galileo*'s staff, of course. Some of them quite attractive. But they hovered on the periphery of Junior's daily tours with Johannsen. Besides, Nordquist was usually close by, close enough to foil any attempts at socializing.

So it was a pleasant surprise one morning when, instead of meeting Johannsen as usual, Junior was greeted in the passageway just outside his one-room quarters by a pair of crewmen.

"Dr. Johannsen asked us to show you the recycling center," said the taller of the two. He was few centimeters taller than Junior.

"It's down this way," said the second crewman, pointing. He was just about Junior's height and—like his partner—very solidly built.

With an accepting shrug, Junior went along with the two of them, down the station's central passageway and then off a narrower tube that led downward, below the station's main deck.

His two companions walked silently with him, one on either side.

After more than a quarter-hour, Junior asked, "How far is the recycling center?"

"Not much farther," said the taller of the two.

A few minutes later they stopped at a heavy-looking hatch. Junior saw instructions printed on the bulkhead alongside it. It was an airlock hatch. Beyond it was the vacuum of space.

Puzzled, he asked, "We're going outside?"

"You are."

"Me? Why? What for? I thought you said—"

The shorter of the two—blond, buzz-cut, the short sleeves of his blouse showing thick, muscular arms—said, "Forget what we said. You're going through that hatch."

Feeling alarmed, Junior demanded, "What's going on?"

The taller crewman said, "You're going to have an accident, pal."

"A fatal one," said his companion. And they grabbed Junior's arms.

"Hey! Wait! What are you doing?"

"We're making an investment in our futures," said the taller one, with a grim smile. And they pushed the struggling Junior closer to the airlock hatch.

Desperate, Junior shouted, "Investment? What are you talking about?"

"We're going to become the owners of three nifty little asteroids," said the shorter of the two.

The taller one scowled at his partner and snapped, "Keep your big mouth shut."

"What difference does it make? He won't be able to tell anybody." Turning back to Junior, he said, "Rockledge made

us a deal. We get rid of you and they give us three whole asteroids. They're worth zillions!"

Junior tried to dig in his heels, but they just slid along the
deck's smooth unyielding surface.

His mind churning madly, Junior gasped, "Three asteroids?
Three of them?"

"Yep. They're worth enough money for both of us to retire
like fuckin' maharajahs!"

"But Rockledge doesn't own them!" Junior shouted frantically. "I do!"

"You'll be too dead to file your claim."

"I've already filed the claim! On all three of them! You can
check it in the IAA files!"

The two of them didn't let go of Junior's arms, but they
stopped in front of the airlock hatch.

"*You* own them?"

"Not Rockledge?"

Trying to keep from hyperventilating, Junior gasped, "My
claim's on file with the IAA. You can check it out. Rockledge
is lying to you."

The two crewmen stared at each other. Junior thought he
felt their grip on his arms easing. Slightly.

"Check it out," Junior insisted. "Those rocks are mine, not
Rockledge's. I'll bet that before you get back Earthside to make
a claim about them, you'll both have fatal accidents."

The taller one muttered, "They're screwing us?"

"And good," said Junior. Quickly, he went on, "If you don't
believe me, just go look up my claim in the IAA files. I'm telling you the truth."

The shorter crewman let go of Junior's arm. "Whattaya
think?" he asked his partner.

His face screwed up with the effort of deciding whether or

not to believe Junior, the bigger one said, "You go back to our quarters and look up the record in the IAA files. I'll keep him here until you get back."

"Okay." And the man started back along the passageway at a trot.

The bigger man, still gripping Junior's arm, reached out and tapped on the hatch's control panel. The heavy, many-layered hatch slowly swung open.

"In you go," he said, pushing Junior into the airlock.

It was the longest wait in Junior's life. Nothing to do. The airlock chamber was bare, utilitarian. Not even a bench to sit on. And beyond the outer hatch, he knew, was the cold, radiation-drenched vacuum of space. *I'll be dead in less than a minute if he opens that hatch*, Junior knew.

At last the inner hatch opened again. The two crewmen wore equally guilty expression on their faces. Breathing a sigh of relief, Junior quickly stepped back into the passageway with them.

"The rocks are owned by somebody named Sam Gunn Jr.," growled the taller of the two.

"That's me!" said Junior.

"I thought your name was Cronkite."

Shaking his head vigorously, Junior said, "That's a phony name I made up. To fool Johannsen."

"Cronkite, Sam Gunn, what's the difference?" the shorter one said. "Rockledge is screwing us. What do we do now?"

Knowing his life was trembling on their decision, Junior quickly answered, "Don't get mad. Get even."

GETTING EVEN

"What do you mean?" asked the taller crewman.

"Rockledge has tried to screw you," Junior quickly replied. "They offered you those three rocks that actually belong to me. You'd be walking into a trap when you tried to return to Earth and claim your reward."

The shorter one shook his head woefully. "Some mess we got ourselves into."

With a wry smile, the taller one admitted, "I guess we're not cut out for this kind of work."

A good thing, Junior thought. *Whoever D'Argent assigned to get me out of his way was a fumbling oaf. Picking out two ordinary crewmen to commit murder.* He shook his head at the sheer lax stupidity of it.

A puzzled frown knitting his face, the taller one asked, "So what do we do? You gonna rat us out to Johannsen?"

"No," Junior snapped. "I'm going to go back Earthside and nail the man who got you into this mess."

"Without telling Johannsen?"

"Without telling anybody." Junior started up the passageway, away from the airlock. The two would-be assassins walked along-side him.

"Before anything else, though," Junior continued, "I'm going to sign over two of those asteroids to you. One apiece."

Surprised smiles bloomed on the faces of the two would-be assassins.

And after that, Junior added silently, *I'm heading back to Earth on the first vessel that's going that way.*

BOOK SEVEN: EARTH

GOING HOME

It took almost a month before a spacecraft that was heading all the way back to Earth docked at the *Galileo* station. Junior spent his time honing the news story he was crafting about the station's study of the life forms inhabiting Jupiter's globe-girdling ocean. He looked up every scrap of information about the Leviathans and the darters that he could find. And he made sure to draw a very flattering view of Director Johannsen, who was so pleased with the draft that Junior showed him that he added a few paragraphs about his childhood life—paragraphs that Junior quickly deleted from the final version.

So Walter Cronkite IV departed *Galileo* at last with Johannsen beaming at Junior while Yolanda Nordquist watched from a distance.

Did Nordquist have anything to do with the assassination attempt? Junior asked himself as he boarded the Earth-bound spacecraft. *Doesn't matter, really. I've seen the last of her.*

I hope.

=====

The spacecraft was named *Ulysses*. Like the ancient Greek hero, it was a wanderer, cruising from Earth to the human bases at Mars and Ceres and Jupiter, endlessly. Once in a while, it was scheduled sunward to the smaller station orbiting the planet Venus.

Primarily a cargo carrier, *Ulysses* still was equipped with a quartet of tight but surprisingly comfortable passenger cabins. The crew was minimal, three men and two lumpy, sour-faced women. Plus a half-dozen robots, which handled most of the housekeeping and maintenance chores. And the vessel's captain, a dour, mostly silent Chinese officer who ran the ship with quiet efficiency.

Perforce, Junior spent his mealtimes with the captain and human crew, in *Ulysses*'s bare-bones canteen: he had to squeeze in at the table between two of the crewmen. The captain, sitting at the head of the table (of course) was bleakly cheerless and mostly silent. Conversation was minimal. *I might as well be in solitary confinement*, Junior said to himself.

He had plenty of time to polish the piece he had written about Johannsen and the people delving into Jupiter's all-encompassing ocean, trying to make meaningful contact with the Leviathans—while avoiding the darters.

The captain had no interest in showing Junior anything of the vessel's accouterments. *Ulysses* was basically a freighter, carrying needed equipment and supplies to the scientists in orbit around Jupiter. Nothing exotic or dramatic about that. The vessel was doing a job, plying back and forth between Jupiter and the stations orbiting Earth, with occasional stopovers in-between. Strictly utilitarian. Nothing glamorous. As far as the captain was concerned Junior was an extra piece of cargo, nothing more.

Junior could feel himself going slowly insane from

boredom. He spent more and more of his time staring at the little viewscreen above his cabin's desk, watching the faint blue speck of Earth slowly, slowly growing into a recognizable arc of glowing blue and white.

Home, Junior breathed softly, silently. *D'Argent is there. I wonder if he'll be surprised to see me?*

He asked himself, *How will I get to see him?*

Then a new thought arose in his mind. *Deborah's there, somewhere. How can I find her?*

———

The day came at last.

Earth hung in a bright blue-and-white curve of warmth and life set against the bleak, dark emptiness of space. Junior sat in his compartment staring at it, tears of joy welling in his eyes.

I should contact Malone, Junior thought. *He's at Selene, on the Moon. He'll be surprised to hear from me. And Big George, out at Ceres. Him too.*

Junior had sent copies of his finished piece about the Jupiter team's work (and Johannsen's leadership) to every news outlet he could think of. So far, no response from any of them.

So much for Walter Cronkite IV's career in journalism, he thought.

As he made his way to *Ulysses's* main airlock, Junior was surprised to see the captain standing by the hatch, smiling genially. Extending his hand, the captain said, "I hope you enjoyed your trip, Mr. Cronkite."

Swallowing the reply that leaped to the forefront of his mind, Junior answered, "It was very restful. Thank you, Captain."

With that, he ducked through the hatch and into the slightly springy tunnel that led to the receiving area of the satellite orbiting Earth. The wheel-shaped satellite was spinning at a rate to produce terrestrial gravity. For the first time in months, Junior felt Earth's full gravity. His knees buckled momentarily, but he straightened up and strode toward the desk where a pretty young woman was waiting, smilingly.

Junior presented his ID card to the woman at the reception desk. She slipped it into the slot on her desktop equipment. Her smile evaporated, replaced by a puzzled frown.

"Gunn?" she asked, looking up at Junior. "But my data says you're Walter Cronkite the Fourth."

Junior shrugged and smiled at her. "I'm Sam Gunn Junior."

"Some screw-up here," the young woman muttered. "You're supposed to be Walter Cronkite."

Still smiling, Junior said, "I had the same problem at the *Galileo* station. Somehow my data has gotten mixed up with this Cronkite guy."

It took a lot of talk, and a quick trip to the station's minuscule medical facility, but at last the highly automated equipment concluded that Junior actually was Sam Gunn Jr. and Walter Cronkite IV was nowhere in sight.

Feeling relieved, almost cheerful, Junior walked swiftly from the reception center and its puzzled female employee to the docking area where the next Earthbound shuttle was taking on passengers.

He couldn't help feeling excited as the shuttle's uniformed crew showed him to his seat in the passenger section and the video screen on the seatback in front of him made its way through the standard safety lecture.

Then, with a gentle puff of thrust, the shuttle departed from the orbiting station and started down toward Boston's aerospaceport.

On Earth.

===

Junior toted his one scant travel bag through the incoming inspection station, then, at last, stepped out onto the sidewalk of busy, bustling suburban Boston. The sky was a perfect blue, dotted with white puffs of cumulous; a fresh, cool breeze was wafting in from the Bay. The sidewalk was crowded with men and women busily hurrying past; beyond them was the street, clogged with slow-moving cars, taxis, buses, and trucks, bleating their horns cacophonously.

Home! Junior pulled in a deep breath. Not much like Nevada, but the very air smelled of home. He felt a thrill of recognition. Just standing on the sidewalk without needing a protective suit, just breathing the tangy air, was a joyful pleasure.

Then he remembered two things: First, he had in his meager travel bag a certified check for slightly more than six million New International Dollars: the payment for the asteroid he had held the claim to. Second, he had to find Pierre D'Argent and tell the scheming head of Rockledge Industries that he was going to destroy him, one way or another.

For a moment, the weight of his goal almost pressed the breath out of him. But only for a moment. Squaring his shoulders and straightening to his full height, Junior stepped into the line of arriving shuttle passengers who were waiting for a taxicab.

Where to? he asked himself. *To the best hotel in Boston,* he answered. *Where else?*

THE COPLEY PLAZA

From the window of the taxi, the hotel looked shabby. Heading toward its third century of existence, the Copley Plaza reminded Junior of an elderly man he had known back in Nevada: wrinkled, poorly dressed, but too proud to accept anyone's help.

"I got this far on my Air Force pension," he would say. "Guess it'll carry me the rest of the way."

Junior wondered what had happened to the old guy since he'd left Nevada. He thought that if he himself lived that long, he'd take advantage of every life-extension technology the medical profession offered.

But you need money for that, he told himself. *Better start a retirement fund.*

Inside, the Copley Plaza was in much better condition than its exterior showed. The registration desk looked sleekly new, gleaming polished mahogany and green-streaked marble, with a combination of human and robotic staff to take care of newly arrived guests. Junior had no reservation, but that caused little difficulty, especially when he asked for "a small suite. I'm a writer of sorts, and I need a quiet nook where I can work in peace."

Within minutes a team of one robot and one assistant

manager showed Junior to a mini-suite on one of the hotel's upper floors.

"You can see the bay from here in the bedroom," said the assistant manager, with a professional smile, as the robot deftly deposited Junior's paltry bag on the suite's sumptuous king-sized bed.

Nodding his approval, Junior handed the youngish man a good-sized tip and nodded smilingly to the robot.

Once they left Junior alone in the suite, he swiftly booted up the computer on the desk in the second bedroom and started searching for anything he could find that bore the name of Pierre D'Argent.

There were only a few news stories about D'Argent, mostly under the business category. But there were several more about his latest wife, a Boston blueblood who was apparently quite active in the city's social life.

After nearly an hour of trolling the news stories, Junior found what he wanted: Mr. and Mrs. Pierre D'Argent were hosting a charity dinner and dance event at—of all places—the Copley Plaza Hotel! This very evening.

———

Wearing a newly rented conservatively cut white tuxedo, Walter Cronkite IV made his way down to the hotel's main ballroom, just a few minutes after 10:00 p.m. Junior had phoned the dinner's reception desk and asked to be included at the last minute on their guest list. The young woman to whom he spoke had no idea of who Walter Cronkite IV was, but the addition of *the fourth* made him sound important enough for her to agree to add his name to the guest list.

Besides, Junior realized that the woman must have been close to his own age, and perhaps she would appreciate having someone at this dinosaur's gathering with whom she might socialize.

He stepped into the ballroom, just off the hotel's main lobby. It was half-filled with mostly older couples, gray-haired but beautifully dressed in shimmering evening gowns and freshly pressed tuxedos. A live five-piece orchestra was playing nostalgic songs, so softly that Junior could barely make out their tunes over the quiet chatter of the guests. None of the gray-haired couples were dancing.

The young woman who had added Walter Cronkite's name to the guest list was nowhere in sight, but on the other end of the quietly buzzing ballroom, Junior spotted Pierre D'Argent, with a familiar-looking young woman at his side, wearing a low-cut midnight-black evening gown. On his other side was an older woman, decked in a sky-blue gown of much more modest style, glittering with jewelry.

She must be his wife, Junior thought, *and the younger one must be*—Junior's eyes went wide with sudden recognition—*Linda Venture!*

So she's attached herself to D'Argent, Junior said to himself. *Or more likely he's attached himself to her. Mrs. D doesn't seem to mind.*

Accepting a long-stemmed cocktail glass from the robot waiter trundling through the muted meager crowd, Junior slowly worked his way toward Pierre D'Argent, keeping behind the Rockledge president as much as possible. *Surprise is always a good weapon,* he told himself.

At last he stepped to D'Argent's side and, with a bright smile, extended his right hand. "Mr. D'Argent! How good to see you again!"

For a flash of a second, D'Argent's face went ash-white, his eyes bulged.

But he quickly recovered his composure and grasped Junior's hand—a bit weakly, Junior thought.

"S-Samuel!" D'Argent gasped. "What are you doing here?"

Instead of drifting through empty space, dead, Junior thought.

Aloud, Junior replied, "I couldn't resist joining your little party. It's good to see you again."

Glancing beyond Junior, searching for his security people, D'Argent temporized, "How have you been? I thought you were out at the Jupiter station."

"I was," said Junior, still smiling, "but a couple of your people convinced me to come back home."

"My people? I don't have any employees at the Jupiter station."

With a shrug, Junior replied, "Maybe I was mistaken. But they did use your name."

"How . . . very strange."

"Yes, isn't it?"

His aplomb almost completely recovered, D'Argent said to the little crowd around him, "People, I'd like you to meet Sam Gunn Junior."

A sort of gasp puffed from the onlookers.

"Sam Gunn *Junior?*"

"I thought the man was dead."

"You're his son?"

But Junior had shifted his attention to Linda Venture. Still standing at D'Argent's side, she looked shocked, struggling for breath. In the low-cut gown she was wearing, her struggle was worth studying.

"How are you, Linda?" Junior asked.

"I . . . I'm fine, Sam. Good to see you alive and well."

Junior's smile widened a little. "That's good to know."

A couple of burly men in tight-fitting tuxedos stepped up to D'Argent's side.

"Sam," the Rockledge president said, his forced smile gone, his eyes stony, "you should come see me at the office. We have a lot to talk about."

With a curt nod, Junior said to the crowd, "Pierre and I have put together an outstanding museum on Mars, all about how we Earthlings have pictured Mars and its inhabitants." Turning slightly back toward D'Argent, he asked, "How's the museum doing, Pierre?"

Obviously unhappy with Junior's using his first name, D'Argent said, through gritted teeth, "Not as well as we hoped. It's a long way to travel, just to visit a museum."

Gesturing toward Linda, Junior said, "Even with Linda's posing as Dejah Thoris?"

With a quick glance at his wife, D'Argent answered glumly, "Even so."

Taking Linda by the wrist and pulling her toward himself, Junior told the little group, "It's worth a trip to Mars to see this beautiful woman posed as a princess of Mars."

That started everyone talking at once. Leaning even closer to Linda, Junior asked, "How's he treating you?"

"Just fine," she replied, in a flat, emotionless tone.

One of the bodyguards that D'Argent had summoned said to Junior, "You'll have to leave now."

The other one grasped Junior's forearm. "Don't make a fuss. Just go quietly."

Smiling at him, Junior asked, "Or you'll break my arm?"

"If I have to."

"In front of all these nice people?"

The bodyguard frowned and looked toward D'Argent, who had turned his attention to his wife and the couple standing next to her.

"Come on now, kid. No fuss. No trouble."

With a shrug, Junior said, "Okay. But you guys stay here. I can find the exit by myself."

"Good."

As Junior walked through the crowd, he thought, *Okay, you've shown D'Argent that you're alive and well. But how long is that going to last?*

REPERCUSSIONS

Stretched out on the sumptuous bed in his hotel suite, Junior tossed uneasily, waiting for sleep that refused to come to him.

So D'Argent's here, just as you thought he'd be. So what? How are you going to get to him? How are you going to prevent him and his goons from getting to you?

The sky outside his bedroom window was starting to turn pearly gray before his eyes closed at last and he drifted into a troubled sleep.

He dreamed.

It was a confused, disturbing dream with D'Argent and a host of unknown demons chasing him. Junior was struggling up a steep mountain slope, somehow knowing that Deborah Salmon was waiting for him at its distant, snow-covered peak. But despite his exhausting exertions, he could not reach her. And D'Argent and his beast-like minions were on his tail, growling and snarling, constantly getting closer.

Junior's eyes popped open. He was safe in his bed, the sheets tangled around him, soaking wet with perspiration.

Bleary eyed, Junior uncoiled himself from the sheets and shambled into the bathroom. His image in the mirror over the sink looked woebegone: dark circles beneath his eyes, red hair tangled and sweaty.

Once he had showered and let the hot-air blowers dry his dripping body, Junior stepped back into the bedroom and saw that the message light on his bedside telephone was blinking.

Wondering who might have called, he commanded the phone, "Answer, please."

Big George Ambrose's thickly bearded face filled the wall screen.

"Hi, kid. Give me a buzz when you get a minute, will ya?"

Junior stared at George's face, frozen on the screen. *How'd he know I'm here?*

Punching the phone's *reply* button, he called out, "George! How'd you know I was here?"

And then he waited, knowing that it would take at least an hour for his message to reach Ceres, out in the Asteroid Belt, where George was. Junior phoned room service and ordered breakfast, then dressed. He was just finishing the last of his coffee when the phone beeped again.

"Answer!"

Big George Ambrose's red-bearded, tousle-haired face filled the screen. "'ello, mate," he said cheerfully. "How're the bots bitin'?"

"I'm fine, Georgie," Junior replied. "But how did you find me?"

It was almost lunchtime before George's answer reached Boston. "Saw the piece you did about Dr. Johannsen and the creatures in Jupiter's ocean. The byline was for some bloke named Water Cronkite, but the photo was you. From there on in it was just searchin' data bases, lookin' for either name."

"You're a blooming detective, Georgie!"

Their conversation limped along, each message traveling more than an hour before it could be answered.

It was while he was waiting for George to reply to him

that it hit Junior. *He saw my interview with Johannsen? It's been published? By whom?* And immediately Junior asked himself, *Why haven't they paid me?*

George told Junior his article about the Jupiter station's work—and people—had been published in an electronic journal called *Interplanetary News.* Junior immediately looked it up and, sure enough, there was his piece about Dr. Johannsen and his team's work among the denizens of Jupiter's all-encompassing sea.

CONTACT!!!

SCIENTISTS ORBITING JUPITER MAKE FIRST CONTACT WITH GIGANTIC JOVIAN CREATURES.

TEAM'S DIRECTOR BELIEVES IMMENSE CREATURES ARE INTELLIGENT.

Accompanying the article was a photo of Junior, identified as Walter Cronkite IV, together with a brief biographical article about the original Walter Cronkite, back in the twentieth century.

Feeling both pleased that his article had been published and annoyed at not being paid for it, Junior looked up the contact information about the journal's top editor, identified as "Norm Quill."

Quill? Junior asked himself as he told the phone the number given beneath Quill's name. *Obviously a pen name.* And he broke into a grin at his unintended pun.

A photo of a stern-looking middle-aged man filled the computer screen, with a message that spelled out a standard "Leave your name and a contact number and we'll get back to you as soon as possible."

Somewhat testily, Junior said, "This is Walter Cronkite IV, and I want to know why you haven't paid for—"

The image of the editor's chiseled features disappeared from the screen, replaced by a young woman's pert, wide-eyed face.

"You're Cronkite?" she asked, breathlessly. Before Junior could reply she went on, "Yes, of course you are! I've been searching and searching for you! You're a hard guy to find!"

Edging back a little in the desk chair he was sitting on, Junior said, "Sorry about that, but here I am, in Boston. I'd like to speak to Mr. Quill."

"We owe you for the payment on your article, right?"

"Right," said Junior. "If I can talk with Mr. Quill—"

"*Ms.* Quill," the young woman corrected. "That's me. I'm Norma Quill. I run the *Interplanetary News.*"

"You? But the picture—"

"That's my grandfather. When he died I took over the sheet."

"Oh."

"So you're in Boston and you want your money."

"Where are you?" Junior asked.

"Not far. Suburban Philadelphia, in a town called Yeadon."

"I guess I could hop an air taxi and come see you."

"No need. I'll wire the money to you. Where are you, what's your address?"

"I'm at the Copley Plaza Hotel."

Norma Quill's eyes went round. "You can afford the Copley Plaza and you're hounding me for a measly hundred New Dollars?"

Junior felt his brows knitting. "It's the principle of the thing, not the amount involved."

"What are you, some kind of millionaire?"

"Not exactly."

"How're you related to the original Walter Cronkite?" Quill pressed. "I couldn't find anything about his family in the news feeds. Or about you."

Junior temporized, "It's a long story."

"I'm all ears."

"Not on the phone . . ."

"Okay, then come on down here to Yeadon. I'd like to meet you in the flesh."

"Why don't you fly up here to Boston?"

"I can't. I've got responsibilities here in Yeadon: the *News*, family, that sort of thing."

Her pert young face had taken on a stony expression. Junior recognized the look. She wasn't going to budge.

"You can afford the taxi fare," she coaxed.

Junior thought, *I might as well get out of this hotel. Don't stay in one place long enough for D'Argent's goons to get their hands on you.*

So Junior agreed to fly down to Yeadon, Pennsylvania, wherever that was. He checked out of the hotel, walked to the nearest bank, and personally deposited his certified check, then found an air taxi terminal and booked a ride to Yeadon, Pa.

━━━━━

The taxi was smallish, built to seat three passengers. It flew in automation mode, although a skinny young human driver sat up front, his full attention focused on a thud and blunder video about modern pirates and the gallant military men and women who scoured the seas to hunt them down.

Completely under ground-based control, the taxi weaved through fairly thick air traffic and eventually landed on a quiet suburban street lined with neat, well-tended three-story houses.

The taxi drove away and took to the air, leaving Junior standing on the tree-lined sidewalk, checking the address Norma Quill had given him. It was a sizable three-story house, not appreciably different from the other houses lining the quiet street on both sides.

With a puzzled shrug, Junior walked up the flagstone pathway that led to its front door. Before he could find the button for the bell, the door swung open, revealing an elfin, smiling young woman. In a powered wheelchair.

"Walter Cronkite the Fourth," she said, without preamble.

Shrugging slightly, Junior confessed, "Not exactly."

Norma Quill's smile turned slightly quizzical. "Come on in, Walt." She backed her wheelchair away from the door and Junior stepped in. He saw that she had no legs. Both of them ended in stumps slightly below her hips.

Junior followed her wheelchair through a perfectly normal-looking entryway and living room, and then into a smallish room that had been turned into an office. A desk, bookshelves filled with magazines and news sheets, a couple of leather-covered chairs, a painting on one wall of the man Junior had seen identified as Norm Quill, and a window that looked out on the front lawn and a sprightly young birch tree in full green bloom.

"It's not much but it's home," said Norma as she wheeled behind the desk.

Junior nodded and sat in one of the chairs. It creaked comfortingly.

"So," said Norma, still smiling at Junior, "the *News* owes you a hundred New Dollars."

Junior nodded, still taking in the room's accouterments.

She opened one of the desk's drawers and yanked an old-fashioned checkbook out of it. "Make it out to Walter Cronkite IV?"

"Uh, no," said Junior. "To Sam Gunn Jr."

"Sam . . . Not *the* Sam Gunn?"

"He was my father."

"Really?"

"Really."

"Wow! Now, that's a news story!"

Junior heard himself blurt, "What happened to your legs?"

For just an instant Norma's face flushed slightly red. But she controlled the reaction and replied, "Auto accident. I'm supposed to be getting bionic replacements, but there's some hang-up with the paperwork."

"Oh."

"They tried to kill me," Norma said in a flatly unemotional tone, but Junior saw the bitterness in her face.

He blurted, "Who tried to kill you?"

Norma shrugged. "The wise guys."

"Wise guys?"

"The mob. Organized crime."

Little by little, Norma explained the situation. She had started work on an article about how electronic "distance learning" had changed schools in America. "You know," Norma explained easily, "the kids stay home. Desktop computers replace printed books. Or laptops."

Junior listened as she spoke of how she stumbled on evidence that organized crime had infiltrated school systems in Pennsylvania and many other states, siphoning off money supposedly budgeted for teachers and other staff.

"Then the mob got into the school books. They got rid of any unfavorable references to crime and criminals. The texts started to look like *Dick and Jane* stories for kindergartners! Kids graduated without learning anything, just shoved up and out of the system!"

"So you were going to publish an exposé."

"Until a goddamned sixteen-wheeler pushed me off the

road," Norma said, with some heat. "I wrote the piece while I was in the hospital, but nobody would publish it! And now they've screwed up the replacement legs I was supposed to get . . ."

She bowed her head, fighting back tears.

Norma's little office went totally silent. Junior sat in front of her desk, watching her struggle to control herself, wondering what he could do to help her.

At last he broke the silence. "I'll get your piece published, Norma."

"How?"

"But not on Earth."

"Not on Earth?"

"On Ceres, the Rock Rats' base."

She frowned at him. "What good will that do?"

Grinning at her, Junior explained, "Lots of the Rock Rats have children they send back here to Earth for their education. And relatives here on Earth. A piece about the schools published in Ceres will get picked up by the Earthside news outlets."

"You think so?"

"I'm sure of it," Junior enthused. "But you better put a pen name on it. That'd be safer."

"Whose name?"

"Walter Cronkite IV."

"Yours?"

"It's an alias I've used."

"Then they'll come after you!"

Junior shrugged. "Old Walter the Fourth doesn't really exist. They'll never find him."

"You think so?"

"I'm sure." But Junior knew he wasn't as confident as he wanted her to believe.

SEARCHING

So Junior moved into Norma Quill's house. It was nearly empty. Her parents were dead, and her two-year-old brother had been taken to Arizona by one of her two older brothers, who both lived in that state.

Junior sent Norma's article to Big George, out at Ceres, together with an explanation of what had happened to Norma.

Nearly two hours later, George huffed, "Damn' near killed her, did they?"

Nodding at the redhead's glowering image on Norma's computer screen, Junior confirmed, "They tried, all right. That's why we're using the Cronkite persona."

After the usual time lag, George reappeared on the computer's screen. He dipped his shaggy head in agreement. "We got no organized crime out here," he said. "Some petty theft and such, but otherwise most folks out here are on the up-and-up."

"Good," said Junior.

====

While they waited for Norma's article to be published at Ceres, Junior realized he could ask her for a favor.

"I'm trying to find someone," he told Norma, as they sat in her snug little office. "I don't where she's gotten to."

"She?"

"She seems to have just plain vanished," Junior said, not noticing the slight frown that wrinkled Norma's brow. "Do you think you could do a search for her?"

Norma hesitated a moment, then replied, "Sure. Why not?"

Grinning at her, Junior said, "And I'll return the favor."

"You will? How?"

"I'll get your legs for you."

Her eyes widened for an instant. Then she asked, "How are you going to do that?"

"Watch," said Junior.

———

He started with the Health Service flunky that Norma had been working with.

"This is Walter Cronkite IV," Junior said, in his sternest, most authoritative voice. "I'm doing a story about problems in the Health Service's replacement limb program."

The bony face of the young woman on Norma's computer screen showed more annoyance than apprehension.

"And who do you represent, Mr. Cronkite?" she asked, in a voice like a dentist's drill.

Junior replied firmly, "The American taxpayer."

That started an upward-flowing cascade through the bureaucracy of the Health Service: from the thin-faced flunky to her section manager, from the manager to the department chief, from the chief to the division head, and at last to the director of the Health Service's public relations department.

He was an inoffensive-looking middle-aged man, with a smiling round face, receding hairline, and chubby fingers that drummed incessantly on his desktop.

"And just who do you represent, Mr. Cronkite?" he asked pleasantly.

"At the moment I'm working on a story about a young woman who has been waiting patiently for replacement legs. She lost her legs in an automobile accident more than a year ago, and your agency's sluggishness in getting her a replacement set is hard to understand, sir."

The PR director's pleasant expression didn't falter for a moment. "If you'll give me the young lady's name and her Health Service identification number, I'll be happy to look up her file for you."

Junior gestured to Norma, who wheeled next to him and spoke her name and ID number to the computer.

The PR director smiled and nodded as the information appeared on his screen. "Very good. This will only take a minute." He turned slightly away from the screen and peered at a different computer.

Junior leaned back in his typist's chair.

It took more than a minute, but at last the bureaucrat broke into a toothy smile and said, "Ah, yes. Here it is. The young lady's replacement limbs have been held up by a labor dispute in Bethesda." Before Junior could respond to that, he went on, "But that's been all cleared up. She should be getting a call from the clinic in a day or two to set up a time for her procedure."

Junior glanced at Norma, who was wreathed in a big smile, then said sternly to the PR director, "A day or two?"

"Tomorrow," the man gulped. "I will personally see to it that the clinic calls her tomorrow. Without fail!"

Keeping an unsmiling stern face, Junior said, "Our conversation has been recorded, of course. If she doesn't hear from the clinic by the end of business tomorrow—"

"Oh, she will! You have my word on that!"

"Very good. Thank you."

"You're entirely welcome," said the PR man. "Now, tell me, please, which news outlet do you represent, Mr. Cronkite?"

With just the beginning of a grin, Junior replied, "The biggest one, of course."

"Of course," repeated the PR director.

Junior thanked him politely, ended the call, and turned to Norma. "I remember a line from an ancient television show that I watched when I was a kid."

"What line?" Norma asked.

Lowering his voice to a dramatic resonance, Junior recited:

"The freedom of the press is like a flaming sword: Hold it high. Use it wisely. *Guard it well.*"

REX KLAMATH

Sure enough, the next day Norma received a call from the Health Service, setting up an appointment for the surgery that would fit her with new legs. She happily agreed to come to the hospital in Philadelphia, grinned as she tapped the keyboard button that ended the call, then wheeled her chair around her desk and threw her arms around Junior's neck.

"You did it, Sam!" she gushed.

Feeling his face reddening, Junior mumbled, "It wasn't so tough."

And, despite his instinctive drive, he kept his hands to himself.

Early the next morning he went with Norma in an air taxi to the hospital, then left her in a semiprivate room and taxied back to Yeadon.

Alone in the big, empty house, Junior picked up on the computer search for Deborah Salmon. Her last known residence was at an aunt's home in California, just north of San Francisco Bay. The aunt, scowling suspiciously at Junior's image on her screen, told him that Deborah had visited with her for more than a week, then abruptly packed her travel bag and left for parts unknown.

"You have no idea of where she might have gone?" Junior asked, plaintively.

"'Fraid not," said the aunt.

Junior thanked her and cut the connection. *Dead end*, he thought. *I'll never find her.*

Later that day he got a call from Big George. The massive redhead looked grim. "Found your dwarf."

Sitting at Norma's desk, Junior felt a pulse of excitement. "Rex! You've found Rex Klamath?"

More than ninety minutes later, George nodded somberly, "He's dead."

Junior's innards seemed to drop away. "Dead?"

"One of the prospectors—out on the far edge of the Belt, he was—picked up the wreckage of a vessel. It was Klamath's ship, the *Idaho*. Looks like it was sliced up by laser beams."

"Who . . . ?"

George shrugged heavily. "Dunno. Must've happened a few weeks earlier, at least."

"And Rex?"

"No sign of 'im. Must've been blown out of the ship when it was hit."

"Hit by a Rockledge kill team," Junior said.

"No way to tell," said George, morosely. "Happens sometimes, out here. Things can get rough."

"Rockledge killed him," Junior insisted. "D'Argent killed him."

With a shake of his head, George replied, "Try provin' *that* in a court o' law."

Junior said nothing. But he thought, *I'm going to get that slimy bastard. If it's the last thing I do, I'm going to get him.*

And he realized that, in all probability, it *would* be the last thing he did.

━━

Still seething with frustrated anger, Junior tried to reach D'Argent on the phone. It wasn't easy. He had to scuffle his way through a small army of underlings. The first ones he encountered frowned with displeasure as they sing-songed that "Mr. D'Argent is a very busy man. If you'll tell me your business, I'll see that the message reaches him promptly."

To which Junior replied, "This is a very personal matter between Mr. D'Argent and me. I must speak to him face-to-face."

And up a layer of the Rockledge bureaucracy he would advance, until finally he was speaking to D'Argent's personal assistant, a sleek-looking young woman with long chestnut hair and smoky eyes.

She started with the same tired line, "Mr. D'Argent is a very busy man—"

"So am I," Junior snapped. "You tell him that Sam Gunn Jr. wants to see him, or you'll be looking for a new job before the close of business this afternoon."

The long-haired assistant blinked once, then put on a thin smile. "I'll see if he's available."

Junior sat at Norma's desk and stared at the Rockledge logo on the computer screen as he counted to himself, *One, one thousand; two, one thousand; three . . .*

Before he reached ten, the screen cleared to show Pierre D'Argent's face, smiling dimly.

"Samuel! How nice of you to call."

Forcing himself to smile back, Junior said, "Let's have lunch, Pierre."

"By all means! Would tomorrow be good for you?"

"Fine."

"Excellent. I'll call my club—"

"No," Junior interrupted. "I'll pick the restaurant."

His smile fading a bit, D'Argent replied, "Very well. Where?"

"I'll call you tomorrow."

"Very well. But Rockledge will pick up the tab, so make it a decent place."

"Certainly," Junior said, with a genuine smile.

"Good," D'Argent said. "And make the reservation for three. I'll bring along a friend."

A bodyguard? Junior wondered. *Or an assassin?*

TOP OF THE HUB

It was one of the oldest restaurants in downtown Boston, sitting on the top floor of a skyscraper that had dominated the city's skyline for more than a century.

Most of the customers crowding the Top of the Hub looked like tourists to Junior—visitors with children who had come to the old city to see Bunker Hill, the Old North Church, and other landmarks of the American Revolution.

Junior got a window seat where—on a clear day—you could see all the way out to the green hills of New Hampshire. The weather was indeed crystal clear, but Junior paid scant attention to the view.

He arrived a bit early and followed a rather cute waitress wearing a miniskirt to the table he'd reserved for himself, D'Argent, and whoever D'Argent was bringing with him.

The restaurant was abuzz with chatter and children pointing to landmarks they recognized from the printed maps that served as place mats. Junior ordered a non-alcoholic drink and as the waiter was depositing it on his table, he saw Pierre D'Argent making his way following the same waitress toward his window-side table, accompanied by the stumpy dwarfish figure of Rex Klamath!

Junior popped to his feet and held both his arms out for his erstwhile partner.

"Rex! You're alive!"

Klamath glanced up at D'Argent, then half-smiled and replied, "Sort of."

D'Argent's smile was cold, hollow. "I thought I'd reunite the two of you."

"How are you, Rex?" Junior blurted as the dwarf clambered onto the chair that the waitress had pulled out for him.

As Junior and D'Argent took their chairs, Junior asked excitedly, "How'd you get here? How are you?"

"Like I said," Klamath answered, "I'm alive."

"Thanks to Rockledge's medical department," said D'Argent. "He was frozen solid when my people located him. Like a block of ice. It took our best medical talent to revive him and save his brain cells. Otherwise, he would have been a blank, a newborn."

"Thanks, Pierre. You've saved his life."

"At a very hefty cost. My accounting people are still toting up the New Dollars of the procedures we've had to do."

Without hesitation, Junior said, "S. Gunn & Company will reimburse you."

With a nod and the beginning of a smile, D'Argent replied, "That will be as good a way to bankrupt you as any."

———

It was a tedious luncheon. Rex Klamath looked healthy and normal, except that he was dressed in an odd sort of plain gray one-piece outfit, studded with little bumps up and down his arms, legs, and torso. And he glanced at D'Argent every time before he spoke. *Like a trained animal that looks to its master before it does anything*, Junior thought.

"So I was sitting in my ship eating dinner when all of a sudden it starts to blow apart. I hardly had time to pull on a pressure suit before I got blasted out into space."

D'Argent sat smiling coldly through Rex's narration. "A Rockledge ship happened to cruise past the site of the accident."

Junior felt his teeth clench at D'Argent's terming the incident an accident, but he forced himself to remain silent.

"Our vessel picked up our little friend as he was tumbling through empty space. He was quite unconscious, frozen like a popsicle, almost dead."

"And they revived him," said Junior.

"No, they didn't have the facilities nor the trained personnel for that," D'Argent replied, quite matter-of-factly. "They checked with our people in the Jupiter station and brought him there. That's where he was revived."

Rex sat between them, his head swiveling back and forth as D'Argent explained what had happened, and Junior asked questions.

At last D'Argent smiled down at the dwarf and said, "You're a lucky little man, Rex."

"He would have been luckier," Junior grumbled, "if your ship hadn't attacked him."

"Our ship?" D'Argent put on an expression of wounded innocence. "Really, Samuel. We've gone to great expense to save his little life and you accuse us of trying to kill him?"

"Who else would try to?"

D'Argent looked down at Klamath. "What do you think, Rex?"

The dwarf glanced at Junior, then quickly turned back to D'Argent. "I owe you my life, Mr. D'Argent," he said, in a voice that sounded pitiable to Junior.

"You see?" D'Argent said to Junior.

Junior didn't know how to respond, what to say, what

to do. The three of them finished their luncheons in tense silence.

When the check came, D'Argent made something of a show paying it. Then he pushed his chair back and got to his feet. Rex Klamath scrambled out of his chair and stood up beside the Rockledge president. Junior rose slowly, unsure of what he should say.

"For your information," D'Argent said airily, "I've made Rex here my personal assistant. He'll have a position with Rockledge for as long as he lives."

Junior glanced down at Klamath, who seemed to be writhing like a man afflicted with some loathsome disease.

"That's good," said Junior tonelessly. "Lots of luck, Rex."

"Yeah," said the dwarf. "Thanks, Sam."

D'Argent put on a satisfied smile and said, "I'd like to see you in my office tomorrow morning, first thing. We have a few things to discuss."

Junior nodded wordlessly, then watched D'Argent walk away from their table, toward the restaurant's exit, with Rex Klamath trotting along beside him like a well-trained puppy.

D'ARGENT'S OFFICE

Junior knew his meeting with D'Argent was going to be tense, unpleasant, but he saw no way to avoid it. *The Rockledge president has Rex in the palm of his hand*, Junior realized. And Rex looked miserable. *How to free him?*

Good question, Junior said to himself as he rode in a half-filled elevator to the top floor of the Rockledge Building in Boston's financial district.

D'Argent was all smiles and good will as his slinky assistant showed Junior into his office. It was a huge room: two walls were made entirely of floor-to-ceiling windows looking out on Boston's busy streets and the glittering Bay beyond. The other walls were covered with bookshelves and fine reproductions of famous artworks.

And there was Rex, standing in a far corner of the oversized room, in front of the big refrigerator/freezer combination that towered over his dwarfish figure. Still wearing a one-piece outfit studded with those odd protrusions.

Once Junior had seated himself in front of D'Argent's handsome wide desk, the Rockledge president said, with a snake's smile, "Samuel, you and Rex have euchred

Rockledge out of three rather valuable asteroids. We want them back."

"Back?" Junior retorted. "You never owned them. My claim was approved by the IAA, and—"

"Never mind the song and dance," D'Argent snapped. "I want those rocks. Now."

Junior grinned at him and shrugged. "I don't own them anymore. Two of them I gave to the two goons your people hired to murder me. The third I've sold off through the IAA's normal procedure."

D'Argent's smile stayed in place, but his eyes went cold.

He said, in a thin, bitter voice, "Then we want payment for them. I'll call up the exact figures—"

With a curt shake of his head, Junior replied, "You're too late, Pierre. Legally, Rockledge never had a claim on those asteroids."

"That's because you and your friend, here," D'Argent nodded in Klamath's direction, "screwed us out of them."

"It was all strictly legal," Junior insisted. "The IAA saw nothing wrong—"

"I don't care what the IAA thinks!" D'Argent snapped. "I want those rocks, or their monetary value."

Junior heard the unspoken, *or else*. He pushed his chair back and started to get to his feet. "I don't think we really have anything to discuss, Pierre."

Jabbing a forefinger in Klamath's direction, D'Argent hissed, "What about our little friend?"

Sinking back onto his chair, Junior half-whispered, "What do you mean by that?"

With a cold smile, D'Argent turned to Klamath and called out, "Rex, roll over."

Obediently, Klamath went into a clumsy, makeshift roll.

"Now hop, skip, and jump."

Klamath did as he was told.

"Would you like to see more?" D'Argent asked, smiling thinly. "He'll do whatever I tell him to. I can make him jump out the window, if you like."

Slowly Junior rose to his feet. "You are a first-class son of a bitch, Pierre."

His smile widening, D'Argent said, "I can be, when it's necessary." Suddenly his smile disappeared. His expression icy, hard, the Rockledge president snarled, "I want payment for those rocks. Now. This very day. Otherwise, your little friend will suffer for it."

Junior let his shoulders slump. "I . . . I'll see what I can do."

"You do that."

With a sorry glance at Rex Klamath, Junior walked slowly across the big room's deep carpeting and left Pierre D'Argent's office.

===

Boston was never a very large city. Busy, yes. Not as frenetic as New York, but quite hectic in its own special way. As junior walked from the Rockledge tower back toward the Copley Plaza Hotel, he racked his brain trying to think of how he could free Rex Klamath from D'Argent's control.

All he could come up with was Mickey Finn.

So, after doing some research on his computer, he went to the nearest pharmacy and asked for a dose of chloral hydrate. The thin-faced druggist behind the counter gave him a suspicious scowl and asked to see a prescription for the drug.

Shrugging innocently, Junior said, "I don't have a prescription. I need it for my dog; she's having trouble giving birth and I thought this would ease her pain."

The druggist—gray-haired, hard-eyed—said, "You need a doctor's prescription."

"I don't have time for that!" Junior pleaded. "It's just to make her birthing easier." And he pulled out his wallet and yanked a credit card from it.

The druggist frowned, but said, "Gonna cost you more than the regular price."

"I don't care!" Junior cried. "I just want to ease poor Daisy's pain!"

And Junior left the pharmacy with a small plastic pouch of chloral hydrate: the knockout ingredient of a Mickey Finn.

=====

It was late afternoon when Junior returned to the Rockledge building. The sun was low in the west; the high-rise towers of Boston's financial district were already in shadows. The wind coming in off the Bay bore a distinctly chilly nip.

Junior rode a crowded elevator to the top floor and was immediately ushered into D'Argent's spacious office. The Rockledge president sat behind his desk, smiling widely. Rex Klamath was still standing by the refrigerator/freezer unit, as if he hadn't moved since Junior had left the office earlier.

"Welcome back," D'Argent called happily as Junior trudged across the carpeting to his desk.

Pulling an envelope from his jacket, Junior tossed it onto D'Argent's desk. "That's just about every penny I have in the world," he said, with what he hoped was a properly defeated air.

D'Argent scooped up the envelope and hefted it, as if weighing it. "Ahh," he oozed, smiling. "The rich get richer."

Junior let his head droop slightly. Klamath didn't move at all.

"Thank you, Samuel. And let this be a lesson to you: don't tangle with your superiors. You'll always lose."

"I suppose so," said Junior, contritely.

D'Argent laid the envelope carefully on his desk and pushed his chair back, getting to his feet. "I think our business is concluded now," he said, his smile showing teeth.

Keeping his voice low, servile, Junior said, "I could use a drink."

Standing behind his desk, D'Argent's face brightened even further. "A drink? Yes! Something to celebrate with." And he strode toward a cabinet set into the wall next to the refrigerator/freezer combination.

Turning in his chair, Junior watched D'Argent open the cabinet and pull a pair of Martini glasses from the shelves. Klamath skittered out of his way, the expression on his face utterly blank. *Like all the life's been drained out of him*, Junior thought.

As the Rockledge chairman busied himself mixing the drinks, Junior slipped the slim plastic envelope of chloral hydrate from his pants pocket. Rex Klamath's little face twisted into a frown. Junior put a finger to his lips to silence him.

D'Argent carried the two Martinis back to his desk, passing Klamath as if the dwarf were an inanimate piece of furniture. He placed the two glasses side by side on his desktop, then went around and dropped down onto his high-backed swivel chair.

"Have you ever had a Martini before, Samuel?"

Junior shook his head negatively.

"Then you're in for a treat," D'Argent said, as he reached for his glass.

Suddenly Klamath shouted, "What was that?"

Junior turned toward the dwarf. So did D'Argent.

"What?"

"Out the window there." Klamath pointed a stubby arm.

D'Argent frowned slightly. "What did you see?"

"I don't know what it was," said Klamath. "Looked kinda like a kid's kite. Brushed by the window."

D'Argent got up from his chair and strode toward the ceiling-high window. "A child's kite couldn't get up this high," he muttered. "But a surveillance snoop . . ."

As D'Argent peered through the window, Junior swiftly emptied the chloral hydrate into one of the Martini glasses, then picked up the other one and put it to his lips.

"I don't see anything," D'Argent muttered.

Junior said, "Maybe you should call your security people."

"And tell them what?" D'Argent scoffed. "That my dwarf assistant had a hallucination?"

He strode back to his desk, sat down, and picked up his Martini. "Confusion to our enemies!" D'Argent toasted, lifting his glass high.

"Amen," said Junior.

Smacking his lips noisily, D'Argent put the glass back on his desktop. "Samuel, what are your plans now that you're broke?"

Junior shrugged. "I had hoped that you'd let Rex go free."

"Free?" D'Argent giggled. "No way. I like having the little man with me. Don't you, Rex?"

Klamath dutifully answered, "Yes, sir, Mr. D'Argent."

"There. You see?" His smile turning sinister, D'Argent asked, "How would you like to be one of my ashinstons . . . er, assistants?"

"Thanks," said Junior, suppressing a shudder. "But no thanks."

D'Argent's expression turned cold once more. "Oh, I suppose you think you're going to . . . to . . ." His voice trailed off.

Junior leaned forward in his chair, staring at the Rockledge chairman.

D'Argent smiled beatifically and sighed. "I'm very sleepy." He put both his arms down on the desktop and laid his head upon them, knocking over his Martini glass in the process.

ESCAPE

Junior got to his feet slowly. D'Argent seemed blissfully asleep, his breathing deep and regular.

Klamath took a hesitant step toward the desk. "Is he . . . ?"

"He's unconscious," Junior said. "He'll be out for a while. Come on, let's get out of here."

Klamath made a beeline around the desk, his face twisted with fury, and kicked D'Argent in the shins as hard as he could. The unconscious Rockledge president didn't budge.

"Let's kill the son of a bitch," said the dwarf.

"No. Let's just get ourselves out of here."

Junior saw tears in Rex's eyes. "I'd like to kill him!"

"Come on," Junior repeated. "Don't put yourself in more trouble."

Klamath still glared at the slumbering form. "I'd like to slice him up in little pieces!"

"Then you'd be just as bad as he is. Let's just get away while we can."

"And go where?"

"Out of here."

Junior scooped up the unopened envelope that still lay on

D'Argent's desk, stuffed it back in his jacket pocket, and, with Klamath trailing behind him, started for the door.

"Not there," Klamath warned. Jerking a thumb toward another door, behind the desk, he said, "This way. It's private."

Junior nodded once and changed course. "You've learned a lot about this place."

"More than I ever wanted to know," whispered Klamath, his tone hot as molten steel.

The door opened onto a short empty hallway. Klamath led Junior to the end of it. "Private elevator," he muttered, barely loud enough for Junior to hear him. "Goes up to the roof."

"Roof?"

"Air taxis," explained Klamath.

"Good," Junior said, with a grin.

The building's roof was indeed a helicopter pad, with several of the ungainly whirlybirds sitting off to one side of the landing area as another one lifted off and clattered away into the crisp afternoon.

One of the landing crew recognized Klamath. With a smug grin, he shouted over the noise of the departing 'copter, "Hi, Shorty. Where's the boss?"

"He's busy," Klamath snapped. "Told me to take Mr. Gunn, here—" he hiked a thumb in Junior's direction—"to his place in the Berkshires."

The technician's grin widened. "Lettin' you off the leash a little, eh?"

"Yeah," said Klamath, with just a touch of his old pugnaciousness.

Pointing to one of the idle choppers, the tech asked, "Where's Mr. Dee?"

"In his office," snapped Klamath. "Not to be disturbed."

Looking mildly surprised, the tech shrugged and said, "Okay, my little man. Have a good flight."

Junior saw Klamath's expression tighten at the *little man*, but Rex controlled his surge of anger. The two of them clambered into the rear compartment of the helicopter while the technician called for a crew. Two people in gold coveralls—a young man and younger-looking woman—came running out of the office structure off to one side of the landing pad.

It wasn't until they lifted off from the roof that Junior let out the breath that he hadn't realized he'd been holding in. *We're out of the Rockledge building,* he said to himself. *We've made it.*

Then the chopper pilot turned in his seat and hollered through the transparent screen separating him from the passenger compartment, "Where do you guys want to go?"

Before Klamath could reply, Junior answered, "Logan Aerospaceport."

The pilot nodded and said to his female copilot, "You heard the man. Logan."

Junior sat back in his seat and let some of the tension ease out of his shoulders. He looked down at Klamath, who was worming his arms out of the sleeves of the studded coveralls he was wearing.

"Once we get over the Bay, I wanna throw this goddamned straitjacket out the friggin' window."

Keeping a straight face, Junior said, "That would be polluting the Bay. You could get in trouble with the environmental police."

"Fuck 'em," Klamath growled.

———

The coveralls that Klamath fairly ripped off his body were studded with electromechanical receivers, the dwarf told Junior, that stimulated the muscles of the wearer's body.

"He could make me do whatever he wanted," Klamath explained. "Turned me into his personal mother-lovin' trained seal."

As he listened to the dwarf's tale Junior glanced at the plastic partition separating the passenger seats of the helicopter from the pilots' places.

"Make me roll over like a goddam' dog. Make me . . ." Klamath seemed to run out of breath. He gasped, "Make me . . . make me . . ." He burst into tears. "The dirty son of a bitch! I wanna kill him!"

Junior gently patted Klamath's shoulder. "It's all over, Rex. He's not going to bother you anymore."

"He looks smooth and elegant," Klamath muttered as he wiped his eyes with the backs of his hands. "But he's a slimeball. Underneath that slick exterior of his, he's a real bastard."

Junior slid his hand around Klamath's minuscule shoulders and let the dwarf sob uncontrollably. He felt some of the pain that Klamath was radiating. And he realized that Rex was right: D'Argent was truly a slimy bastard.

LOGAN AEROSPACEPORT

Junior's first stop at the noisy, crowded aerospaceport was an automated bank teller, where he converted the check he was carrying into cash. It was a considerable wad of bills.

"Christmas bells!" Rex Klamath blurted. "Stuff that into your pocket! Don't let anybody see you carrying that much cash."

Nodding his agreement, Junior pushed the money into his pants pocket. It made a pleasantly thick load.

Then he and Rex went to the gigantic electronic board that listed departures and arrivals.

"Where we going?" Klamath asked. Shouted, actually, over the rumble of the crowd surging past them.

"I'm not sure," said Junior. "Somewhere far from here."

Pointing a stumpy finger at the board, Klamath said, "Cruise ship heading for Saturn! Let's take that one."

Junior glanced down at the little man. "Saturn," he mused. "I've always wanted to see those rings."

"Come on," Klamath urged. "The cruiser's in orbit and there's a shuttle heading for it in half an hour."

Nodding his agreement, Junior told himself that D'Argent

wouldn't be able to send his hired killers all the way out to Saturn after them so quickly. So he and Klamath found the counter where passengers were being boarded for the shuttle, ready to purchase a pair of tickets.

The pert young woman at the counter gave Junior a congenial smile, but said, "I'm afraid that the tourist seats are totally sold out."

"Are there any other classes available?" Junior asked, with one eye on the electronic clock on the wall behind her.

Her smile fading into a concerned little frown, she replied, "This is a special flight. The Reverend Wilmot has booked the entire tourist section. He's bringing a whole shipload of his flock to Saturn. They're planning to set up a permanent colony there!"

Frowning back at her, Junior asked, "Does that mean that there aren't any accommodations available at all?"

"I have a few first-class seats still open, but I'm afraid they cost—"

"We'll take 'em!" Klamath snapped.

Junior grinned, nodded, and pulled his wad of banknotes from his pocket.

The woman went wide-eyed for a flash of a moment, then smiled and said cheerfully, "Two first-class tickets, all the way out to Saturn."

"Fine," said Junior, as he peeled off bills.

The shuttle flight was uneventful, like taking a bus. The vessel was nearly empty. The shuttle's lone flight attendant—a rake-thin male with a perfunctory smile—stood by the hatch and watched the few passengers troop aboard and find their seats without his help.

Junior felt nervous, though, as he listened to the automated safety lecture sing-songing on the display screen above his head. *A whole shipload of religious fanatics*, he thought. *Ought to be interesting. Interesting*, he knew, was a euphemism for *troublesome.* Or worse.

Liftoff was uneventful, although the thrust of the rocket engines rattled the compartment and pushed Junior deep into his thickly cushioned reclining seat.

Sitting by the small, oval window, Klamath stared outside as the nearly cloudless blue sky swiftly turned deep black. Junior focused on the video screen set into the chair back in front of him and saw the ground falling away. Within minutes he could make out the fishhook shape of Cape Cod and then much of the continent's eastern coast.

His arms floated off the seat's rests and his stomach started to climb up toward his throat. *Relax!* Junior commanded himself. *You've been in zero-g before.*

Looking over at Klamath, he saw that the dwarf was still staring out the window, although there was nothing to see now except the endless blackness of space.

Suddenly Klamath tapped a finger against the window's triple-paned Glassteel. "There's the cruiser!"

Junior leaned over the dwarf's stumpy figure and saw a huge globular spacecraft floating serenely out there. He made out the name painted on its curving flank: *Saturnalia.*

The pilot's voice came over the intercom, flat and calm as if discussing the weather. "*Saturnalia*'s dead ahead. We'll link up with her in about eight minutes. You'll feel a sense of gravity return, so you won't need your whoopie bags any longer."

As if in reply, Junior heard someone gagging and then upchucking noisily. It made his own stomach churn unhappily.

═══

True to the pilot's word, the shuttle mated with the huge *Saturnalia*, and a feeling of gravity returned to the vessel. Junior could swallow normally again; he felt relieved. Klamath hadn't seemed to be troubled by zero-g. *He was too excited to pay any attention to it*, Junior realized. *Like a kid on a fairground ride.*

The flight attendant, still wearing his professional smile, nodded to the passengers as they got up from their seats and shuffled to the hatch. Without saying a word to anyone.

═══

The *Saturnalia* was luxurious, almost sumptuous. Each first-class passenger was shown to a small but comfortable private cabin by a set of happy-faced young women in short skirts and perky little hats. Junior and Klamath had adjoining cabins, with a connecting door between them.

The flight attendant who escorted them to their cabins sing-songed, "The ship has shops that can provide you with fresh clothing, bathing and shaving accouterments, all your personal needs."

Junior smiled at her. And saw through the open doorway between their cabins that Klamath merely nodded, as if he wanted to be rid of her as quickly as possible.

Junior glanced over his cabin. Full-sized bed, cabinets, private bathroom with a shower, desk with a sizeable viewscreen over it. *Not bad*, he thought, realizing that this was going to be home for him and Rex for slightly more than two months. *Should be an interesting flight.*

"Ordinarily," said the flight attendant continued, her expression going more serious, almost apologetic, "we have a full complement of entertainers for the passengers' enjoyment. But Reverend Wilmot scratched that. He says his people will find their entertainment in prayers and atonement."

Junior felt the breath gush out of him. He glanced at Rex, who stood by the bed in his compartment, transfixed by the news. And he realized that *interesting* probably meant *catastrophic*.

BOOK EIGHT: SATURN

LEAVING EARTH

Junior sat alone in his compartment, staring in silence at the visibly dwindling image of Earth on the viewscreen above his desk. The blue-and-white hemisphere glowed against the blackness of space, a haven of warmth and life set against the cold, indifferent emptiness.

We'll just stay at Saturn long enough to make sure we haven't been followed by any of D'Argent's thugs, Junior told himself. *Then we'll come back home.*

But he knew that there were a thousand ways that his plan could fall through, leaving him and Klamath stranded nearly ten times farther from the Sun than the Earth is. *And Deborah is back there, somewhere on Earth, hiding from me.* He realized the truth of his thought. *She's hiding from me. She's deliberately avoiding me.*

With a sigh, he told himself, *Maybe I'll stay at Saturn. Try to find something to do out there.*

There was only a handful of other passengers in the first-class section of *Saturnalia*, most of them engineers heading for a two-year contract at the station orbiting the brightly ringed planet. No brilliant conversationalists among them. Junior and

Rex stayed clear of them for the most part, despite Junior's growing sense of isolation.

"You know what they say about engineers," Klamath jeered one evening, over the dinners that the ship's robots had brought to Junior's cabin.

Looking up from his tray of bland, inoffensive, unappetizing food, Junior said, "No, Rex. What do they say?"

With a rare smile, the dwarf replied, "Most engineers are so narrow-minded they can peek through a keyhole with both eyes!"

Junior grinned; it took an effort.

"Come on, big guy!" Klamath wheedled. "Perk up!"

With a small shrug, Junior promised, "I'll try."

"There's a couple of decent looking women among the engineers, you know," Klamath said. "Might be worth a try."

Junior shrugged again.

Shaking his head, Klamath grumbled, "We shoulda had you frozen and carried aboard as cargo. Cheaper."

Junior admitted, "I guess I'm not much company."

"Not much. That's for sure."

Once they had finished their dinners and the robot waiter had taken their trays away, Klamath got to his feet and jerked a thumb toward the door of Junior's compartment. "I'm heading for the bar."

Junior recognized the invitation. Or the challenge. Getting up from his chair, he said, "I'll go with you."

Klamath grinned at him. "Attaboy!"

———

Saturnalia's bar was only half filled, mostly with untalkative men nursing tall drinks and three rather plain-looking women who sat huddled together, like wildebeests trying to protect themselves against prowling carnivores.

Junior ordered a scotch on the rocks from the robot bartender; somewhere he had heard that that was a man's drink. Klamath asked for a Bloody Mary. Conversation among the others was low and sparse, mostly mutters and grumbles.

Klamath, perched on one of the bar stools, scrambled to his feet atop it and lifted his drink high over his head.

"How many lawyers does it take to change a light bulb?" he shouted.

The others looked up at the dwarf, plainly startled by his outburst, their mouths hanging open, eyes wide with surprise.

But no one answered Klamath's question.

Grinning, Klamath answered it himself: "Six lawyers. One to screw in the bulb, and the other five to screw the first one!"

Dead silence, until one of the women—a lanky young brunette with oversized teeth—broke out with, "I get it! They're lawyers!"

She giggled, and the other two women at her table tittered halfheartedly.

Otherwise, the bar was totally silent. Junior, thinking as fast as he could, asked loudly, "How many psychiatrists does it take to change a light bulb?"

One of the engineers, a short, sturdily compact gray-haired man, grinned and answered, "I know that one! Only one psychologist—"

The guy standing beside him at the bar interrupted, "But the light bulb's got to *want* to change!"

That brought a guarded burst of laugher. One old joke followed another, and soon all the bar's patrons were giggling and talking to one another. Klamath got down from his stool and hustled over to the women's table. Junior got involved in a conversation with several of the engineers.

But as he exchanged pleasantries with the engineers, Junior found himself admiring his companion. *Rex did it,* he told himself. *He broke the ice.*

Several hours later, when Junior finally left the bar and made his way back to his cabin, he realized that Rex was nowhere in sight. Neither was any of the three women.

I'll be darned, Junior said to himself. *The little guy has made off with all three of them!*

=====

Junior was sleeping when Klamath finally made it back to his own compartment. Junior was awakened by girlish giggling coming through the half-open door between his quarters and Rex's.

"Ssshh," he heard Klamath whisper. "Don't wake him up." And Junior heard the door separating their rooms click softly shut.

Junior turned over and eventually drifted back to sleep. He dreamed of Deborah.

SATURN PRIME

Saturnalia finally arrived at *Saturn Prime* and took up orbit within a hundred yards of the station circling the planet just beyond its outermost ring.

In his stateroom, Junior stared at the image of the ringed planet on the viewscreen above his desk. It was magnificent: the planet itself, slightly flattened at the poles, gleaming against the utter blackness of space with streamers of muted amber, grayish pink and dull white racing across its face; and those impossible rings hovering about the planet's middle, bright as new snow, just floating there.

Off in one corner of the screen hung their destination, *Saturn Prime*, the space station that already housed several thousand exiles—*no*, Junior corrected himself, they're not exiles. They've chosen to come out here, ten times farther from the Sun than the Earth is, chosen to build a new life for themselves in a new world.

Their space station doesn't look very impressive, Junior thought. He focused the screen's view on it. It looked like a length of sewer pipe several kilometers long. Junior could make out blisters and protrusions along its length, like metallic pustules infesting the tube's length. He could see that the station was rotating slowly along its long axis, like an immense log rolling across the face of the planet Saturn.

As the *Saturnalia* edged closer to the station, Junior began to make out tiny specks of spacecraft buzzing around the giant stovepipe: maintenance and construction vehicles, busy as bees swarming around a hive.

Then he realized that there was another structure hovering near the station, a new construct, barely more than a set of rings connected by long slim metal rods, with a bevy of construction vehicles congregating around it.

They're building a second station, Junior realized. *They're expanding their habitat.*

===

Saturnalia took up orbit close to the stovepipe figure of the completed space station, and the PA system in Junior's compartment announced, "Boarding for first-class passengers is now ready. Please proceed immediately to the first-class debarkation port."

Junior hefted his slender travel bag and headed for the door. Rex Klamath was already in the passageway, toting a bag that was much larger than Junior's.

"Bought myself some duds," he explained as they headed for the debarkation port. "I wanna look decent, for a change."

Smiling down at his little friend, Junior recited a line he remembered from an ancient motion picture, "Baby, you'd look good in a shower curtain."

Klamath did not laugh; he didn't even crack a smile.

===

The debarkation procedure didn't take long, but as Junior and Klamath stepped through the hatchway that led them into the station's surprisingly spacious reception center, a squat robot trundled up to them and asked, "Mr. Gunn? Mr. Klamath? Follow me, please."

"Where we going?" Klamath inquired.

"Professor Wilmot wants to talk with both of you," the robot replied, without inflection.

Junior asked, "And who is Professor Wilmot?"

Without a microsecond's hesitation, the robot replied, "The leader of this community."

The robot led them along a bewildering assortment of passageways until they stopped at a door that bore the name-plate, *James Colerain Wilmot*. Nothing else.

Junior felt his brows knitting as the robot opened the door and gestured them inside.

James Colerain Wilmot sat at a modest-sized desk, smiling benignly at his guests. Junior stared at the man. *Santa Claus!* he said to himself. *The man looks like Santa Claus!*

Wilmot was chubby. His cheeks were not like roses, but he was smiling from behind a snow-white beard. His sapphire-blue eyes sparkled as he gestured Junior and Rex to the seats in front of his desk.

"Welcome to *Saturn Prime*," he said, in a cheerful deep voice. "Please make yourselves comfortable."

Wilmot was wearing a long-sleeved blouse of bright scarlet; his expression was joyful. Junior could not help liking him.

Klamath was a little more circumspect. "Whattaya want to see us for?"

JAMES COLERAIN
WILMOT

For an instant, Wilmot's good-humored expression darkened.
But only for an instant. He made a smile for Klamath and said,
"Neither of you two put down a job specification on your entry
forms. Why did you come here? What are you looking for?"

Klamath looked up at Junior, who was staring silently at
Wilmot. Silence stretched for several eons-long moments. At
last Junior replied, "We're seeking refuge."

Wilmot's bushy white eyebrows climbed up his forehead a
centimeter or so. "Why didn't you put that down on your entry
forms? *Saturn Prime* is filled with refugees."

"It is?"

"Of course," said Wilmot. "That's what this habitat was
created for: to take refugees who cannot live on Earth. We are
fulfilling an ancient promise: 'Give me your tired, your weak,
your poor, your huddled masses yearning to breathe free . . .'"

Klamath said sourly, "I heard this habitat was a kinda prison,
a place where troublemakers get sent to."

"Troublemakers," Wilmot growled. "People who will
not—cannot—live under the restrictive regimes that control
almost every nation on Earth."

"Exiles," said Junior.

"That's right," Wilmot agreed. "The kind of exiles that Britain expelled to the New World from its Merrie Olde land. The kind of exiles who built a new nation of freedom and human rights."

"That's what you're doing here?" Junior asked.

With a faint smile, the white-bearded Wilmot said, "Actually, this habitat was started as an experiment. This space habitat has given us—the human race, that is—an opportunity to deliberately create a new environment for human communities, a new world in which human beings can build their own society, fresh and pristine."

"But why—"

Wilmot cut off Junior's incipient question with a brusque wave of his chubby hand. "The original motivation behind this habitat was to create a testing ground for an interstellar mission. To see if a few thousand ordinary, cantankerous men and women could live in a sealed community for the several generations it would take to cross the lightyears between our solar system and another."

Junior heard Klamath let out a low whistle.

"But it didn't work out that way, of course," said Wilmot. "The experiment needed the best and brightest, the most highly motivated men and women. But the various governments on Earth saw *Saturn Prime* as an ideal dumping ground for the kind of people who were dissatisfied with their governments—the kind of men and women they labeled as troublemakers, malcontents, rabble rousers."

"And that's what they sent you," Junior said, in a near whisper.

"Pretty much. *Saturn Prime* became a dumping ground for the people who were unhappy with the way their nations were being governed."

"By the New Morality," said Klamath.

"And the other religiously oriented movements that have captured most of the governments on Earth," Wilmot agreed sadly. "This habitat of ours has become a modern-day Chateau D'If. If Jean Valjean were alive today, he'd be here, among us in *Saturn Prime*."

"But the people here aren't criminals, are they?" Klamath asked. "They're not murderers or thieves or . . . or . . ."

A wan smile touched the corners of Wilmot's lips. "No, we've managed to refuse taking on hardcore criminals. Most of our so-called troublemakers are nothing more than malcontents, idealists who want to live in a free society."

"And that's what you're building here," said Junior.

His smile fading, Wilmot said, "It's not easy. But we're trying."

Silence settled over the three men.

Wilmot broke the hush with, "So the question is still: where do the two of you fit into our community?"

Junior said, "We don't intend to stay here long. Just 'til the next ship arrives."

"We wanna get back home, to Earth," Klamath added.

With an understanding nod, Wilmot said, "I see. But I'm afraid the next ship won't be here for many months. What do you propose to do during that time?"

"Many months?" Junior squeaked.

"At least."

Klamath muttered, "Crapola."

His mind racing, Junior suggested, "We could start a tourist operation. You know, see the rings of Saturn first-hand."

"Yeah!" Klamath agreed.

But Wilmot shook his head. "*Saturn Prime* is a haven for the dispossessed, not a tourist attraction."

"But—"

"No tourists," said Wilmot, with great finality.

"Then what?"

"You tell me," Wilmot replied. "Your entry applications had no information about your job interests or qualifications. None at all."

Junior realized he had no qualifications for any job he could imagine. None at all.

MENIAL LABOR?

Junior sat before Wilmot's desk, his mind racing, but finding nothing that resembled an employment possibility. Klamath was silent, also, as Wilmot stared questioningly at the two of them.

At last the professor broke the tense silence with, "I suppose we'll have to put you into one of the menial labor groups."

"Menial labor?" Klamath asked, almost in a growl.

"There's lots of work to be done maintaining this habitat," Wilmot explained. "Everything from repairing faulty equipment to looking after the recycling systems."

Cocking a doubtful brow, Klamath muttered, "Sounds like taking care of the garbage."

Wilmot nodded. "There's a surprising amount of manual labor involved, despite all the automated systems."

"Not for me," said Klamath flatly.

With a melancholy shrug, Wilmot replied, "I'm afraid you'll have no choice in the matter. It's the recycling job for both of you."

Holding up a restraining hand, Junior said, "Wait a minute. There must be something better than that. Something more interesting."

"And less stinking," Klamath added.

"You tell me," Wilmot challenged.

Junior looked around the director's office. *Something,* he thought. *There's got to be something. Anything!*

His wandering glance stopped at the viewscreen across the office that showed Saturn hanging against the black of space, its broad rings gleaming brightly.

"The rings," he murmured. "They could be a major tourist attraction. People would pay . . ."

"No tourists," Wilmot said flatly. "We can't have tourists coming here. This habitat—and its successors—will be for the poor souls who've been exiled from Earth. Plus the handful of scientists who are studying Saturn and its moons."

Junior grinned at him. "Okay. So we can't bring tourists to the rings. But we can bring the rings to the tourists."

Wilmot fixed him with a skeptical eye. "What do you mean by that?"

With a joyful grin, Junior explained, "We could set up 3-D camera systems all around Saturn. Have them watch the rings, twenty-four seven."

Nodding unconsciously, Wilmot murmured, "The rings are dynamic . . . constantly changing."

"Lots of people Earthside already have 3D viewers in their homes," Junior said.

"This'd boost the sales of new ones!" Klamath added.

"And it wouldn't interfere with habitat, hardly at all," Junior continued. "Just a small team of technicians to set it up and monitor the system."

Wilmot said, "We could probably recruit the talent we'd need from our existing population."

"It could be a source of income for you!"

Wilmot's smile of joy faltered. "You'll need to get the scientists' approval for your scheme."

"Why shouldn't they approve it? We won't be tinkering with the rings, just looking at them. Helping them study them!"

His face dead serious, Wilmot said, "Scientists can be queer ducks."

"But this would be helping them and their work."

"We'll see." And Wilmot reached out and touched a button on the console of the phone on his desk. "Connect me with Dr. Wunderly, please."

"Dr. Wunderly?" Junior asked.

"She's the scientist who heads the studies of the rings. Almost won the Nobel Prize last year."

NADIA WUNDERLY

The face that appeared on Wilmot's desktop screen was younger than Junior expected. Rather plump, with large gray eyes and brick-red hair falling just short of her shoulders. She quickly agreed to come to Wilmot's office, and within a few minutes, Junior heard a timid tap on the professor's door. Wilmot touched a button on his desktop and the door slid open.

Nadia Wunderly stepped in. She was short, stumpy, obviously too heavy for her height. But her gray-eyed face radiated intelligence. Junior got to his feet as Wilmot introduced him and Rex Klamath.

Junior stepped to the round conference table in the corner of Wilmot's office and pulled out a chair for her while Klamath sat and stared at her.

From his desk chair, Wilmot said, "These gentlemen," waving a hand at Junior and Rex, "want to set up a system of cameras about the rings and beam the pictures to ordinary citizens on Earth."

Wunderly blinked. "Why . . . ?"

"Show business," said Klamath.

"We want to let the people Earthside see the dynamic, ever-changing rings of Saturn," Junior elaborated.

Wunderly's rotund face pulled itself into a skeptical frown. "They can already see the rings. We send continuous synopses of our observations on a regular basis."

"Scientific reports," Wilmot elaborated.

Klamath said sourly, "Who the hell looks at scientific reports?"

Junior quickly explained, "The imagery we send Earthside would be continuous, twenty-four-seven imagery of the rings. It would show their dynamic, ever-changing condition."

Softly, Wilmot added, "It could stir up lots of interest in the work you're doing, Nadia. Might even get the IAA's astronomy board to show more interest."

"I mean," Junior took up, "I had no idea that the rings were so dynamic. I just thought of them as sitting there, passively circling around Saturn. But no, well . . . it's almost like they're alive."

"They *are* alive," Wunderly said, almost in a whisper.

"They are?"

"That's what I'm trying to prove to the astronomy board, back in Copenhagen." Wunderly's face took on an intense, almost outraged expression. "The particles in the rings are living creatures! I'm sure of it."

Wilmot began to say, "But the board—"

"The board is composed of blind men!" Wunderly snapped. "Old men who look at the data I've sent them and see nothing! Half-dead old has-beens who refuse to see the truth!"

Before Wilmot could react, Junior said, "Then the imagery we send back to Earth will show the world's population that you've discovered a new life form."

"And stick it to the old farts," Klamath added gleefully.

Wilmot held up his hands placatingly. "Let's not get carried away, now."

But Wunderly asked Junior, "What do you need to accomplish what you intend to do?"

Thinking fast, Junior replied, "We'd need to set up a minimum of three remote cameras just outside the limits of the ring system. Four or five would be better."

"We can build the camera systems here," Wilmot said. "Together with the rocket boosters, you'll need to establish them in orbit."

Nodding, Junior said, "I'll have to contact the television networks Earthside, work out contracts with them."

"Count your fingers when you shake hands with those bastards," Klamath warned. But he smiled as he said it.

"I can help you contact the networks," Wilmot offered.

But Wunderly said, "You'll need approval from the IAA, of course."

Surprised, Junior blurted, "Why? We're not going to interfere with your work or anyone else's. We'll just be photographing the rings."

"You should get a blessing from the IAA," agreed Wilmot. "I'll be able to help you with that too."

Feeling suddenly uneasy, Junior said, "I want to go ahead with this. I don't want to have it tied up in IAA politics."

"It'll be better if you get the IAA's go-ahead," Wilmot coaxed.

After several long moments, Junior reluctantly agreed, "I suppose you're right."

The next five weeks sped past in a blur. Suddenly, Junior was involved with engineers, technicians, rocket designers, all the different experts he needed to get a cluster of unmanned satellites into orbit just outside of the rings of Saturn. Klamath was unexpectedly helpful, serving as Junior's aide, finding the people he needed to talk to, arranging meetings with the supervisors who controlled job assignments.

Wilmot spent much of his time working his way up the IAA's chain of command, until finally he and Junior were speaking with the head of the organization's astronomy board, Dr. Marlon Ingersol.

"Keep the rings under constant surveillance?" asked the narrow-faced astronomer. "What on Earth for?"

Tempted to remind Dr. Ingersol that Saturn was more than a billion kilometers away from Earth, Junior instead answered calmly, "Two reasons, sir. One, to show the people of Earth the most spectacular sight in the solar system in real time. And second, to provide enough data to determine if those ring particles are actually alive."

It took nearly two hours for Ingersol's answer to reach them. With a sour expression, the astronomer grumbled, "Alive? Is this Dr. Wunderly's doing? Is she trying to prove her ridiculous theory about the ring particles?"

Before Junior could respond, Wilmot answered, "No, this proposal was originated by Mr. Gunn, here, and I think it's good enough for us to go ahead with it." He left unsaid, *Whether you approve of it or not.* But Junior heard the threat in the tone of his voice.

Turning to Junior, Wilmot said, "Now we wait for another couple of hours."

Klamath jumped down from his chair. "Gotta hit the men's room."

Junior got to his feet also. "I ought to talk with the head of the surveillance imagery team."

Wilmot nodded understandingly. "I'll give you a buzz when Dr. Ingersol calls back."

═══════

It took several days of phone discussions—interrupted by the hours it took for messages to travel back and forth between Saturn and Earth—before Wilmot at last smiled and said, "Ingersol has no objection to your plan, Samuel."

Sitting before Wilmot's modest desk, Junior broke into a hearty grin. "Good! We're already testing the first batch of three satellites."

Smiling back at Junior, Wilmot said, "I know. It's something of a leap forward that the IAA bureaucracy has acted faster than our own engineers."

Junior laughed politely, then sobered. "Now I've got to find a TV network executive who'll take our imagery and broadcast it worldwide."

Wilmot leaned back in his comfortable swivel chair. "We all have our crosses to bear, don't we?"

MANUEL GAETA

Junior picked at his dinner while he watched Klamath eating as if this might be his last meal. The two of them were sitting in Junior's compartment, where they usually took their meals. Wilmot thought it best if they didn't mingle too closely with the habitat's regular population.

Pushing his tray aside, Junior muttered, "I never thought it would be so hard to sell the idea."

His cheek bulging with the steak he was chewing on, Klamath replied, "Still no bites?"

"Not even a nibble."

"Tough."

With a disappointed shake of his head, Junior complained, "I thought all the networks would jump at the chance to show live coverage of Saturn's rings."

"Nobody's jumping, huh?"

"Nobody."

"Tough to sell science to the network big shots."

"Tell me about it. The kindest reply I got from any of the network execs was, 'It'd be like watching a merry-go-round. After the first cycle or two, who the hell cares?'"

Klamath returned his attention to his reconstituted steak. Junior pushed his chair back and slowly rose to his feet. "There's got to be some way to get them. Got to be."

Klamath made a tiny shrug. "What about the stuntman?"

"Stuntman?"

Frowning with concentration, Klamath said, "Manny something-or-other. He dove through the rings a couple years ago. Big TV coverage of that."

"Manuel Gaeta!" Junior recalled. "He's here? On this station?"

"I think so," said Klamath. "He retired from doing stunts, got married, and settled down here on *Saturn Prime*."

"I wonder if I could talk him out of retirement?"

With a toothy grin, Klamath replied, "Couldn't hurt to ask him." Then the dwarf reached for Junior's plate and the untouched steak on it.

———

Manuel Gaeta was indeed living in *Saturn Prime*, with his wife, Nobel laureate Kristin Cardenas. He agreed easily enough to have dinner with Junior and Klamath, and that evening the four of them sat at a table in *Saturn Prime*'s best—and only—restaurant.

As their robot waiter brought the drinks they had ordered, Manuel Gaeta asked casually, "So what do you want to talk to me about?"

Gaeta's voice was soft, almost musical. He was on the small side, slightly shorter than Junior but solidly built, burly. Lots of hard muscle beneath his casual open-necked Hawaiian-style shirt. His face was hardly handsome. His nose had obviously been broken, perhaps more than once; his heavy jaw made him look somewhat like a bulldog. But his deep-set dark eyes seemed friendly enough, and his grin was disarming.

Sitting beside him was his wife, Dr. Kristin Cardenas, the Nobel laureate nanotechnology expert. Despite her calendar years, she looked no more than thirtyish, a pert sandy blonde woman with bright cornflower-blue eyes, a swimmer's shoulders, and a strong, athletic body. That was because her body teemed with nanomachines, virus-sized devices that acted as a deliberate, directed immune system that destroyed invading organisms, took apart plaque forming in her blood vessels atom by atom, and rebuilt tissue damaged by trauma or aging.

Cardenas had won a Nobel Prize for her research in nanotechnology before the fundamentalist governments of Earth succeeded in banning all forms of nanotech on the planet. She had carried on her work at Selene for years, helping the lunar nation to win its short, virtually bloodless war against the former world government. But because she had taken nanomachines into her own body, she was not allowed to return to Earth, even for a brief visit. She lost her husband and children because they dared not come to Selene and risk being exiled from Earth with her. Cardenas bitterly resented the short-sighted attitudes of the "flatlanders" who had cost her her children and grandchildren, a bitterness that haunted her until she fell in love with daredevil Manual Gaeta.

Junior put down his glass of juice and answered Gaeta's question, "You dove through the rings once, didn't you?"

Gaeta grinned softly and replied, "That was my last stunt. I retired after it." With a glance at his wife, he added, "I got married and settled down."

Junior nodded, but asked, "What would it take to get you to do it again?"

Gaeta shook his head. "I'm retired."

"But—"

"Ever hear of the law of averages?" Gaeta asked. "I've risked my butt all across the solar system. Climbed Mt. Olympus on Mars and skied down the other side of it. Risked my butt dozens of times doing other stunts. If I keep on doing that, sooner or later the law of averages is going to catch up with me."

Dr. Cardenas added, "Manny's retired. Alive."

Junior stared at the two of them, sitting side by side across the table from Rex and himself.

"What are you trying to accomplish?" Gaeta asked, a friendly smile on his rugged face.

"I want to show the people back on Earth that Saturn's rings are exciting, dynamic, maybe alive."

"They are alive," Gaeta agreed, with a nod.

Klamath snapped, "The science people Earthside don't believe that."

"They haven't been there. Those little *fregados* were walking all over my space suit, right across my goddam faceplate. I saw them! Covered my whole frickin' suit, they did!"

A blaze of excitement flashing through him, Junior asked, "Did you get any imagery of that?"

Gaeta's face went sour. "Nah. The little bastards covered me in ice, cut off my link with my controllers. No data got through."

"So it's your word against the bigshots back Earthside," Klamath grumbled.

"Yeah. One stuntman against the whole passel of the IAA's scientists. Guess who they listen to."

Junior muttered a heartfelt, "Shit!"

GLOBAL NEWS

Junior felt stymied by the television networks' haughty rejection of his offer of real-time coverage of Saturn's rings.

"It'd be like watching paint dry," was one of the more polite responses he got.

He was sitting at the desk in his compartment, reviewing a report on the progress the technical team was making on the camera systems that would take twenty-four-seven imagery of Saturn's rings, feeling somewhere between depressed and defeated, when his phone chimed.

"Call from Global News Network, New York City, Earth," said the phone's crisp tenor voice.

"Global News?" Junior blurted.

"Call from Global News Network—"

"Connect!"

As usual, it took slightly more than two hours for Junior's command to reach Earth and Global News Network's call to reach Saturn, but at last Junior was looking at the image of a clean-shaven blond young man smiling at him.

"Mr. Gunn?" he asked, in a surprisingly deep baritone voice.

Nodding, Junior replied, "Sam Gunn Jr."

Two hours later the young man broke into a pleasant smile. "My father knew your father. I'm Tom Freeman."

Tom Freeman didn't look like a newsman to Junior. He had a fresh, youthful face—thin, almost scrawny—with light-blue eyes and a slightly lopsided grin. Junior saw none of the hard, almost feral expression that he associated with newsmen.

Junior asked, "How did your father and mine know each other?"

And then the interminable wait. Junior spent the time reading the tech team's progress reports off his screen.

At last Freemen replied, "Long story. Too long to go into now, with the corporation paying the phone bill."

"Okay," Junior said. "What can I do for you, Mr. Freeman?"

Again, the wait. At last Freeman said, "Tom."

"Tom," Junior agreed.

Some two hours later Freeman answered, "This proposal you've sent out, about observing Saturn's rings . . ."

"I don't think I sent one to Global News."

"You didn't send one to Global News," Freeman said, while Junior's words were crossing the gulf between Saturn and Earth. "But I got a copy of it from a buddy at International. Looks kind of interesting."

Junior felt his eyebrows climbing toward his scalp. "You think so?"

After the inevitable wait: "Yeah. It's not the sort of thing we usually do, of course, but Global has an affiliate for school kids, Education, Inc. I think they'd be willing to run your imagery of Saturn's rings. I think they'd love it."

For school kids? Junior asked himself. Is that the best that I can do?

Their time-lagged conversation limped along until Freeman explained, "Here's the plan: We start running your footage of

Saturn's rings on the education channel, and here on Global we give it big coverage. We stress the idea that the ring particles might be alive. We put together panels of experts, have them debate the idea. Make it a hot news item!"

It took more than a day before Junior happily agreed to let Global News carry the ball.

═══════

At last *Saturn Prime*'s technical team was ready to launch half a dozen small TV satellites into orbit around Saturn's rings. The tech leader—a graying fugitive from the stern restrictions against nanotechnology research anywhere on Earth—invited Junior to the team's makeshift control center, down in the bowels of the huge space station.

Junior sat in front of a desktop TV screen that showed a view of the rings seen from the space station. He saw a vast field of gleaming white particles, most of them as small as his fist, a few others as big as a good-sized house. They weaved back and forth in an intricate, never-ending, almost hypnotic ballet.

Suddenly, the view on his screen changed. He was looking at the ring particles as if he were actually out there among them. Fascinated, Junior watched the particles shift and maneuver, work their way upstream through the teeming assembly of gleaming lustrous particles.

"They're live," said a woman's voice, from behind him.

Junior turned and saw Nadia Wunderly staring at the screen as if hypnotized by the endless, constant dance of the myriads of snow-white particles.

With a nod, Junior agreed, "We've got to capture some of them, so you can study them in your lab."

Wunderly gushed a heartfelt sigh. "Tell that to the assholes back in Copenhagen."

———

Junior was surprised when he glanced at the clock clicking away at the bottom of his screen. Nearly an hour had passed since he'd first sat down at this makeshift observation post.

He remembered Frederick Malone's telling him about the old-time sailors and the "raptures of the deep."

This is like the raptures of the deep, he told himself. *Watching the dance of those rings is hypnotic.*

It took a deliberate, almost painful effort to push his chair back and get shakily to his feet. *Maybe we shouldn't be showing this to schoolkids,* he thought. *It's too damned fascinating.*

Wunderly, still standing beside him, also pulled her gaze away from the screen, with an obvious effort. Blinking several times, she said, in a near-whisper, "It gets to you, doesn't it?"

"It sure does," Junior agreed.

Together they walked past the other desks, each one occupied by a man or woman staring at a TV screen that showed an endless parade of gleaming, glittering, dancing ring particles.

Suddenly someone shouted, "Hey, look at this!"

Junior saw one of the female technicians—chunky, gray-haired—leaning forward in her chair, staring intently at her screen. He hurried to her desk, with Wunderly close behind him.

Pointing at the screen, the tech said excitedly, "That rock just coasted into the ring. Must've been chipped off one of the moons orbiting near the ring plane."

Her screen showed an irregular chunk of grayish rock, maybe as large as a living-room sofa, being swiftly covered by ice particles.

"They're smothering it," said the tech.

"They're *eating* it!" Wunderly cried, and she actually clapped her hands together, lost in wonder and admiration.

Junior muttered, "Show that to the big wheels in Copenhagen."

"Damned right," agreed Wunderly.

═══════

The displays shown by the TV monitors were mesmerizing, spellbinding. Junior and Wunderly stared at the desktop screens for hours more, watching the ring particles move, maneuver, swarm over any piece of rock that entered the ring plane.

At last, feeling weak with excitement, Junior pulled himself away from the technicians' desks and made his way slowly, reluctantly, toward the door that led out to the station's main passageway.

Wunderly, beside him, kept whispering, "They're alive. They're alive."

Nodding his agreement, Junior said, "You've got to send this footage to Copenhagen. Right away."

Her eyes showing disappointment, despair, Wunderly retorted, "And they'll file it with all the other disks I've sent them."

A PARTY TO THE CRIME

Junior and Wunderly shared a bleak, quiet dinner, then went to their separate quarters. When Junior stepped into his compartment, he saw that the message light on his TV screen was blinking.

"Tom Freeman," he read aloud, "Global News Network."

Sitting at his desk, Junior pressed the reply button on his keyboard.

Freeman's lean face was grinning. "Got an idea, Sam. Call me soon as you can."

Without bothering to check on the time in New York City, Junior punched the reply button again.

Freeman's face shifted minutely on the screen, then his image said, "I'm recording this message to you, Sam, so don't bother to reply until you've heard it all."

The newsman appeared to take a deep breath, then he began, "Why don't we sponsor a contest among the schoolkids? Are those ring particles really alive? The best explanation for what they're seeing on the views of the rings gets a free ride out to Saturn, to see them in real time! Global will pay for the trip. It'll generate a lot of interest, and we'll set up interviews with top scientists to discuss what your imagery is showing and the schoolkids' ideas about it!"

Freeman was clearly excited. "It'll get lots of interest from everybody—schoolkids, their parents, scientists, the big shots in the IAA. It'll be sensational!"

Junior felt Freeman's excitement stirring his own fervor. *A contest!* he thought. *Why didn't I think of that?*

And he heard himself saying to the recorded image, "Why restrict the contest to schoolkids? Why not include parents, ordinary people, scientists, everybody?"

Freeman's image did not reply. It just sat there, grinning like a self-satisfied cat who had just swallowed a delicious canary.

Junior glanced at the clock's numbers at the bottom of the screen: it was a few minutes past 3:00 a.m. in New York. With a self-deprecating little laugh, he blanked his screen. *Have a good sleep, Tom,* he said to himself. *I'll talk to you in the morning. Greenwich Mean Time.*

═══════

Freeman was just as enthusiastic when he and Junior finally linked up. Even with the long lags in their conversation, it was clear that the Global News executive was excited about the idea of a contest.

"Sure!" he enthused. "Make it a contest with several different divisions: kids, grownups, scientists, witch doctors, everybody!"

Junior would have been just as enthusiastic, but he saw the message light was blinking on his screen. Professor Wilmot wanted to speak with him.

As quickly as he decently could, Junior finished his time-lagged conversation with Freeman. Tom was smiling widely and promised to keep Junior "in the loop" as he made arrangements for Global News' global-wide contest.

Professor Wilmot was much less enthusiastic.

OLD IRONSIDES

Junior could see from the grim expression on Wilmot's face, glowering on his tabletop's screen, that the professor was upset. His message was succinct:

"Come to my office as soon as you can."

Trouble, Junior recognized. He hurried to Wilmot's office.

As soon as Junior stepped through the doorway, Wilmot grumbled, "I overheard the discussion you had with that newsman. What's this about a contest? You want to turn the work our scientists are doing into a silly contest?"

As he went to the chair in front of Wilmot's desk, Junior answered, "Yessir. And it's not silly. It's a good way to draw attention to the work the scientists are doing." *And make some money out of it*, he added silently.

Shaking his head doggedly, Wilmot said, "I can't allow you to turn a very sensitive scientific investigation into a children's game. It's out of the question!"

"But it won't be just a children's game," Junior protested. "There will be separate contests for adults, another for scientists—"

Wilmot interrupted, "And another one for a wild-eyed interlopers who have no respect for proper decorum!"

Biting back the reply that leaped into his mind, Junior sucked in a deep, calming breath, then replied, "Have you ever been to Boston, sir?"

Clearly taken aback, Wilmot groused, "I was born and raised in Boston. What's that got to do with this?"

"Have you ever visited the *USS Constitution*? She's docked somewhere in Boston harbor."

"What of it?"

"The *Constitution* helped the United States win the War of 1812 against Britain. They nicknamed her *Old Ironsides* because she was so stoutly built that cannonballs bounced off her. She was a very famous ship, back then."

"I know that," Wilmot huffed.

"Later in the Nineteenth Century," Junior continued, "the United States Navy decided to scrap the *Constitution*, break her up and destroy her."

"That's ancient history," Wilmot snapped.

Undeterred, Junior went on, "Do you know why the ship was never destroyed? Why she's still on the Navy's rolls as an active member of the fleet?"

Without waiting for Wilmot to respond, Junior went on,

"Because a Boston physician wrote a poem called *Old Ironsides.*" Rising to his feet, he began to quote, "It starts, 'Ay, tear her tattered ensign down! Long has it waved on high—'"

"I know the poem," Wilmot rumbled, motioning with both hands for Junior to sit back down. "What's that got to do with the situation here and now?"

Working hard to keep from smiling, Junior answered, "That poem started a movement. Children all over the United States sent in money—pennies, mostly—to save *Old Ironsides*. And it worked. The ship is still there."

"I still don't see—"

"Great things can be accomplished from small beginnings," Junior said. "We can get the IAA to recognize that the ice particles in Saturn's rings are alive. A new life-form. That would be quite an accomplishment, wouldn't it?"

For several moments Wilmot did not reply. At last he said, "If they really are alive."

"Dr. Wunderly is certain that they are," said Junior.

"But her superiors back on Earth are not."

"These contests that we plan to run will bring teams of scientists here, to Saturn," Junior said. "You'll be their host, their director. Quite a feather in your cap, Professor."

Wilmot's irritated scowl slowly morphed into a tentative smile. "That would be quite an accomplishment for the people of *Saturn Prime*," he admitted.

And Junior thought he heard his father's voice approving, "Make the victim a party to the crime."

THE CHILDREN'S CRUSADE

It's like an avalanche in slow motion, Junior said to himself as he watched the latest analysis of the various contests that were being sponsored by Global News.

ARE THE PARTICLES IN SATURN'S RINGS REALLY ALIVE? blared across his viewscreen, the question that formed the basis of the contests. So far, the results showed that children of school age voted an overwhelming yes, with 87 percent in favor. Their parents were less sure, but still showed 68 percent voting in favor. Among professional scientists the results were more conservative, at 26 percent positive, 19 percent negative, 55 percent unsure.

Regardless of the various counts, the contests were the biggest thing on newscasts all around the world. From the United States to Tasmania, from Yakutsk in Russia to Cape Town in South Africa, from the Maldive Islands in the Indian Ocean to Martinique on the edge of the Caribbean Sea, everyone from seven to ninety-seven seemed to have an opinion.

Tom Freemen was harried, overworked, pressured by his superiors and his equally harried and overworked staffers—and happy as a man who had just discovered a gold mine.

"I can't believe it!" he enthused to Junior. "It's fantastic! *Everybody* wants to get in on this parade."

Junior smiled, but in the back of his mind he wondered how happy Wilmot was going to be when a shipload of tourists set sail for *Saturn Prime*.

He didn't have to wait very long.

Two months after the contests started, Freeman decided to tote up the votes and pick the winners. There were several million votes to count.

"Looks like you'll have a shipload of visitors heading your way in a few weeks," he told Junior, grinning from ear to ear. Then he added, "And I'm getting a promotion: as of Monday I'll be heading Global's marketing division!"

Junior grinned back at Freeman's image on his viewscreen. "Congratulations, Tom!"

But Freeman was not finished with his message. He kept right on talking, "And I'll be coming out there on the same ship as our prize winners. Plus a gaggle of scientists and other adults with the parents and kids who've booked passage to your station!"

Swiftly calculating the number of prize-winners from the various contests, Junior said, "Sixty-some people coming here? Including about a dozen children?"

Junior knew it would take a couple of hours before he heard Freeman's answer. And he realized that whatever the answer was, it was going to stir the wrath of Professor James Colrain Wilmot.

═══════

.

"No!" Wilmot fumed. "We can't have it! A dozen-some runny-nosed children and their parents? Plus more than two dozen other people? Never! I can't allow it!"

Junior countered, "But among the adults will be half a dozen top-ranked scientists. They're coming here to see the rings for themselves and decide if Dr. Wunderly is right and the ring particles are alive."

"The scientists can come," Wilmot answered, "but not the others. Not a shipload of children and out-and-out tourists!"

Junior closed his eyes and silently counted to ten. He thought, *If Wilmot bars the kids and the non-scientists from coming, the whole scheme collapses. We'll have gone through all this for nothing.*

As reasonably as he could manage, Junior pleaded, "Look, Dr. Wilmot, this is an opportunity to show the people back on Earth the work you've been directing. Show them how productive, how successful you've been in taking in the exiles from Earth and helping them to build a thriving, successful community for themselves out here, more than a billion kilometers from Earth."

Wilmot's frown eased a fraction.

"And," Junior added, "how you're accomplishing significant scientific research, here on the edge of human settlement of the solar system."

"There's another colony being established around Uranus," Wilmot said, in a low voice. "They're farther out than we are."

"But they're not sponsoring significant scientific research, the way you are. Under your direction, Dr. Wunderly may have made the biggest discovery since we first started digging up the remains of the extinct civilization on Mars!"

"True enough," Wilmot muttered.

"We'll play host to fewer than a hundred people," Junior coaxed. "A few of them will be children, sure enough, but a handful of others will be top-notch scientists from the IAA."

Wilmot leaned back in his swivel chair and raised his eyes to the ceiling. For eternally long moments, he spoke not a word. At last he sighed and focused once more on Junior.

"Mr. Gunn, you are a silver-tongued devil."

Junior barely held back the response that popped into his mind, *Thank you, sir. I appreciate your appreciation.*

═══════

Thus, it was that on the thirty-first of October—Halloween back on Earth—the spacecraft *Normandie* established orbit around Saturn, liked with the *Saturn Prime* space station, and began offloading its passengers.

Junior was at the docking port as the first passengers entered the station. They were children, each of them firmly in the grip of an adult.

"Hello," Junior said cheerily to them. "Welcome to *Saturn Prime.*"

The newcomers did not reply. They were too busy goggling at the station's reception area. In total silence the adults filed up at the security desks and presented their ID chips. The children stared wide-eyed at the reception area's inspection arches.

The men and women manning the inspection booths spoke to the new arrivals in hushed whispers. The arriving adults replied in equally low tones. The three teenagers among the arrivals kept glancing around at the booths and the inspection arches. The younger children squirmed unhappily, like hooked fish trying to wriggle free.

As the newcomers made their way slowly through the inspection arches, one of the smaller boys wrestled his arm free of the adult who was holding him and bolted for the open hatch that led to the station's central passageway.

Before Junior could react, a half-dozen other children broke free and followed the youngster who was already through the hatch.

Chaos erupted.

The reception area was suddenly filled with children running, hollering, shrieking—while their parents and guardians raced after them, yelling for them to stop.

Junior bolted for the hatch, knowing that Wilmot was watching all this from his office and probably having the beginnings of a stroke.

"No! No!" Junior bellowed. "Come back!"

A few of the kids stopped running—mostly the teenagers—but the smaller, younger children continued racing down the passageway, yelling happily, glad to be free to explore.

It took the better part of an hour to round up the escapees and return them to their guardians. As Junior carried the last of them—a wriggling, squalling boy of about nine years old—to his obviously mortified father, he wondered what Professor Wilmot was going to make of this mini-jailbreak.

———

Wilmot was obviously furious, his face smoldering red as he sat behind his desk and glared at Junior.

"Five minutes they're on this station and they caused an upheaval!" he snapped.

Trying to calm the professor's wrath, Junior said, "They'd spent two weeks bottled up in the ship that brought them here. They were glad to be free. And to see their new surroundings."

His chest heaving, Wilmot insisted, "I want them all packed back aboard the *Normandie* and shipped back to Earth. Immediately!"

"The scientists who came with them, too?"

"The scientists can stay, of course. But those little monsters have got to go! I want them out of here! Immediately!"

Trying to plan a strategic retreat, Junior said softly, "If that's what you want, sir."

"That's what I want!" Wilmot snapped.

Junior got up and headed for the office's door, thinking, *The* Normandie *is scheduled to detach from the station and start its return flight to Earth as soon as the last of its passengers have passed through the reception routine. If I don't reach the reception center before she undocks . .* ˘

Walking as slowly as he could, Junior made his tedious way back to the reception area. As he stepped through the hatch, he saw that the center was quiet and empty of the newcomers.

He called to one of the immigration inspectors, who was packing up a handful of information chips, "Where is everybody?"

The man gave Junior a baleful look. "The new arrivals are heading for their quarters."

"And the ship?" Junior asked. "The *Normandie?*"

"Her captain pulled out as soon as we processed the last of the new arrivals. Said he was going to enjoy a peaceful trip back Earthside."

Suppressing the smile that blossomed inside him, Junior asked plaintively, "You mean he's gone? Already?"

With a nod, the inspector said, "And he looked damned happy to be getting away from those kids. Said they damn near drove him batty on the trip here."

Junior nodded back and recalled a fragment of the French lessons he had taken back in Jackpot, Nevada. *C'est dommage. Tant pis.*

Too bad. What a pity.

But, knowing that Wilmot was watching, he let his chin slump toward his chest and slowly left the reception center. Inwardly, though, he felt like dancing.

[BARELY]
CONTROLLED MAYHEM

In the weeks that followed, Junior often told himself that Wilmot had been right: the children were agents of chaos.

How could a dozen youngsters cause such pandemonium in a once-orderly and quietly managed space station?

The nine-year-old boy that Junior had chased down on the day that the newcomers had first arrived turned out to be a natural ringleader. He dreamed up adventures for the other children and most of them followed his lead. At first he and the younger children explored the station. Junior had to track them down at the Glassteel dome of *Saturn Prime*'s observation center, where they were staring goggle-eyed at the huge ringed planet glowing against the darkness of space.

The next day Junior responded to a desperate call from the kitchens: the kids had invaded the area and were poking into everything, while the cooks and assistants chased them with brandished cooking spoons and angry screams.

Then the teenagers among the visitors discovered the VR parlors and started running erotic videos on the giant viewscreens there. Junior shut off the displays and rounded up the boys, as well as several young women from the station's regular residents.

One of the young men he located in the women's locker room of the station's gymnasium, fondling the only young woman among the newcomers, both of them half-naked and panting like rhinoceroses in full mating ritual.

A trio of the youngest boys led by a seven-year-old adventurer found their way to the station's chemistry laboratory and had enormous fun filling the lab with mounds of soap bubbles that they manufactured from the lab's unguarded supply closet. Junior got to the lab just in time to stop one of the chemists from strangling one of the kicking, shrieking boys.

"You've turned this station into an insane asylum!" shouted a wild-eyed, thoroughly anguished Professor Wilmot. "I want them out of here immediately! And you with them!"

Junior smiled sympathetically at the professor, who looked close to a hysterical collapse. "We're getting them under control," he replied softly. "Besides, there won't be a ship here for another six weeks."

"Six weeks?" Wilmot bleated. "I'm calling Copenhagen for an emergency rescue mission."

As reasonably as he could manage, Junior asked, "Who would the mission be rescuing, sir?"

"Us! The normal men and women of this station! Get those damned brats out of here! As fast as you can!"

Trying to sound reasonable, rational, Junior said, "We're getting things under control. There hasn't been a—"

Wilmot's phone blared, "Emergency! Emergency!"

The professor fixed Junior with a baleful eye as he shouted to the phone, "Answer, dammit!"

The phone's computerized voice replied in a carefully

modulated baritone voice, "Unauthorized persons have invaded the astronomical center. Dr. Van Maanen wishes to speak to you immediately."

Looking close to a complete physical collapse, Wilmot groaned, "Connect."

The viewscreen flicked to a head-and-shoulders view of the chief of the astronomy group, a man that Junior had often heard Nadia Wunderly describe as "such a straight arrow that he could lead a crusade through purgatory—and hell!"

But Isaak Van Maanen was smiling gently as his image appeared on Wilmot's viewscreen. He was a rather handsome middle-aged man, gray of hair and mustache, with bright-blue eyes that seemed to sparkle. The chief of the station's astronomy group said cheerfully to Wilmot, "Good morning, Professor. How are you this lovely morning?"

"What's happened?" Wilmot snapped. "What are those brats up to now?"

Gesturing to six boys and three girls sitting placidly at man-sized desks, Van Maanen replied, "Oh, you mean the new assistants you sent to me? They are studying the rings." The camera view shifted to show the nine children staring quietly at the viewscreens atop each of the desks at which they were sitting.

Wilmot's eyes nearly popped out of his head.

Van Maanen went on happily, "All they needed was something to occupy their curiosity. They're quite intelligent, you know, if you give them something to engage their minds."

One of the boys raised his hand and started waving it frantically. "Look!" he shouted. "Look! They're covering up a new rock."

Van Maanen pushed himself up from his chair and went to the boy's desk. Bending down, he stared at the viewscreen and smiled benignly. "Yes, my lad, the ice particles are swarming over the new arrival." Straightening up, the astronomer said to the other children, "Set your screens for AB-six. Watch the ice particles chew up the new rock."

Junior turned from the viewscreen to Wilmot's staring face. The professor was just as rapt as the children.

Van Maanen returned to his own desk and sat down heavily. "They are basically good boys and girls. What they need is something to engage their interests, their natural curiosity. That's what science is all about, isn't it?"

Wilmot nodded silently, his mouth hanging open, his eyes glued to the TV image of the ice particles swarming over the once-bare rock.

Junior couldn't help smiling. Van Maanen had found the way to control the kids.

MEETING OF MINDS

Junior looked out at the people filing into the station's largest conference room. The adults—mostly scientists of various specialties—chatted quietly among themselves as they found their seats. Toward the rear of the auditorium-like chamber sat the visiting children and their parents or guardians, most of the kids squirming and fidgeting as they gazed around the big room.

So far so good, Junior said to himself as he sat near the middle row of the audience. But he worried that something might send the kids into a paroxysmal release of pent-up energy.

Dr. Van Maanen sat among the children, chatting quietly with them. By checking Van Mannen's dossier, Junior had learned that the astronomer had been born in Amsterdam, the youngest of twelve children, was happily married and the father of six.

He knows how to get along with kids, Junior said to himself. *If we have a Christmas celebration aboard this bucket, he could play Santa Claus with no sweat.*

The buzz of conversations hushed as Professor Wilmot stepped out of the stage's wing and crossed the otherwise empty platform to stand at the podium.

"Welcome to our meeting," he began, with a tentative smile,

his eyes focused on the children seated toward the rear. "This is an historic occasion, one that will be recorded in . . . in history journals all through the solar system. We are making our report to the International Astronautical Association's board of directors in Copenhagen, back on Earth. We are going to announce our discovery of the fact that the particles composing Saturn's rings are alive, living creatures existing at temperatures far below zero, Celsius."

Junior searched for Nadia Wunderly, seated among the scientists in the front rows. He made out the back of her head, her short-cropped, brick-red hair.

This is your discovery, Nadia, Junior said silently. *Your claim on the Nobel Prize.*

As if on cue, Wilmot smiled down on the scientists sitting before him and called, "Dr. Wunderly, will you please come up here?"

It took some floundering and bumped ankles as Nadia pushed her way out to the aisle and plodded up the steps to join Wilmot at the podium. A big viewscreen slid down across the back of the stage and—after a few moments—it lit up to show the head and shoulders of a pleasantly smiling man.

"Hello to all of you out there at Saturn," he said, in a calm, controlled tenor voice. "I am Dr. Marlon Ingersol, the head of the IAA's astronomy board. I'm happy to be with you this evening."

"And we're delighted you have joined us, sir," said Wilmot, adding, "despite the long time gap time in our conversation due to the distance between Earth and Saturn."

Ingersol's image remained frozen on the screen.

Wilmot went on, "So without any further delay, I present Dr. Wunderly, who has directed our studies of Saturn's rings." Turning and making a slight bow, Wilmot gestured Nadia to the podium. "Dr. Wunderly."

For more than an uninterrupted hour, Wunderly showed TV footage of the ice particles, swarming over bits of rock that had fallen into the rings. Junior watched, entranced, as the tiny creatures scuttled over the bits of bare material chopped off Saturn's copious moons and wayfaring comets that had wandered into the ring system.

"They move, they swarm over new arrivals, they digest them completely," Wunderly said into her microphone. "Conclusion: they are alive. Our next step will be to capture samples of them and investigate them in our laboratories."

Wilmot moved in beside her and, with a smarmy smile, announced, "We are currently preparing a sampling mission that will enter the outermost ring and return to us here at the station a sampling of the ring particles."

"And their inhabitants," Wunderly quickly added.

Junior couldn't take his eyes off the screen and the scrambling, crawling ice particles that were being displayed. *Live creatures*, he said to himself, *living hundreds of degrees below zero. If we could transport samples of them back to Earth, every biologist in the world would want to get his hands on them.*

Should be a healthy market, Junior thought. *And not just for scientists. Ordinary people would want to buy some for souvenirs. And schools! Could be a worthwhile market.*

He tucked the idea away in the back of his mind as the scientists in the audience began asking questions of Nadia and Professor Wilmot.

━━━━━

The visiting scientists seemed to agree with Nadia that the ring particles were alive. But their leader—a lean, lanky Japanese astronomer—insisted that they could not definitely declare the particles alive until they had examined samples of them in the station's laboratories.

Wilmot smiled and nodded agreement. "We are putting the finishing touches on a probe that will dip into the outermost ring and collect samples for study here aboard the station."

Still sitting in the middle of the audience, Junior thought, *Wilmot's going to push Nadia aside and claim as much of the credit for this discovery as he can.* Frowning inwardly, he wondered, *How can I help her to get the credit she deserves?*

He realized that the answer to his question was sitting a few rows behind him: Tom Freeman, the newly named head of Global News Network's marketing division.

INTERVIEW

"Interview who?" Freeman asked.

Junior had invited the newly promoted Global News executive to his narrow compartment for a private talk. The cubicle was cramped, crowded with the two of them in it. Junior had gestured Freemen to the only chair, by the minuscule desk, while he sat himself on the end of his bed.

"Nadia Wunderly," he answered Freeman. "She's the one who really deserves the credit for discovering that the ring particles are living creatures."

Freeman smiled slightly as he muttered, "Living creatures. At several hundred degrees below zero. Who'd've thunk it?"

"Nadia did," Junior replied. "Nobody else believed her—including Wilmot—but it turned out she was right."

"Has she done any interviews with any other networks?"

"No. Nobody out there really knows who she is, or how important she is. She's discovered a new life form! Against the opposition of her superiors. She should get the credit."

"Instead of Wilmot."

Junior nodded.

"Could be interesting," Freeman conceded. "But how will Wilmot react to it?"

"Who cares?" Junior replied. "He wants to hog all the glory for himself, but it's Nadia who deserves the congratulations."

"And the Nobel," Freeman added.

———

Nadia's interview on Global News went well—too well, Junior thought. He had expected that Nadia would be shy, withdrawn, while the network's cameras were pointed at her. Actually, she was just the opposite. Global's pair of news interviewers couldn't get her to shut up!

Junior watched the video broadcast from his tight little compartment, smiling as he saw Nadia run away with her interview.

"This is something totally new to science!" she said, more than once. "Living creatures existing at temperatures hundreds of degrees below zero! It opens up an entirely new field of biological studies."

The female half of the pair of interviewers started to say, "It certainly is unlike anything—"

"It's mind-blowing!" Nadia interrupted. "They're alive! Out in the frozen wilderness of Saturn's rings, these creatures are alive! Nothing we've seen before has been anything like this! It's a whole new area of biology!"

The male member of the team nodded smilingly. "Well, you certainly seem excited about it, Dr. Wunderly."

Jabbing a stubby finger at his chest, Nadia insisted, "You should be too! This is history-making! It's fantastic!"

His smile obviously weakening, the newsman turned to look directly into the camera and said, "And that's the big news from Saturn: living creatures inhabit Saturn's dazzling rings."

The video screen went dark for a moment, then cleared to show a housewife frowning as she watched a round, flat little robot bumping against the leg of a kitchen chair.

"Does your household cleaning 'bot get snarled amongst your furniture?" asked a disembodied female voice. "Time to switch to—"

Junior snapped his fingers and the screen went dark.

———

This place has changed, Junior said to himself.

He was striding along the station's central passageway, heading for Wilmot's office. Thanks to Van Maanen's fatherly shepherding, the children hadn't caused any real uproars in several weeks. Oh, a couple of the younger ones got themselves stuck in one of the station's simulations labs, where they wandered into a sim of Saturn's rings and didn't know how to get out of it. Junior led a "rescue" mission that shut down the three-dimensional presentation of the ring particles and got the kids safely back to their parents before Wilmot even heard about the problem.

Under Nadia Wunderly's careful leadership, the sampling mission into the rings went smoothly. The automated vehicle sailed into the outermost ring, picked up half a dozen of the ice particles, and returned them to the station. Nadia took the heavily insulated box that held them and hurried to the subzero lab she had specially prepared to study the samples. Junior hadn't seen her since she'd closed the insulated door to her lab; she had been alone with the samples for three days now without a peep to anyone outside.

"What's she doing in there?" Wilmot grumbled to Junior. "I tried to get into her damned laboratory, but the door was

sealed, and she wouldn't open it to me. She's been in that refrigerated room for three days straight now. Won't even answer my
calls to her."

Sitting in front of the director's desk, Junior smiled to hide
his own worries about Nadia. "She's in her element," he said.
"She's completely wrapped up with those particles."

"But she can't keep herself hidden in there!" Wilmot
snapped. "For all we know, she could be lying on the floor of
that damned refrigerated lab of hers, dead."

With a shake of her head, Junior replied, "She's been eating
the meals she's ordered. The serving robots have been bringing
food into her lab three times a day."

Wilmot said nothing, he just sat in his desk chair, smoldering like a volcano about to erupt.

As if on cue, Wilmot's desk screen brightened to show
Nadia's face, framed by the fur-lined hood of her winter parka.

"Professor Wilmot," she called, in a shockingly weak voice.

Wilmot hunched forward in his chair. "Yes! I'm here!"

Nadia seemed to take a deep, shuddering breath. Then she
said, almost whispering, "I'd like to make my report about the
ring particles, sir."

"Yes, yes!" said Wilmot. "Go ahead."

"I'll come to your office, if that's all right with you."

"Yes! Of course. Mr. Gunn is here with me."

"Good. Perhaps you could get Dr. Van Maanen, too?"

"Certainly! How soon will you be here?"

"In a few minutes."

"Good! Fine!"

Nadia's image faded away and the screen went dark.

DISCOVERY

Junior struggled to keep himself from fidgeting as he and Wilmot waited for Nadia Wunderly. *She didn't look right*, Junior kept thinking. *She looked dazed, as if somebody had knocked her on the head.*

Wilmot drummed his fingers on his desktop impatiently, his eyes fixed on the door to his office. Van Maanen came in and seated himself beside Junior without saying a word.

"Do you think she's all right?" Junior heard himself ask.

"She's tired, that's all," Wilmot replied. "Probably hasn't slept a wink for days, playing with those particles."

"She's kept her lab refrigerated," Junior muttered.

"That too. She could be—"

The office door slid open. Nadia Wunderly stood there for a moment, her eyes blinking slowly, still wearing the heavy parka, its hood pushed back across her chunky shoulders. Junior jumped up from his chair and went to her. She half-collapsed into his arms.

"Nadia!" Junior cried. "Are you all right?"

Wilmot and Von Maanen shot to their feet also and watched Junior help Wunderly to the other chair in front of the desk.

She sank into it slowly and let the heavy parka slip from her shoulders.

As Junior returned to his own chair and the other two men sat down again, Nadia said in a weak, almost timid, voice, "They're not alive."

Junior heard Wilmot gasp. "Not alive?"

"No."

"Then what . . . ?"

Nadia seemed to be panting, as if she needed fresh air. Junior saw that her face was pale, drawn—shocked.

"They're machines," she breathed.

"Machines?" Wilmot gasped.

Fumbling with her parka, Nadia pulled a small white object from its pocket. It was slightly larger than the palm of her hand.

"Here's one of the ice particles," she said, almost in a whisper, as she laid the object on Wilmot's desk.

It just sat there, a roundish white hump. Inert. Unmoving.

The three men stared at it.

"The temperature in this room is much too warm for it," Wunderly said, her voice gaining some strength. "Back in my lab, in its subzero temperature, they move around sluggishly. They need to be a couple of hundred degrees colder to be fully active."

Wilmot stared at the object. Van Maanen reached out and poked it with his finger. No reaction from it. Junior stared at Nadia. She seemed stunned, her eyes focused on the ice particle. *A machine?* he asked himself. *How could it be a machine?*

His hand trembling noticeably, Van Maanen picked up the palm-sized machine and turned it over onto its back. Its underside was lined with tiny, hair-thin legs.

"I'll be damned," he muttered.

"They're all like this?" Wilmot asked, his voice hushed, awed.

Wunderly nodded. "All the ones we brought back from the ring."

"Machines," Junior heard himself mutter.

Sitting up straighter, Wunderly said, "We've wondered for generations why Saturn had such broad, bright rings while the other big planets—from Jupiter to Neptune—have slim, dark rings." She pointed to the inert object still on Wilmot's desk. "This is why. Saturn's natural rings have been seeded with these machines."

"That's fantastic," Wilmot said. It wasn't an objection or a criticism. His voice was hollow with awe.

Junior's mind moved to the obvious conclusion. "Somebody seeded Saturn's natural rings with these machines."

"Somebody?" Wilmot snapped. "Who?"

Van Maanen answered, "Somebody who was here at Saturn since at least Galileo's time."

"Probably earlier," said Wunderly.

"Who?" Wilmot repeated. "Why?"

"Good questions," said Junior.

"How do we find the answers?" Van Maanen asked.

None of them offered a response.

MYSTERY

From that moment on, Saturn became the focus of a scientific investigation that changed everything. Instead of being a refuge for the discarded people of Earth, the *Saturn Prime* station became the focal point of a study of the planet's ring machines—the palm-sized mechanisms that had built the brightly glowing rings of Saturn and maintained them for centuries, perhaps millennia.

Van Maanen became, perforce, the head of the stream of astronomers and other scientists who flocked to Saturn. Wilmot was jostled aside and actually seemed glad to return his attention to supervising the station's needs and to directing the construction of the second space station, built alongside the original *Saturn Prime*.

Junior found himself drafted into the management of the new station, which the assembled scientists soon named *Cassini*, after the seventeenth-century Italian astronomer who first realized that the puzzling bright objects glowing on either side of the planet Saturn were indeed ring structures.

Van Maanen and Junior shared an office in the unfinished *Cassini* station, where Van Maanen directed the astronomical studies of the rings and Junior took care of all the housekeeping work.

Shaking his head as he sat at his capacious desk, Van Maanen muttered, "The more we study the *verdammt* ring particles, the less we understand them."

Junior looked up from the list of housekeeping supplies displayed on his desktop screen. "It's that bad?"

For the first time since he'd originally met the astronomer, Junior saw bitter frustration in Van Maanen's face. He leaned back wearily in his desk chair and grumbled, "When we try to take the damn machines apart to study their insides, they just go *poof!* and melt into puddles of liquid metal. It's infuriating!"

"Maybe your cryolab isn't cold enough," Junior suggested. "Maybe you should set up a lab in the rings themselves."

Van Mannen stared at Junior for several long, wordless moments. Then, "Maybe I should have thought of that myself."

Junior grinned at him and returned his attention to the list on his desktop screen.

━━━━━

A month later Van Maanen convened a meeting of a tight group of the astronomers' leaders. Wilmot was invited, Junior was not. But—curious—Junior slipped into *Cassini*'s smallish conference room and silently took a seat by the door, half expecting to be asked to leave.

Van Maanen eyed Junior from his chair at the head of the oval table but said nothing.

Suppressing a grin, Junior told himself, *Nothing ventured, nothing gained. Silence means assent.* And he remembered his father's, *L'audace. Toujours l'audace.*

Nearly two hours later, Junior was struggling to stay awake. The meeting was monumentally boring.

"Let me sum up," Van Maanen was saying to the half-dozen other astronomers sitting glumly around the oval table: four men, two women—one stout and flabby, the other rail-thin.

Van Maanen went on, "The machines are based on a cryonic technology that we don't yet understand. We have no idea how they work, what their energy source is, what their *purpose* is."

One of the men raised a hand halfheartedly and said, "We haven't been able to detect any electromagnetic signals out of them. They aren't communicating with anybody, apparently."

"Apparently," echoed the chubby woman, her voice dripping sarcasm.

"They could be using a communications system that's not based on electromagnetics," said the man sitting beside her.

"Like what?"

The astronomer shrugged elaborately.

With a heartfelt sigh, Van Mannen said, "So we have no idea if they're communicating with whoever placed them here."

Shrugs and head shaking.

"And no idea why they're here."

Junior slowly raised his hand.

His expression halfway between irked and amused, Van Maanen nodded at Junior. "Mr. Gunn?"

"If they've been here a couple of million years—"

"We have no way of establishing their age," snapped one of the astronomers.

"I know, I know," Junior acknowledged. "But *if* they've been here for some two million years, they could be connected with the Pleistocene Ice Age on Earth."

Smiling tolerantly, Van Maanen retorted, "Or not. We have no way of knowing."

Junior nodded. "Yeah. I guess not." Then he went on, "But if they've been here since the Pleistocene, they might have been placed here to observe us, to watch the rise of Homo sapiens on Earth and report it back to whoever put them around Saturn."

Dead silence. But Junior could see the skepticism, the disbelief, the outright resentment among the astronomers sitting around the conference table.

At last Van Maanen smiled tolerantly and said, "That's piling assumptions upon assumptions, Mr. Gunn. With no proof for any of them."

Junior muttered, "Maybe so."

The meeting ended soon afterward, with no reasonable ideas about why the machines were placed around Saturn, who placed them there, or what their purpose might be.

REUNION

For the next several weeks, Junior went through his daily routine of managing station *Cassini*'s housekeeping, while his mind stubbornly kept ruminating over the mystery of Saturn's mechanical ice particles.

The news that Saturn had been visited by an alien civilization that seeded the planet with cryonic machines created something of an uproar back on Earth.

ALIENS APPARENTLY VISITED THE SOLAR SYSTEM
AGES AGO!
                                        —*New York Times*

WE ARE NOT ALONE IN THE UNIVERSE
                                    —*Manchester Guardian*

UFO SEEDED SATURN'S RINGS WITH SPY MACHINES
                                        —*Sky Watch Magazine*

THEY'VE BEEN HERE! WHEN WILL THEY RETURN?
                                        —*UFO Observer*

The world government moved with unaccustomed speed—critical voices called it *heedless, reckless* speed—and announced a new branch of the International Peacekeeping Force would be created. Dubbed the *Star Watch*, this new organization would have the responsibility of scanning the heavens, searching for evidence of intelligent extraterrestrial civilizations.

And what was it supposed to do if it found intelligent aliens? No one had a reasonable answer to that question.

Weeks evolved into months, and the worlds spun 'round in their usual orbits. No aliens in sight. No threats to Earth and the other worlds of the solar system materialized.

Life went back to normal . . . almost.

But everything had changed. The human race knew that there were other intelligent creatures somewhere among the stars, intelligent creatures who had seeded Saturn's rings with their machines. Why? What did they want? Would they return?

Humankind's ancient dream of expanding out to the endless spaces of the universe became tainted with the fear of what was out there, waiting, watching, perhaps already on their way, returning to Earth and the solar system. Why? Who were they? What did they want of us?

The ancient dream of reaching the stars became stained with fear. With a deep, unshakeable sense of foreboding. Of dread.

———

On the *Cassini* space station, orbiting brightly ringed Saturn, there were days when Junior almost forgot the shadow of the alien presence. Almost. But it lurked deep in his unconscious mind: alien monsters, capable of wiping out the puny human race.

But why would they do that? Junior asked himself. *Why do we assume that the aliens will be hostile, dangerous, a threat to our existence?*

And each time he asked himself such questions, he recalled Oliver Cromwell's advice from centuries earlier: "Keep your faith in God, my boys, but keep your powder dry."

Hope for the best, Junior thought, *but prepare for the worst.*

Day after day, Junior went through the seemingly endless routines of keeping the *Cassini* station in good working order. He handled everything from incoming scientific personnel to the maintenance and repair of the station's myriad systems and the daily requirements of fresh fruits and vegetables that fed the station's growing population.

Day after day, Junior hid the lurking fear of menacing alien invaders behind endless grocery lists and personnel dossiers. *I've become a clerk,* he told himself, *nothing more than a paper-shuffling clerk.*

He felt tremendously disappointed. Almost ashamed of himself. *I ought to be out there with the Star Watch,* he chided himself, *scanning the heavens for a sign of the aliens. Instead, I'm nothing but a glorified grocery clerk.*

What would my father do? he asked himself. But he found no answer.

———

As he did every day, Junior was sitting at his desk, next to Van Maanen's, scanning a list of new arrivals due to dock at the *Cassini* station in two days. Astronomers, astrophysicists, biologists eager to examine the ice particles of Saturn's rings, cryogenics specialists who hoped to study the ring particles without having them dissolve into useless puddles.

Boring, Junior said to himself. *Here I am in the middle of the greatest discovery—the greatest mystery—of the century and I've got nothing better to do than run through lists of new arrivals.*

But then his eye happened to light on one of the names on the list scrolling along his computer screen:

Deborah Salmon: physical therapist.

Deborah! His heart thumped eagerly beneath his ribs. *She's coming here! Here to Saturn!*

Suppressing a wild urge to leap from his desk chair and shout "Yahoo!" Junior forced himself to remain seated, staring at Deborah's name.

She's not coming here because of me, he said to himself. *It's just a coincidence. She probably doesn't even know I'm here.*

But he slowly got up from his chair, walked very carefully to the office door, and headed for his quarters. He never noticed Van Maanen staring curiously at him as he left.

Junior walked, almost in a daze, to the shuttle that brought him back to the *Saturn Prime* station, and then went straight to the one-room compartment that served as his residence. Like an automaton he went in, softly closed its door, then went to the closet where his clothes hung and picked out the freshest looking set of coveralls he could find. Out of the three that were hanging there.

———

Waiting was agony. Junior rehearsed in his mind a dozen meetings with Deborah. *She'll be surprised to see me here,* he thought. *But I'll tell her it's fate. Kismet. We were meant to be together. The entire solar system wasn't big enough to hide you from me.*

He didn't sleep much that night, and when he did, he dreamed of Debbie.

DEBORAH

Feeling as nervous as a teenager on his first date, Junior paced impatiently across the reception area of the *Saturn Prime* space station. Deborah's ship, the same *Normandie* that had brought (and returned) the visiting children a few months earlier, was due to arrive in another hour. Junior had come to the reception area more than an hour earlier, and spent his time restlessly pacing back and forth while the immigration personnel slowly, quietly arrived at their desks and stared at him as they waited for the *Normandie*'s arrival.

Time stretched endlessly. Junior tried to imagine Deborah's arrival. *Would she be surprised to see me here, in this man-made habitat orbiting many-ringed Saturn? Yes, of course she would*, he told himself. But will she be glad to see me? Or annoyed, disenchanted, unhappy?

A sudden thought almost made his knees buckle. *Maybe she's married to someone else! Maybe she's forgotten about me!* He tried to push that idea out of his mind, but it hung there like an icepick aimed at his heart.

At last the reception area's public address system announced, "*Normandie* has matched velocity with the station. The vessel will mate with *Saturn Prime* in fifteen minutes."

Junior stopped his pacing and turned to face the hatch that would soon begin disgorging the vessel's passengers. His heart thumped so hard that he thought the immigration clerks could hear it, sitting at their stations a few meters away from where he stood.

Standing there as the hatch opened, Junior remembered from his school days a slogan from some long-dead politician back on Earth: "Patience and fortitude."

Patience, he told himself. *And fortitude.*

Passengers started filing through the hatch. Men, mostly. They looked like scientists, in Junior's eyes, come here to Saturn to study the ring particles.

But where is Deborah?

At that moment, she came through the hatch, clutching a small travel bag, glancing around the reception area; almost Junior's height, her dark hair falling to her shoulders, her gray-green eyes sparkling, alert, just as he remembered. She was wearing a simple one-piece coverall, but it couldn't hide the beauty of her slim waist, her graceful long legs, her shapely figure.

Junior tried to call to her, but his voice caught in his throat. Deborah's searching glance stopped the instant she saw him. Her eyes went wide, she dropped her bag, and she shouted, "Sam!"

Junior croaked out, "Debbie!" and ran to her. He swept her up in his arms and kissed her mightily.

"You're here," she gasped, clinging to him. "You're really here!"

"And so are you!" Junior grinned. Other passengers were still streaming past, one whistled admiringly, but Junior paid them no attention. He held Deborah as if his life depended on it. *It does*, he realized. *My life really does depend on her.*

Releasing Deborah at last, Junior bent down and picked

up her travel bag. "Welcome to *Saturn Prime*," he managed to choke out.

As Junior led her to one of the immigration desks, Deborah told him, "Your friend Frederick Malone told me he thought you were here. He wasn't very forthcoming, though. He acted like I was a hired assassin trying to track you down."

Junior laughed carelessly. "Freddie's a suspicious sort. I'm surprised he told you that much."

"I think he thought I was pregnant and abandoned."

"Where would he get that idea?"

Deborah laughed. "From me."

Junior led Deborah through one of the immigration desks and the inspection arch beyond it. The clerk at the desk eyed the two of them curiously, scanned Deborah's papers briefly, then directed her to the arch, where scanning beams swiftly showed that she was carrying no restricted items, such as fresh fruits or hidden weapons.

Grinning happily, Junior led her to the docking station where a transfer vehicle was preparing to ferry the new arrivals to station *Cassini*.

As they boarded the fat little transfer ship, Junior finally worked up the nerve to ask, "So . . . what brings all the way out here, Deb?"

And he trembled to hear her answer.

Sitting beside him in the ship's cramped passenger compartment, Deborah looked into his eyes, smiled shyly, and answered, "You. I wanted to find you, Sam. Once Malone told me he thought you were here, I decided to come out and find you."

For once in his life, Junior was speechless.

Deborah went on, "My mother died, and my baby brother is living with his uncle Stu. My big brothers have wives and families of their own. I'd be a stranger to them, interrupting their lives. And . . ." she hesitated, took a breath, then continued, "And I couldn't get you out of my mind."

"I love you, Debbie," said Junior.

She nodded. "I love you, too, Sam."

Junior felt as if he were zooming across the universe, free and deliriously happy. He slid his arm around Deborah's shoulders, pulled her toward himself, and kissed her. Her lips felt warm and soft. When he released her, he saw there were tears in her eyes.

"Don't cry," he whispered to her. "Be happy."

"I am happy, Sam. Happier than I've ever been in my whole life."

Nodding, Junior choked out, "Me too."

PIERRE D'ARGENT

Hand in hand, Junior and Debbie left the transfer ship and found Deborah's assigned quarters aboard the *Cassini* station. The single compartment consisted of a narrow bedroom, with a closet on one side and a tight little bathroom on the other.

Smiling, Junior admitted, "This is bigger than my place on *Prime.*"

"So you'll move in with me?" Deborah asked.

"In a supersonic flash."

Kismet, thought Junior. *It was meant to be.* He moved in with Deborah, and they lived together as if it had been ordained by the gods.

Junior had never been happier. Except that when he asked Deborah about getting married, she grew hesitant, evasive. "There's plenty of time for that, Sam," she told him. "Let's not rush."

And then the message from Pierre D'Argent arrived.

Junior was sitting at his desk in the *Cassini* station, going through a long list of replacement items that the station needed, when the message light on his screen started blinking: Incoming call from Pierre D'Argent.

Surprised, annoyed, and more than a little curious, Junior

minimized the replacement list and pulled up D'Argent's message.

The Rockledge president was smiling in his usual oily way as he announced, "I thought you'd like to know that I'm on my way to your *Saturn Prime* station, Samuel. With my new bride. I've reached one hundred years of age, which is the mandatory retirement point here at Rockledge Industries. So I'm taking a little jaunt out to Saturn. A honeymoon trip. See you in two weeks! 'Til then, *bon chance!*"

Junior stared at D'Argent's sculpted features frozen on his desktop screen, thinking, *That's his third wife. Or is it his fourth? And he's coming here. Why? What's he up to?*

Feeling halfway between curious and worried, Junior looked up the station's manifest. Sure enough, a Rockledge vessel—the *Ark Royal*, no less—was due to arrive in twelve days.

===

The first thing Junior did was to ask Rex Klamath to have lunch with him. They sat together at a small table in *Cassini*'s only restaurant—a fairly comfortable eatery where the scientists gathered daily.

"The son of a bitch is coming here?" the dwarf snarled once Junior broke the news to him. "Good! Let's shove him out an airlock."

Breaking into a guarded grin, Junior responded, "Not until we figure out why he's coming."

"Who the hell cares," Klamath grumbled. "That bastard turned me into a trained seal. His friggin' pet! Let's kill him. Any two-bit lawyer could get us off on a plea of justifiable homicide."

Junior shook his head. "Calm down, Rex. Calm down."

"Easy for you to say, Sam."

"Revenge is a dish best served cold," Junior quoted.

Klamath repeated, "Easy for you to say."

========

At last the *Ark Royal* arrived at the *Saturn Prime* space station. Waiting in the arrival area, Junior was only mildly surprised to see that D'Argent—with his current wife—were the vessel's only passengers. *Rank has its privileges*, he thought as D'Argent stepped through the hatch and entered the arrival station.

His wife was two steps behind him: tall, slim, and beautiful, with long blonde hair and a fashion model's painted smile, Mrs. D'Argent looked every inch the reward for a man of extraordinary means, a rich man's prize.

D'Argent looked around the arrival area's desks and inspection arches. Then his eyes settled on Junior. He strode up to him, his right hand extended.

"Samuel!" he exclaimed. "It's good to see you again."

"How are you, Pierre?"

"Not bad, for a man facing mandatory retirement." Turning slightly, he gestured to his wife as he said, "Let me introduce the love of my life, Marliena."

Junior bowed politely over her extended hand. "How do you do?"

"I'm fine, thank you." Marliena's voice was thin, high, very controlled.

Junior led them to the only desk that was occupied and through the inspection arch beyond it. Aside from a heavy burden of jewelry, the examination beams showed no problems.

As Junior led the two of them out of the inspection area and into *Saturn Prime*'s central passageway, he told them, "Professor Wilmot, the head of this station, has fixed up a three-room apartment for you here on the station, so you won't have to move in with the scientists aboard *Cassini*."

"How nice," said D'Argent.

"He'd like to meet you, of course. I thought we might have dinner some evening while you're here."

D'Argent nodded his agreement. His wife had nothing to say.

Junior showed them to their apartment, then left them to unpack and settle in. But not before D'Argent asked, "What time will tonight's dinner be?"

"Nineteen hundred hours," said Junior.

"And this station is on Greenwich Mean Time?"

"Same as all the space facilities off-Earth."

"Good."

"Our dinner reservation is for nineteen hundred hours," Junior repeated to Mrs. D'Argent.

With a blink of her sky-blue eyes, she asked, "What time is that, for real?"

D'Argent snapped, "Seven p.m."

"Oh. Okay."

DINNER PARTY

Glancing at his wristwatch as he and Deborah approached *Saturn Prime*'s restaurant, Junior saw it was five minutes before 7:00 p.m.

"D'Argent hasn't come all the way out here for fun," Junior was muttering. "He wants something."

"Wants what?" Deborah asked.

Grimly, Junior answered, "We'll find out soon enough."

D'Argent showed up at the restaurant precisely on time, with his wife, who was decked in a silvery, slinky floor-length gown that showed plenty of bosom, at his side. A robot waiter led them to the table where Junior and Deborah stood up as they approached.

"Ah," said D'Argent, with a smile that looked just a little bit forced to Junior, "you beat us here."

Junior shook hands with the Rockledge president and the two men introduced their women to each other.

As they took their seats at the table, D'Argent sniffed, "Not the fanciest of establishments, is it?"

Junior forced a grin. "It's the best restaurant between here and Mars."

374 | BEN BOVA

D'Argent agreed (reluctantly, Junior thought) with a silent nod.

They ordered drinks and then dinner. D'Argent spoke in generalities about his imminent retirement and Junior listened patiently, waiting for him to get around to his reason for coming out all this way. The two women chatted with each other, about clothes and jewelry and other inconsequential things.

Halfway through their main course, D'Argent at last said, "You know, Samuel, you still owe me for those three asteroids that you and your little friend snookered me out of."

For a moment Junior said nothing. Then, "Pierre, you have a habit of ending sentences with prepositions."

"Don't be facetious," D'Argent snapped.

With a tight smile, Junior said, "Do you intend to go to court over this?"

"No, I have other ways of settling old scores."

"Hired assassins, perhaps?"

"Perhaps."

"Killing me won't get you any money."

His eyes shifting to Deborah, D'Argent muttered, "I wouldn't dream of having *you* killed."

Junior heard the slight emphasis D'Argent put on *you*. For a long moment he said nothing, his mind whirling. Then he slightly misquoted, "'There's no terror in your aspect, Pierre, for I am armed so proof in honesty that your threats pass me as the idle wind, which I respect not.'"

D'Argent laughed. "Very good! Shakespeare, isn't it?"

Junior nodded, poker-faced.

"But the fact remains that you did indeed cheat me out of those three asteroids—"

"Rockledge," Junior corrected. "If anyone was cheated, it was Rockledge Industries, not you."

With a dip of his chin, D'Argent agreed, "Rockledge, yes.

I still work for them, you know. Right up until my birthday, next month."

Frowning, Mrs. D'Argent asked, "What are you two talking about, Pierre?"

Scowling back at her, D'Argent snapped, "Several billion dollars."

"Oh!"

Junior leaned back in his chair. "Let's stop the threats, Pierre. Can't we settle this amicably?"

"Certainly," D'Argent replied, with an oily smile. "You hand me . . . oh, say, three billion New International Dollars and we'll call it even."

"I haven't got anywhere near that much money."

"Then you'd better get it."

Sitting up straighter, Junior broke into a warm smile. "Okay. I will."

"How?"

Spreading his arms wide, Junior said, "It's a big universe, Pierre. Lots of room for lots of discoveries."

"Such as?"

With a seemingly careless shrug, Junior replied, "If I knew, I'd tell you."

Just at the moment Junior spotted Rex Klamath at the entry- way to the restaurant. The dwarf was looking around, scanning the restaurant and the diners sitting at the various tables.

"Uh-oh," Junior muttered.

At that precise moment, Klamath spotted D'Argent sitting at the table with Junior and the two women. He broke into a run, heading straight toward D'Argent's chair.

Junior jumped to his feet so fast he overturned his own chair. With a quick stride, he positioned himself between D'Argent and Klamath, shouting, "Rex! No!"

Klamath was hurtling toward D'Argent as fast as his stubby legs could propel him, his face set in a grim snarl. "Bastard!" he screamed.

Junior intercepted the dwarf and wrapped him in his arms, lifting him off the floor, his little arms and legs churning furiously. Klamath howled, "Lemme go! Lemme get at the son of a bitch!"

D'Argent seemed frozen in his chair, his eyes wide, his mouth hanging open. The two women backed their chairs away from the table. Three robots, the restaurant's manager, and a pair of the human waiters converged on the table while Klamath squirmed and struggled in Junior's grip.

Junior hung onto Klamath until the dwarf suddenly seemed to collapse, all the fury drained out of him.

"Easy, Rex," Junior whispered. "Take it easy."

Puffing, sweaty, Klamath nodded shakily. "Okay, Sam. It's okay."

No one seemed to know what to say, what to do. Junior deposited Klamath gently on the carpeted floor, standing trembling on his stunted legs, his chest heaving, his eyes blazing at D'Argent.

Without taking his hands from Klamath's shoulders, Junior asked softly, "Are you all right now?"

Klamath nodded slowly. "I'm all right." He took in a deep shuddering breath and repeated, "I'm all right."

"Okay." Junior released his grip on the dwarf. Looking at the perplexed restaurant manager he said, "We need another chair."

"Of course," said the manager. He snapped his fingers and one of the human waiters slid a chair from the next table and placed it beside Klamath. The dwarf climbed up onto it, his eyes never leaving D'Argent.

Turning toward the two women, Klamath muttered, "Sorry for the commotion."

D'Argent seemed to relax. Putting on his usual smarmy smile, he said calmly, "I think we'd better call it a night, Samuel."

Klamath sat at the table unmoving, his eyes staring off into space.

"Maybe you're right," said Junior. Then, turning to Klamath, he asked, "Rex, have you had your dinner?"

Shaking his head, Klamath muttered, "I'm not hungry."

Junior looked across the table at D'Argent and agreed, "You're right. Let's go."

Junior, D'Argent and the two women got up from their chairs. Klamath hesitated, then slid off his chair too. The five of them walked to the restaurant's entrance in silence.

Once in the passageway outside, though, Klamath spun around and kicked D'Argent in the shins so hard that Junior thought he heard bone snap. Before anyone could say or do anything, Klamath started running down the passageway, shouting, "I owed you that, you son of a bitch!"

D'Argent, yowling in pain, hopped awkwardly on one foot.

TREASURE HUNT

Junior decided to leave Klamath alone. *Let him walk off his anger,* he thought. Then he added silently, *Hope he doesn't decide to attack D'Argent while he's asleep—if he can sleep, knowing that Rex is somewhere aboard this station, burning for revenge.*

But the night passed with no alarms, and when Junior woke up, he felt almost refreshed from his night's sleep.

He got to the office aboard *Cassini* that he shared with Van Maanen ahead of the astronomer, as usual, and plunged into his daily routine of checking the status of the station's supplies. *Busywork,* he complained to himself. *A robot could be doing this job.*

When the astronomer finally arrived at the office (nearly an hour after Junior) he slid onto his desk chair with a happy smile on his face.

"How's it going?" Junior asked, by way of a greeting.

Van Maanen was already peering at his desktop video screen. He muttered, "I'll let you know . . . in just . . . a moment."

His eyes widened and he sat up straighter in his desk chair. "Ah! They're working!"

Curious, Junior asked, "What's working?"

Glancing at him, Van Maanen broke into a pleased grin and replied, "Put your screen on A-22."

Voice control of the computers could get seriously snarled when two people shared an office, so Junior tapped on his keyboard and the image on his desktop screen shifted to show a close-up of one of the gleaming metallic white particles that made up Saturn's rings. It was gripped in a robot's metal fingers.

"We've captured several dozen of the ring particles," Van Maanen explained. "Out there in the rings themselves. In their natural environment."

"And?" Junior prompted.

"We're starting to study them, remotely. Robots are doing the work, following instructions from our scientists here on the station."

"And?" Junior repeated, his voice rising a notch.

Van Maanen's grin went wider. "Take a look."

Junior stared at his screen. The robot held the ice particle in one hand, then used a long, slim metal probe to pry its gleaming white hump of a cover off its back.

Van Maanen sighed like a man who had just seen a vision of paradise.

"Look!" he whispered. "Look!"

Junior saw the insides of the ice particle, a tiny assembly of minuscule shapes blinking and winking. It looked like a miniaturized city, flashing busily away.

"It's signaling!" Junior exclaimed.

"Signaling who? Why?" Van Maanen whispered.

Junior had no answer.

━━━━━━

For more than an hour, Junior and Van Maanen sat in awed silence as they watched the robots disassembling the ice particles they had captured. Their insides glowed and blinked purposively.

At last Van Maanen shook his head, as if trying to wake himself from a dream. "They're signaling, all right. I'd bet my teeth on that."

"But how?" Junior asked. "You've scanned up and down the spectrum. There's no emission from them."

"They're not using the electromagnetic spectrum."

"Then how—?"

His face twisting with frustration, anger, Van Maanen snarled, "If I knew, I'd tell you! This is beyond anything we understand!"

Junior had a thousand more questions he wanted to ask, but he saw that they would merely upset the astronomer's normally good-natured disposition even further, so he kept his mouth shut. For nearly another hour the two men watched the video views in total, frustrated silence as the robots took one after another of the ice particles apart.

At last Van Maanen switched off the video and slumped back in his desk chair. With a sigh, he admitted, "Whoever seeded Saturn's rings with those machines has a technology way beyond ours."

"Not beyond ours," Junior maintained. "Different from ours."

Van Maanen nodded silently, but the expression on his face showed more than disappointment. It showed defeat.

Rolling his desk chair closer to Van Maanen's, Junior said, "We've got to study those machines, whatever they are. Try to find out about their technology."

"Play the blind men and the elephant," Van Maanen said, almost in a whisper.

"Play science!" Junior snapped. "You've got an opportunity

to open up a whole new field of study. And maybe make contact with an intelligent extraterrestrial civilization."

Strangely, Van Maanen smiled. A little. "The optimism of youth," he murmured.

Junior grinned at him. "Somebody once said, 'When life gives you lemons, make lemonade.'"

Van Maanen almost laughed. Almost.

SURPRISES

The next day, D'Argent invited Junior to lunch. For once, the Rockledge president was already waiting at the restaurant's entrance when Junior arrived—precisely on time.

As they followed the robot waiter to their table—next to one of the oversized wall screens that showed views of Saturn and close-ups of its rings—D'Argent smilingly announced, "I'll be leaving tomorrow."

Junior felt his brows hike up. "So soon? You've only been here a few—"

Sighing as he sat down, the Rockledge president said, "This has been a sort of honeymoon trip for us, you know. She's a hopeless romantic."

Junior allowed a small smile to curve his lips. "You're a very lucky man, Pierre."

"Not lucky. Wealthy."

Sensing deep water in that direction, Junior changed the subject. "So what will you be doing in your final weeks at Rockledge?"

With a small shrug, D'Argent replied, "Showing the intricacies of management to my successor. Then bowing out gracefully."

"And?" Junior probed.

"We've bought a small island in American Samoa. Marliena is there now, directing the team that's building our dream home."

"Sounds wonderful."

Leaning slightly closer to Junior, D'Argent hissed, "I still want the three million you owe me."

"Owe you?" Junior said, putting on a surprised, puzzled expression. "Or Rockledge?"

"Me. The company won't miss the money, but it's a matter of principle to me."

With a slow smile, Junior said, "Well, you'll have to be patient, Pierre."

"I'm willing to wait . . . providing you promise to pay me."

Nodding, "I'm negotiating with Aldrin Aerospace for a vehicle that I can go exploring with."

"Exploring? Where?"

"The Kuiper Belt. Out beyond Uranus. Much bigger than the Asteroid Belt between Mars and Jupiter. There are thousands of icy bodies out there. Millions, more likely. That means water, the most precious commodity in the solar system. It's going to be the new Bonanza out there."

"And you intend to get there first."

Smiling, Junior replied, "If I can."

D'Argent smiled back. It looked like the smile of a slithering cobra, to Junior. "Just like your father," the Rockledge president murmured.

"I'll be taking Rex Klamath with me," Junior added. "I think it'll be best to keep him as far away from you as I can."

D'Argent nodded his agreement. Then he asked, "What about your lady friend? What's her name? Deborah something, isn't it?"

Junior's smile widened. "It'll be Deborah *Gunn* in another week. We're getting married."

"Indeed?" D'Argent broke into a smile that almost looked genuine. "Congratulations. Maybe I'll stay around for the wedding."

"That'd be fine."

Leaning closer, D'Argent asked in a near whisper, "Is she pregnant?"

Junior fought down the surge of anger at the question. He took in a deep breath, then answered flatly, "Not yet."

D'Argent's smile turned thoughtful. "Ah, well, you're both young. Plenty of time."

Junior said nothing.

The Rockledge president leaned back in his chair, reminiscing, "Marriage. That's something your father never got around to."

Junior thought, *And you have, three times. Or is it four?* With a curt little nod, Junior replied aloud, "I'm not my father."

D'Argent seemed to eye Junior in a totally new manner. "No, you're not, are you? You're your own man, Samuel. Bright. Tough. A lot like the old Sam, but much better in many ways."

Junior could feel his cheeks flushing. "By God, Pierre, you're becoming civilized!"

D'Argent look surprised for a moment. Then his usual sneering, smug, superior expression returned to his face. "It must be your influence, Samuel."

Shaking his head, Junior said, "I doubt that."

D'Argent shrugged nonchalantly. For a longish moment, the two men sat across the table from one another, both of them smiling.

Then D'Argent said, "I should give you a wedding present, shouldn't I?"

With a shake of his head Junior started to reply, "No, that's not necessary—"

"If it were *necessary*," D'Argent snapped, with some of his usual venom, "I would resent it. But I really feel I should give you two children a present."

Junior objected, "But—"

"How about a spacecraft for you to go scouting through the Kuiper Belt?"

Despite himself, Junior gasped with surprise. "A spacecraft?"

"Yes. A wedding gift from Rockledge Industries. And from me."

"That . . . that would be awfully generous, Pierre."

"It will be worth it, if you can keep that maniac dwarf away from me! Besides, why should Aldrin Aerospace make money off you?"

AND MORE SURPRISES

The following week was a blur of busy activities for Junior. True to his word, D'Argent handed Junior the ownership papers for a sleek, small spacecraft for exploring the Kuiper Belt.

"Your honeymoon hideaway," said the Rockledge president as Junior ogled the computer diagrams of the vessel's interior. "I wonder if it's wise to bring that dwarf along."

Junior glanced at D'Argent, sitting beside him in his office, then said, "Rex will be okay."

"You're sure?"

"I'm positive."

With an exaggerated sigh, D'Argent said, "Very well. It's your honeymoon."

Junior nodded as he thought, *You have a dirty mind, Pierre.* But he said nothing.

As the days passed, Junior grew calmer, more assured of himself, while Deborah seemed more and more excited with the details of the wedding and the reception she was planning to follow it.

Frederick Mohammed Malone arrived from Selene two days before the wedding, his dark face wreathed in smiles for the happy couple, bearing a pair of wedding rings for them. "Cut from the only vein of gold we've found on the Moon, after all the years we've been exploring the old lady."

Junior admired the twin golden circlets, and when he showed them to Deborah she broke into happy tears.

Then Big George Ambrose arrived from Ceres, huge and shaggy with his flaming red hair and beard. Junior flung his arms around George's massive frame when he stepped into *Saturn Prime*'s reception center.

Gorge gave Junior a statuette of two lovers holding hands, carved from meteoric iron.

"Best I could find," he said, almost apologetically, as he handed the gift to Junior.

"It's beautiful," Junior said, surprised and pleased.

Once George had passed through the inspection arch and handed his papers to the inspector, he said to Junior, "Got somethin' else too."

"Oh?"

As they left the reception area and started down the station's central passageway, George said, "Y'know, we've applied for membership in the IAA."

Junior grinned. "About time you Rock Rats joined the rest of the human race."

"Yeah, I know. Had some opposition, y'know. Lotsa the Rats don't want to be civilized."

"But you convinced them?"

"I hadda bang a few heads together," George said, as serene and unruffled as a dozing lion, "but they finally saw th' light and we applied for IAA membership just before I started out for here."

"You won't have any trouble being voted in, will you?"

"Shouldn't. People I dealt with at IAA headquarters seemed pretty happy that we're finally joining the organization."

Junior grinned. "Bringing the Rock Rats into civilization. That's quite an achievement, Georgie."

"Yeah. Guess so."

They had reached the guest quarters, where one of the doors bore a sparkling new name tag: George Rockne Ambrose.

Junior goggled at the middle name. "Rockne?" he asked.

Looking somewhat embarrassed, George muttered, "My father was a Notre Dame football fan."

The door slid open when George leaned his heavy hand on the identification plate. The two men stepped inside. It was a one-room compartment that looked comfortable enough to Junior, although he wondered if the bed was big enough to hold the big redhead.

George seemed unconcerned about the furnishings. "One thing about joining the IAA, though," he said, as the door slid shut behind them.

"Oh?"

"We've gotta send a representative to Amsterdam. To be our man on the Council."

"So have you elected someone?" Junior asked.

His red-bearded face furrowing into a frown, George replied, "Yeah."

"That's good."

"It's you, Sammy."

Thunderstruck, Junior shrieked, "ME?"

George nodded. "Nobody else would take the job. I tried, believe me. None of the Rats, o' course. But none of the reg'lar staff at Ceres, either. Nobody wanted the responsibility!"

"But I'm not even a citizen . . ."

With an almost ashamed nod, George interrupted, "Yes you are. I appointed you an honorary citizen in absentia. I got th' papers in my briefcase."

Feeling close to panic, Junior pleaded, "But George, I'm not a bureaucrat. I can't be your representative on the IAA's Council."

More firmly, George replied, "Your name's been sent to them and they accepted it. You've got to help us, Sammy. Please!"

"I'm going out to the Kuiper Belt," Junior pleaded.

"Can't you postpone that? Send Rex out by himself? Or with a crew?"

Junior sagged down onto the king-sized bed. "I'm not a diplomat. I don't know anything—"

George interrupted. "It's not that difficult. You listen to what the rest of 'em say and then either vote no or abstain. Simple."

Shaking his head, Junior replied, "That's ridiculous."

"Ridiculous or not, the Rock Rats need you to represent 'em. *I* need you, Sammy! Don't let me down. Please!"

WEDDING DAY

Thus it was that Sam Gunn Jr. accepted—reluctantly—his appointment as the Rock Rats' representative on the IAA's Council.

To Junior's surprise, Deborah was delighted by the turn of events.

"We'll be going to Earth!" she exclaimed when Junior asked her how she felt about the appointment. "You'll be an ambassador! An Important Man!"

"But we were going to go to the Kuiper Belt," Junior pleaded.

"Let Rex handle that. He can hire a crew, can't he?"

"I guess," said Junior.

Without another word, Deborah went straight to the phone console and began to look up real estate agents Earthside.

Klamath was surprised but agreeable. "Sure, I can handle the ship," the dwarf said, with a tight smile. "No sweat. Got a couple of guys in mind to help crew the bird."

And that was that. Klamath stayed at *Saturn Prime* long enough to stand as Junior's best man for the wedding, then started out for the Kuiper Belt. Big George headed back to Ceres and Frederick Mohammed Malone returned to Selene, on the Moon.

Junior and Deborah flew to Earth on a Rockledge vessel on a low-energy trajectory that took several weeks to reach Earth, most of the time in zero-gravity.

It was a stupendous honeymoon.